PICKING UP THE GAUNTLET

BELOW THE SALT
BOOK ONE

ELIZABETH ROSE

OLIVERHEBER BOOKS

Copyright © 2023 by Elizabeth Rose

Published by Oliver-Heber Books

0 9 8 7 6 5 4 3 2 1

 Created with Vellum

CHAPTER I

BLAKE CASTLE, ENGLAND, 1374

D ogs. There were at least two of them in the distance and they were headed her way!

Lady Raven Blake's head shot up as she listened closely from her secluded spot in the forest. It was just past daybreak, but she was sure she'd heard the low, deep barking of canines, and it was getting louder.

How had they found her so quickly?

"My lady, it sounds as if the castle hounds are searching for you, and on your trail," announced Albert, the thirteen-year-old page who was one of the two boys assisting her today. Albert was a tall, skinny lad with deep-set eyes as dark as his scraggly hair that hung down to his shoulders. The other boy with her was Harold, the squire of Raven's twin brother, Rook.

Harold was the opposite of Albert, having blond hair and a good build with muscles. At eighteen years of age, he was far from actually being a boy anymore. Harold was in training to someday become a knight. He sat atop his horse at the other end of the makeshift tilt that would separate them as they

1

jousted. By rights, this should be a wooden fence, but Raven had to be resourceful since she was practicing in the woods. She'd used a rope and tied it between two branches that she'd stuck in the ground. All she really needed was something to depict lanes, so this would work fine.

Harold gripped his lance, ready to joust, but looked more than nervous to actually do it. She'd seen him joust many times when he'd practiced with Rook. He'd never seemed as nervous as he did now. The young man actually had nothing to worry about. He was good at the sport. Raven learned a lot about the joust just by watching the knights and other men but had never really tried it.

"I am well aware of the dogs on my trail, Albert," Raven answered with a sigh, mounting her horse and collecting her shield from the boy. She knew exactly which dogs were pursuing her because of the sound of their barking. They were her own dogs, Copper and Brindy. There was no doubt that her brother, Rook, was involved in this. Raven had purposely sneaked off to the woods at sunrise to practice the joust, since she wasn't allowed to do so back at Blake Castle. She had hoped to return before anyone noticed she was missing. That plan, sadly, wasn't working.

"Perhaps it would be best to leave now." Harold flipped up the visor on his helm, glancing nervously towards the sound of the barking dogs in the distance. He wore armor, as was required of the sport, but Raven didn't have any. "Your father isn't going to like this, my lady. I don't want him angry with me." Harold tried to talk her out of this, but Raven was a fighter and wouldn't give up so easily.

"You're worried about what my father will say?

Really, Harold," said Raven, with a *tsking* noise from her mouth. "I'd think you'd be more concerned with what Lord Rook will do to you, rather than Lord Corbett. After all, you are Rook's squire."

Raven found it odd that Harold had come to her, eagerly offering his services yesterday, when she hadn't even asked him for his help or told him her plan at all. He said he'd heard about it from Albert, even though Albert denied telling a soul. Well, she should have known right then and there that something was rotten. Instead of turning him down, she'd accepted his help since she needed someone familiar with jousting to go up against. Plus, Harold had access to the jousting equipment, and wouldn't be questioned about borrowing a few lances. If she or Albert tried to sneak them out, someone surely would have stopped them.

"I–I am concerned, that's all." Harold wasn't usually so uptight. "I mean, of course I'm worried about what Sir Rook will say or do to me. I am, my lady." The boy fidgeted with his lance and wouldn't look directly at her when he spoke. She'd seen this action before, but it had usually been from her three brothers when they were growing up. She hadn't seen her younger brothers, Tolin and Daegel, for some time now, since they were both off being fostered by other lords. She missed them dearly. Being around Albert and Harold helped to fill that void.

Harold's lack of eye contact right now meant he was lying. She was sure of it. It also told her that what she'd suspected was true. Rook was behind the search party headed this way. Her twin brother always gave her trouble. Well, Raven no longer cared. She wanted to learn to joust, and Rook was not going to stop her.

"Bid the devil," she spat, looking back over her shoulder for the approaching search party. She could hear at least one rider crashing through the woods, traveling with the dogs. "Why did they have to bring the mastiffs?"

Raven collected the oversized helm from Albert, donning it and fastening the buckle under her chin. It was awkward and she found it amazing that anyone could wear this heavy thing, and still be expected to joust, or even fight with it upon their head. "Hand me the lance, Albert. Hurry. I only have enough time for one pass before they find and stop me." Raven was skilled with weapons of every kind and even had her own sword. She liked a challenge, and the joust by far was the most challenging thing she'd probably ever do.

Jousting was a sport for the nobles, and only the men. No proper lady was ever supposed to do that! That's why she had to practice in secret.

"My lady, I agree with Harold. I think it would be wise to return to the castle now." Albert shifted from foot to foot, biting his lip and looking back toward the sound of the approaching party. She supposed the boys had reason to be worried. They could lose their positions over this, or even be put in the pillory. The pillory was a wooden device where their head and hands were locked through small wooden openings. It was a device to shame people who had done wrong. Usually they got hit by rotten fruit thrown by the serfs and peasants. She, on the other hand, wouldn't be punished. Her father favored her since she was his only daughter. Raven had used this to her advantage many times, and today would be no different.

"Give me the lance, and that's an order." Raven's

hand shot out and she waited. "Harold, are you ready?" she called out to the squire, glancing over to see him lower his visor and give a slight nod. Her palms were moist with sweat under her leather gloves. She also found it hard to breathe with the heavy helm weighing her down. The sound of her rapidly beating heart thundered in her ears, mixed with the barking of the mastiffs getting closer and closer. It was now or never. Raven wasn't going to quit. This might be her only chance. She would do it or die trying.

"Thank you, Albert." Raven took the long wooden pole from the boy, slipping the grapper, the ring attached to the lance, into the arret—the hook she'd sewed onto her padded gambeson since she was wasn't wearing armor. The grapper and arret worked together to steady the lance and keep it from sliding backwards upon impact. This was risky and not much protection, but no armor made for a man would ever fit her. A mail coat would have been beneficial, but was much too heavy and bulky for her frame. So, clothed in her brother's old tunic and trews and with only a padded vest for protection, this would have to do.

Now that the lance was supported, she lowered her visor, barely able to breathe or see a blasted thing. God's eyes, how did knights do this?

Raven was tall for a lady. Her physical strength exceeded any woman's two-fold, since she grew up wielding a sword. She was nothing like the rest of the frail doves that spent their time sewing, weaving, and gossiping all day long. Instead of partaking in these activities, Raven had been involved in archery, throwing daggers, or swordplay. She wanted excitement, challenges, and the ability to do what she pleased in life. Just like that dark bird she was named after, she was confident, inquisitive, and pretty much shunned or feared by the rest of the ladies of the castle.

"Go on. Give him the signal to start," she told Albert, itching to try the joust before she was stopped in her tracks. She gripped the lance securely while her horse danced restlessly beneath her. The sound of the barking in the woods became louder, doing nothing to calm any of them.

Raven's mastiffs barely ever barked. It made her wonder why they were making such a fuss now. Perhaps they were warning her that they were coming. That thought made her smile. She had a connection to her dogs like none other. She loved her pets but didn't want to see them right now.

Until today, she'd only practiced the joust on a quintain—a wooden arm that swung around when hit, and had a sandbag attached to the other end. She wasn't any good at it, and tired of fighting against a wooden object. Today would be her first time to go up against a man.

"Go!" shouted Albert, swiping his hand through the air, hitting her horse on the back end to send it running.

Raven shot forward with a jerk, trying her best to keep her lance high and steady as her horse thundered over the ground, making its way toward Harold. It was hot under the heavy helm. Her breathing made it slippery from inside. As she propelled forward, her helm slipped down and she had to raise her chin just to be able to see out the slit in the visor.

Her heart raced faster than the steed beneath her. Raven was excellent on a horse and always rode astride, although it upset her parents. Excitement coursed through her body as she moved closer and closer to her opponent.

She knew better than anyone that the joust was dangerous and that she should be frightened for her safety. Instead, she saw it as a challenge, pushing her fear away. Just as she approached Harold, her helm slipped again, covering her eyes completely. She could no longer see where she was going. Before she could even try to straighten the helm, she felt the tip of Harold's lance hit against her chest.

"Oh!" she exclaimed in surprise, not quite ready for this, since she'd just been trying to see. It wasn't a hard blow, but certainly enough to set her off balance. Her body shifted to the side, causing her to lose her grip on the lance as well as the reins of her horse as it continued to run. As hard as she tried, she was not able to right herself.

The pole fell from her grasp, making a loud thunking noise as it hit the ground. She fought to retrieve the reins, but without being able to see properly, it was impossible to do. Raven could no longer hold on to the horse. She fell, striking the ground hard. Her horse ran off without her.

"Ooomph." She'd had the air knocked from her lungs and struggled to breathe. This had not gone at all as planned.

"My lady, are you all right? I am so sorry." It was Harold. Or at least she thought so. Everything was muffled and all she could see was a slit of sunlight coming in through the visor, as well as the trees high above her head. She lay there, unable to move.

"Lady Raven, I knew this wasn't a good idea," came the voice of Albert next, along with the sound of his feet pounding the ground as he ran to help her. "Lord Corbett is going to kill us when he discovers his only daughter has been knocked off her steed."

Then she heard the panting of her dogs as well as the sound of somebody slowly clapping their hands together. Looking up out the opening in the visor she saw Brindy, her male mastiff curiously staring down at her. The dog slobbered as he tried to lick her face but instead got the helm. When the hound moved to the side, she saw her brother Rook sitting atop his horse clapping, looking down at her with a smirk on his face.

"Rook!" She tore off the visor in anger. When she did, Copper, the female mastiff, reached over and licked her face. Both dogs were big, each weighing more than she. They had square-shaped heads, floppy black ears, and black muzzles. The male was a beautiful brindle color with black and brown stripes that looked to have a golden hue to them when illuminated by the sun. The female dog was a little darker than the normal light fawn color of mastiffs. The color was called apricot, but reminded her of shiny copper. That is how the dog got its name.

Copper lay down next to her, resting her head on Raven's chest. Brindy kept pushing up against her, nudging her with his nose, examining her to make sure she wasn't hurt. They were both cute and cuddly and also good watchdogs. They weren't apt at running long distances, but were still taken along on the hunts because of their tracking abilities. Not only could they follow the scent of an animal, but as this proved, they could follow the scent of a human, too.

"All right, that's enough. Get the hounds off of her," Rook commanded, making Raven realize that Daniel, the kennelgroom, was there as well. He was an older man, and traveled on foot while Rook rode his horse. The kennelgroom usually accompanied the men on the hunts, holding the dogs back with leads until they were ready to be set loose to chase down the prey.

"Aye, my lord," answered Daniel, pulling the heavy dogs off Raven, hooking leads on their collars to control them.

Raven pushed up to a sitting position, scratching Copper behind the ears. "Do you think it's wise to take her away from the castle while she's pregnant?" she asked the kennelgroom.

"She's in no danger, my lady," answered Daniel, trying to gain control of the dogs. "You weren't far into the woods, and a little exercise is good for her. She's not birthin' the pups for at least a few more weeks yet."

"Still, there was no reason to bring my hounds at all." She looked up and glared at her brother, knowing this was all his doing.

"Well, little sister, have you learned your lesson yet?" Rook asked with a chuckle. His dark hair lifted in the warm spring breeze. His hair was black, the same as hers, and nearly as long.

"Quit calling me little," spat Raven. "I'm the same age as you and you know it." True, they were twins, but Rook had been born two minutes before her and would never let her forget it. "And what do you mean, *did I learn my lesson?*" she asked.

Still sitting, she pulled off her leather gloves one by one, throwing them on the ground. Copper and

Brindy took the opportunity to pick them up, thinking she wanted to play. Daniel busied himself trying to pry the gloves out of the animals' mouths.

"You knew this would happen, didn't you?" asked Raven, before her brother had a chance to answer. "You wanted this to happen," she said, seeing it all so clearly now. "That is why your squire came to me offering his help. You told him to do it, didn't you?"

"I'm sorry, my lady," blurted out Harold, coming to her side while Albert collected Raven's horse. "I was only following orders. I didn't hit you hard at all, I swear." His head jerked around to look at Rook. "I only gave her a tap just like you instructed, my lord. I had no idea she would fall from her horse or I never would have done it."

"Rook! You swine," hissed Raven through gritted teeth. "How could you?"

"Hopefully, this little lesson knocked some sense into you," said Rook. "Besides, it would serve you right if you ended up a little bruised. It's no one's fault but your own. This is a sport for men, not women. It is time you get these silly notions out of your head and start acting like a lady."

"Stop being so mean to me," snapped Raven. "We always sparred together growing up, and I can handle any weapon. You know that."

"True," said Rook, dismounting his horse and walking over to her. "You just can't joust and this is proof of it. Now give me your hand and I'll help you up. Let's get back to the castle." Rook reached out for her, offering his assistance.

She took it, but as soon as she was on her feet, she used her leg to try to sweep Rook's feet out from under him, the way she always did when they fought as youths. Rook saw it coming. He moved to the side, grabbed her arm and twisted it behind her back.

"Don't think that little trick is still going to work on me."

He released her.

"Get away from me," she said, slapping his arm.

"I was only trying to help."

"I don't want your help and neither do I need it. I don't need anyone's help, for that matter." Raven felt a little light-headed. She rubbed her aching shoulder, wondering how bruised she was going to be, come the morrow. When Brindy jumped up on her, wanting to play, she was knocked off-balance by the dog's motion and weight. Rook reached out and caught her before she fell.

"Daniel, take those damned dogs back to the kennel," Rook told the man.

"Aye, my lord," answered the kennelgroom. "Right away."

"Harold, make sure the horses are stabled and tended to properly," Rook called out. "I will also hold you and Albert responsible for the equipment getting back to where it belongs."

"Of course, my lord," answered Harold.

"Aye," added Albert, as they collected the lances and headed back toward the castle with Daniel and the dogs leading the way.

When they were out of earshot, Rook spoke to Raven. "Stop playing these silly games and start acting like the lady you were meant to be."

"Never!" she answered defiantly, brushing the dirt off her clothes. "And you can't make me."

"Mayhap I can't, but our father can," he reminded

11

her. "I assure you, he won't just ignore what's happened here today, Raven."

"Then don't tell him," she said with a sniff. "He doesn't need to know."

"You can't honestly believe that he doesn't already know. Father is lord of the castle and privy to everything that happens there. I'm sure not only he but everyone knows by now that you're missing. It's no secret you've been sneaking off to the woods to practice with your weapons for a while now."

"Well, if Father knows and he hasn't stopped me, I hardly think this will be any different. After all, he's the one who gave me my sword, so he won't mind."

"Raven, that was when you were younger. And he does mind, I promise you. You are twenty-two years old now, but you're acting like a child. It's time you start embracing your status and title."

"I don't care about it, and I don't think you have a right to tell me what to do."

"It doesn't matter what you think. Father has found a way to make it happen."

"He has?" she asked. "What do you mean? Make what happen? Tell me, Rook."

Rook chuckled playfully and shook his head. It was obvious that he wasn't going to tell her. Angry with him, Raven beat her fists against his chest. Rook only laughed louder, grabbing her wrists in his large hands to stop her. Or rile her, was more like it. She twisted out of his hold and elbowed him hard in the ribs.

"Ooomph!" That stopped his laughing at least. Rook reached out, grabbing her around her waist to keep her from running. Raven moved her foot backward, trying once more to sweep his feet out from under him but Rook didn't let it happen. He quickly released her and moved away. Instead of hitting his leg, she kicked at air, which caused her to lose her balance and fall to the ground for the second time that morning.

"What's going on here?" came a deep voice from behind her. Raven's head snapped around to see her father, Lord Corbett Blake, riding toward them. Devon, Raven's mother, was on her own horse right behind him. "Raven, get off the bloody ground before someone sees you," growled her father. He stopped his horse and dismounted and then proceeded to help his wife.

It was just like her father to worry more about what others would think, not even asking if she was hurt first.

"Raven, are you injured? What happened?" Devon rushed over to Raven, putting her arm around her as Raven got to her feet.

"Nay, Mother, I am fine. And thank you for asking." She glanced over at Rook and her father who were standing there, looking at her as if she'd lost her mind.

"When your handmaid said you weren't in your bed this morning when she arrived at your room, I was afraid you'd been abducted," said her mother. "What are you doing out here in the woods? Especially at this time of day?"

"Mother, you know I don't like having a handmaid. I wish you'd tell Emma she's not needed."

"Answer your mother's question," commanded her father, using the tone he used when reprimanding his soldiers.

"I'll answer it for her," offered Rook. "Raven had

the hare-brained idea that she was going to joust. I knew she was sneaking away before sunup to the woods to practice. That's why I told my squire to offer to help her."

"You did what?" gasped their mother. "Rook, why didn't you try to stop her instead? She could have been hurt. What is the matter with you?"

"Me?" Rook's hand slapped against his chest and confusion clouded his face. "I was only trying to teach her a lesson so she'd stop this silly nonsense."

"Rook, you should be protecting your sister, not sending your squire into the woods with her so she can do something that might have caused her to get hurt." Corbett echoed his wife's concern.

"I was only trying to discourage her from wanting to act like a man," protested Rook.

"You don't need to worry about that anymore," Corbett told him. "Did you tell your sister what I've decided?"

"Nay, he didn't tell me anything," Raven interrupted. "Father, what is going on?"

"Tell her, Corbett," said Devon softly. "She has a right to know."

"Raven, I'm doing this for your own good, even though I know you're not going to like it," said Corbett.

"What won't I like?" asked Raven.

"I've been more than patient with you over the years, but I can no longer condone your obnoxious behavior," continued Corbett. "It's gotten way out of hand."

"Obnoxious?" Raven had never heard her father talk this way to her before. "What does this all mean?

14

I am not a child anymore, so please stop being so secretive."

"Nay, you're not a child. I agree," mumbled Corbett, with a slow shake of his head. "You are a woman now, Raven, as well as a titled lady. Not to mention, my only daughter."

"Tell her," whispered Devon, growing impatient with him.

"Raven, I've decided it is time for you to marry," announced Corbett, standing up straighter and lifting his chin, almost as if he were throwing down the gauntlet and not expecting her to pick it up in challenge.

"M-married?" That shocked her so much that she found herself tongue-tied. Raven thought he would possibly take away her weapons for a week, or mayhap confine her to the ladies' solar for a spell, if he even reprimanded her at all. But this was something she never expected. It had to be the worse punishment of all.

Raven never thought her father would betroth her without talking to her about it first. In hindsight, she should have known it was coming. Raven was well past marrying age. In reality, she should have been betrothed during childhood and birthing babies by the age of sixteen at the latest, but it hadn't happened. She had told her father on more than one occasion that she never wanted to marry. Somehow, she thought he understood, but apparently not. She didn't like this in the least. The last thing Raven wanted was to be married to a man who was sure to make her put down her weapons and instead wear frilly dresses and sew or weave all day long, barely stepping foot outside in the sun. This isn't at all what she wanted to hear.

"Now, Raven, you know I've always respected your wishes, but this time, I have to agree with your father," said her mother, shocking her even more since she hoped at least her mother would be on her side. "It will be for the best, dear." Devon put her hand on Raven's back, rubbing her fingers in small circles, trying to comfort her the way she did when Raven was a child and having a bad dream. Actually, this was a bad dream. All Raven wanted to do was to wake up and discover that none of it was even real.

"Who?" she pushed the word from her mouth, still finding it hard to speak. "Whom am I to marry?" was all she managed to say. It felt hard to breathe again. This time it had nothing to do with falling from a horse or wearing a heavy helm.

"I can't say," answered Corbett, running his hand over his horse's head. Raven could tell this decision upset him as well as it did her, since he couldn't seem to look at her when he spoke.

"I have a right to know," she retorted.

"He's not keeping it from you," interrupted her mother. "Your father just doesn't know yet whom you'll be marrying." She tried to explain, but still, Raven didn't understand.

"So, I'm not betrothed yet?"

"Nay, not yet," said Corbett. "But soon."

This should probably have made her feel more at ease, but it only prolonged the agony.

"I've decided there will be a tournament at the castle in three weeks' time," her father told her.

"A tournament?" That took Raven's interest. She loved tournaments. Secretly, she always wanted to compete in one. "Tell me more. What is the occasion? This doesn't have something to do with my betrothal, does it?" Part of her felt excited about the tournament, but she was also afraid this might have something to do with her upcoming marriage since her father changed the subject so quickly. That only made her stomach queasy.

"Oh, do let me tell her," said Rook, eagerly wanting to give her bad news even though she couldn't drag information from him a few minutes ago.

"Go ahead." Corbett held out his arm.

"Father is holding a tournament, and the winner gets the prize," said Rook.

"The p-prize? What prize?" Raven asked, but was afraid she already knew the answer.

Rook opened his mouth to tell her, but Corbett stopped him this time.

"Nay. I'll tell her," said Corbett, still petting the horse. "It's my responsibility. I should have taken measures long before now. Raven. Daughter," he said, leaving the horse and coming and gently placing his hand on her shoulder. "It is time you marry a nobleman. I don't want you to fight me on this anymore."

"God's eyes, nay!" She backed away from him, holding her arms around her. "Please don't tell me I'm the prize for the winner of the tournament."

"You are," said Rook, flippantly. "Although, I can't say the winner will consider you a better prize than a gold cup."

"Rook, stop it," scolded their mother.

"How can you do this to me?" she asked her parents, feeling her body shaking with anger. "At least let me have a say about whom I wed."

17

"It doesn't work that way, Sister," said Rook.

"Well it should," she ground out. "If men get to choose their brides, why can't a woman choose her own husband?"

"Because, knowing you, you'd probably choose someone that Father doesn't approve of," Rook blurted out. Raven could see in her father's eyes that this was exactly how he felt.

"Tell me. What do you know about the men who will compete?" she asked. "Mayhap you won't approve of them either," Raven pointed out, fighting for her life now.

"Your father has already sent out the missives to all the eligible bachelors this side of the Scottish border, as well as an invite to our connections in France," explained her mother.

"You mean to all the eligible *nobles*, don't you?"

"It's important that all my children, nephews, and nieces marry nobles," explained Corbett. "I tried for years to bring back honor to the family name that was sullied by my father, who married the illegitimate daughter of the vicar. You know that. I am finally accepted again by the King and nobles, and I will not risk losing respect once more."

"So then," said Raven, her lip quivering as she raised her chin in challenge. "Whoever wins the tournament will win my hand in marriage, no matter who that competitor might be?"

"That's right," said Corbett with a nod. "I'm sorry, but this is the way it's going to be."

"Then so be it," said Raven, turning on her heel, already devising a plan in her mind to get around her father's stupid decision.

CHAPTER 2

Jonathon Armstrong stopped fixing a dent in the helm and looked up as the bells over the door to the blacksmith shop jangled and two men entered the outer room.

"Lords Blake," he said, surprised to see Lord Corbett Blake and his son, Rook, at his shop, since he'd just repaired their armor recently. He put down his hammer and the helm, quickly wiping his hands with a rag. Without removing his leather apron, he hurried away from the forge and over to greet the nobles.

Jonathon's family's shop was visited by the nobles often. He not only made and fixed armor, but was a skilled swordsmith, too. Since there was no blacksmith in town, he and his father handled large as well as small and menial jobs.

Jonathon spent years as an apprentice learning the skills of the forge until he worked his way up to journeyman and returned home. Now, he'd put in his time and all that was keeping him from being a master at his trade was completing one impressive masterpiece that would earn him the respect of the guild. If so, they would accept him and he'd hopefully gain his title of master, just like his father.

Working so much with weapons also gave Jonathon the opportunity to use them on occasion. Over the years, he'd taught himself to fight, and was damned good at it. Many times, Jonathon even hired out his own sword, acting as a mercenary or guard for the nobles when they needed an extra soldier. Even though Jonathon was naught but a commoner, his services were needed in more ways than one. The nobles paid well, making Jonathon's family the highest paid craftsmen in town.

"Good morning, Jonathon," said Lord Corbett with a quick nod. His eyes scanned the room. Jonathon realized he wanted to talk in private.

"I'm the only one here right now, my lords," he assured them. "Did you perhaps wish to speak to my father?"

"Nay, it's you to whom I wish to speak," answered Corbett.

Normally there was enough work to keep Jonathon, his father, another journeyman, as well as an apprentice busy. However, lately, the work had slowed and their income suffered greatly because of it.

"I hope you weren't dissatisfied with my latest repair of your armor."

"Nay. Not at all," said Rook. "Your work is exquisite as always."

Hearing this made Jonathon release a breath of relief that he hadn't even been aware he'd been holding. The lords Blake and their knights brought much work to Jonathon's family's little shop. He would hate to lose business over one dissatisfied noble. Thankfully, that didn't sound to be the case.

"What brings you to town today?" Jonathon asked curiously. "Do you need me to repair one of your weapons? Or fix a link in your chain mail perhaps?" Jonathon was skilled when it came to the forge. There wasn't anything he couldn't do. He served as blacksmith, swordsmith, and armorer, too.

"Nay, we're here for another reason altogether," said Rook, moseying around the shop, picking up a hammer and testing its weight.

"My lords?" asked Jonathon, not understanding what they wanted.

"I have a tournament planned in three weeks' time," Corbett informed him. "There will be knights and nobles coming from all over the country."

"Oh, I see." Jonathon nodded, thinking he knew what they wanted after all. "I will be ready if any of the competitors need anything, my lord. You know you can count on me."

"Where is your father?" asked Corbett, looking around the forge.

"He doesn't work in the forge much anymore since he is getting older, my lord. He usually stays in the rooms above stairs with my mother unless his help is needed."

"So he's unable to do the work?"

"Nay, not at all. It's just that I like to handle the brunt of the work myself. He's worked hard his whole life, and I'm happy to let him rest and spend more time with my mother."

"So, you're the only one working here?" This seemed to bother Corbett.

"Aye, right now I am. We do have another journeyman as well as an apprentice," he told him. "Since work has been slow lately, I gave them some time off. But I assure you, my lord, I will be ready for the tournament should my services be needed."

"Aye. That's good." Corbett nodded, then looked down and fidgeted with fixing the gloves on his hands.

"Is there something else?" Jonathon knew Corbett well enough to realize there was something he was hesitant about asking. Usually, Corbett wasn't shy about anything, so whatever it was, Jonathon could tell it bothered him greatly.

"My father will need extra guards during the tournament," said Rook. "You've worked for us in the past and we'd like to hire you again."

"Really?" Jonathon was taken aback. Usually when he served as guard, or even mercenary, it was in the slow times of winter, and only done to make extra money. He didn't usually take this position in springtime, since business would be picking up again soon. Plus, there was a tournament about to happen. This would prove to be one of his busiest times yet. Still, he couldn't say *no* to a noble and it was an honor to be asked at all. "Well, you know I am interested, and thankful that you would even consider me, my lord. However, I must point out that it'll be a busy time at the forge with everyone arriving for the tournament. Unless your own blacksmith will be handling the brunt of the work, that is."

"Nay, I'm afraid he won't. You see, my blacksmith died recently, and I've yet to replace him," explained Corbett.

"Then all more reason I should be here to help out

with the work the tournament will bring. I mean, I'm not sure it's a good idea for me to leave."

"Nay, you don't understand. I want to hire you now, not for the tournament only," said Corbett.

"My lord?" Jonathon looked from one man to the next, not understanding at all what they wanted.

Rook put down the hammer and walked over to him. "You know my twin sister, Raven, don't you?" he asked.

"Aye, of course, my lord," said Jonathon, remembering the fetching girl. "I've met her once or twice through the years, but I'm not sure she'd remember me since it was only in passing." Raven was a beauty who had always caught Jonathon's eye. He also remembered that she was the furthest thing from a lady, and known to be very rebellious in nature. The townsfolk called her a shrew behind her back. But hell if he'd offer up that information right now. "Lady Raven is a lovely girl and admired and respected by all," he lied through his teeth.

Rook chuckled softly. "Well, I don't know if I'd go that far, but thank you for your vote of confidence."

Corbett gave him a nasty look. Rook cleared his throat and refrained from saying more.

Corbett continued, "Jonathon, I'd like to hire you on several accounts, actually."

"My lord?"

"First, I'd like to employ you as my blacksmith until after the tournament, when I'll have more time to find and hire a new one."

"You want me as the castle smith?" he asked in confusion. "I am foremost an armorer, my lord. Surely you know that I've grown our business here and that I will soon be a master, opening my own shop. Or at least that is what I hope."

"This will just be temporary, of course," said Corbett. "Until after the tournament. You will live at the smithy. There is a room in the back that you can occupy during your stay. That way you'll be closer when your services are needed during the tournament."

"Of course," said Jonathon, trying not to be disrespectful, but less than excited about this opportunity. He'd seen the forge at the castle. It was small and lacked much to be desired. "I'd have to bring along my tools, since I'm not sure your blacksmith possesses the supplies I'm used to having."

"I'll provide you with whatever you need," said Corbett. "That's not a problem."

"You'll have enough people to cover the work here in your absence?" asked Rook.

"I believe so, my lord." Jonathon started feeling anxious. He had planned on spending this slow time creating his masterpiece to present to the guild masters. It was a project that would determine if he was good enough to become a master and own his own shop. Now, this would put him far behind schedule. The guild masters would be at his door soon. If he wasn't ready, they wouldn't return again until next year. This was very disheartening. Still, he couldn't say no to a nobleman, and wasn't sure what to do. He supposed he could create his presentation piece at the castle forge, but it would be challenging since it was such a basic shop.

"Then it's settled," said Corbett. "You'll move into the smithy within the castle walls anon. And don't worry about the pay, I'll compensate you well. My blacksmith had an apprentice who will be there to help should you need it."

"Thank you. I don't mean to sound rude, but I'm used to my own apprentice and journeyman," he told him.

"Then you are welcome to bring yours over if you'd like. When the tournament starts, things will get busy." Corbett nodded in finality.

"Thank you, my lord." Jonathon bowed slightly. "Did you say you wanted to hire me for... another job as well?" he asked, only having heard of the one so far. "Or did you mean you wanted me to act as guard and smith both during the tournament?"

"Well, not exactly," said Corbett, clearing his throat and glancing over to Rook. "You see, I'd also like to hire you to be my daughter's guard until the tournament starts. Her personal guard, actually."

"Pardon me, my lord? Did you say... personal guard?" Jonathon was more confused than ever, and thought mayhap he'd misheard the man.

"The tournament is being held to find a husband for my sister," explained Rook.

"Really." If he wasn't so shocked to hear this, he might have chuckled aloud. There had to be a reason why the wench was twenty-two years old and still not married. He figured every nobleman in England must have heard of her bad reputation.

"The winner of the tournament gets her hand in marriage," said Corbett.

"I see," answered Jonathon, wondering if this was really a prize or just an answer to a problem. After all, no man wanted a woman who could outfight him.

Jonathon would never understand the way nobles did things. To him, marriage was sacred and entered into when two people fell in love. It was a lifetime commitment. Falling in love was something that had never happened to him personally, but he hoped it would someday. He'd been too hard at work to even court a woman properly. Nobles, on the other hand, often married for alliances. Or in this case, Lady Raven was to be naught but a prize. The idea disgusted him but he stayed silent since he had no right to question anything a noble decided. "I still don't understand how any of this involves me, or why Lady Raven requires a personal guard."

"We need you to watch over her. We're worried she might try something stupid," said Rook bluntly.

"Rook, please," growled Corbett. "What my son means is that we'd like someone to keep a close eye on her and report back to us if she is up to anything."

"Up to anything?" asked Jonathon. "Like what?"

"Anything not suited for a lady, and should I say, out of the ordinary," added Corbett. He exchanged worried glances with Rook.

Jonathon had heard of Lady Raven's escapades. She often used her sword to fight, and liked to challenge any man to spar with her. She rode astride, sometimes wearing trews instead of a gown, and acted more like a man than a lady. He pitied the poor man who got her as his bride. She'd probably wrestle him to the ground and sit on him every time he tried to speak. Or mayhap she'd slug him in the jaw or hold a blade to his throat if he criticized her hair or clothing. Jonathon felt anxiety course through him. He didn't fancy this job in the least.

What attracted Jonathon to a wench was femininity. He wanted a woman to look to him to support her and for her protection. Lady Raven, he was sure, would never want any man trying to protect her when she would rather do it herself. How could he ever be her personal guard? She wouldn't want him doing it, and she certainly didn't need it. It was already evident they wouldn't get along.

Nay, he really didn't want this job but couldn't risk anything happening that would turn Lord Corbett against him. The Blake family was Jonathon's biggest and best customer. He needed that to continue, especially now that his family was struggling. The last thing he wanted to do was to lose Lord Corbett's support.

"I must say, I am more than honored, and I respect you choosing me, my lords, even if I don't understand why you'd want me."

"We feel you are the perfect man for the job," said Rook.

"Actually, I am sure that I'm not the right man for the job at all. I am only a commoner. Shouldn't someone more respected, or possibly one of the castle soldiers have the job of guarding a noblewoman?" Jonathon tried to get out of this suicidal mission gracefully, but it wasn't working to sway them at all.

"No, no, we've already decided on you," insisted Corbett. "I've known you and your father for a long time, Jonathon. I trust you with this job more than even my own soldiers."

"Plus, we know you will tell us if my sister is doing something she shouldn't—which she always is," added Rook.

"But I–"

"The job pays well, and I'll even fund you to pay for another man at your shop here in town, should you need one in your absence."

"Thank you, my lord," said Jonathon with a slight bow. "If you don't mind, I'd like to bring my brother along with me to the castle while I serve as your temporary blacksmith. He is a journeyman here, but will be a valuable asset." His younger brother, Avery, always wanted to work at a castle. Plus, Jonathon wanted someone with him whom he could talk to freely about this troubling task. "His skills are amazing and he will be beneficial when the tournament starts."

"Fine, then. Bring him along. I'll pay to add another man to replace him in his absence as well," said Corbett.

"Thank you," said Jonathon, meaning for allowing his brother to join him, and for the temporary job as castle blacksmith. However, Lord Corbett seemed to think that meant that Jonathon had agreed to the other job involving Lady Raven as well.

"Good. It's settled then," said Corbett. "I'll expect you to move into the smithy in the next day or two. Finalize plans here, and report to my son as soon as you arrive. He'll instruct you as to what's required of you, pertaining to guarding my daughter each day, all day long."

"Your daughter," repeated Jonathon, wanting to hit himself in the head for being so careless. Now that Lord Corbett had been so generous with him, how could he disappoint him by telling him he wanted nothing to do with the castle shrew?

"After the tournament, you'll be free to go," said Rook. "After all, Raven will then be her new husband's problem, not yours anymore." Once more he received a nasty glance from Corbett.

Jonathon was in a bind. The last thing he wanted

was to be reporting Lady Raven's doings to anyone. If she got word of it, she'd probably physically hurt him. On the other hand, she was a beautiful woman and it would be exciting to be with her all day long. Perhaps this wouldn't be as bad as he thought. He also no longer had a choice... he had to accept the job.

"Will I be able to work in the forge at night?" he asked. "I have a very important project to plan and will need time to do it."

"Yes," said Corbett. "That's fine. Lady Raven isn't allowed outside the castle walls at night, and I'll be seeing to her then. You will only need to keep watch over her during the daytime hours. The night is yours to work in the forge."

"I see." Jonathon was at a loss for words, thinking this was all a little odd.

"While you're at the castle, you are welcome to eat and drink all you want," said Rook.

"That's right," agreed Corbett. "You are also allowed to use your weapons in the practice yard, and spar with the knights or other soldiers, including myself and my son. Your brother is invited to join in these opportunities, too."

"My lords, that is too generous of you," said Jonathon, knowing he'd never get a chance like this again. Avery would be excited to hear this, and probably never stop thanking Jonathon for suggesting him. This would be a good opportunity for both of them. Jonathon wanted to polish his fighting skills, but none of the commoners were a match for him. To be welcomed in, fed, and given the grand treatment is something that usually didn't happen to someone like him—a mere commoner. Perhaps, he decided, he could put up with the troublesome wench for a few weeks after all. At least he'd get his foot in the door, and hopefully impress Lord Corbett with his skills. With any luck at all, mayhap he would even be offered a permanent position at the castle someday. It would be a good secondary plan should he not get accepted as guild master and have the opportunity to open his own shop. He was sure the pay and opportunities of working at the castle would be grand, even if owning his own shop was his dream.

"Then it's finalized," said Corbett, holding out his hand to shake on the deal.

Jonathon looked from Rook to Corbett once more, and nodded. "Of course, thank you, my lords," he said, shaking first Corbett's hand and then Rook's, feeling like a king, since nobles didn't usually make deals or shake hands with commoners. "I mean, after all, how much trouble could one girl possibly be?"

"You'd be surprised," mumbled Rook, as they headed for the door.

"Oh, I almost forgot," said Corbett, turning back around. "I don't want Lady Raven, or my wife, or anyone else to know why you are really there or what you've been hired to do."

"So... I'm just going to follow Lady Raven around, and she won't wonder why?" asked Jonathon.

"Of course she will, and she's going to hate it," said Rook with a chuckle.

"Then, what will I tell her?" asked Jonathon, feeling suddenly panicked. "What am I going to say as an excuse to be near her?"

"You're right, that won't work. I'll just have to tell her you're there as her personal guard for security purposes, and not to give you any trouble," said Corbett, following Rook out the door. "Hopefully, having a guard at her side all day long will fix our little problem."

Jonathon stood there with his mouth hanging open, watching the Lords Blake mount their horses and ride away.

"Jonathon?" came his father's voice as he hobbled down the stairs. "Is that the Lords Blake riding away? Were they just here?"

"Aye, Father," Jonathon answered, still staring out the window in a daze.

"Well, what did they want?" He looked around the room. "I don't see that they left any of their armor to be repaired."

"It's not armor they want me to fix this time." Jonathon turned around and headed back to the forge. Now, even the blazing flames from inside the hearth seemed mild, compared to what he was about to face.

"If not, then what do they want you to fix?" asked his father, following him.

Jonathon picked up the hammer and slammed it down against the anvil, making a loud clanking sound that rang out through the room.

"I've just agreed to a job that I honestly wish I hadn't."

"I don't understand." His father came closer, cocking his head and squinting one eye.

"Let's just put it this way," said Jonathon, not wanting to break his promise of not telling anyone about the real reason. "The Lords Blake want me to fix something that is most likely too damaged to ever be repaired."

CHAPTER 3

Two days later, Raven awoke to a knock at her solar door. Usually, she was up early to work with her weapons before any of the men got to the practice yard, but she was too distraught lately even to do that. After the chastising she received from her father and brother, she was rebelling in her own way. She barely spoke to them, and decided she wouldn't even show up in the great hall this morning to break the fast.

"Who is it?" she mumbled, pushing up in bed and looking over at the door. The slight stream of light coming into the room from the crack in the shutter told her it was probably already late morning.

The door swung open and her handmaid, Emma, hurried into the room, followed by someone else. It was too dark to see who it was. Raven rubbed her sleepy eyes, yawned, and lay back down.

"Lady Raven, your father sent me up here to wake you," announced the handmaid.

"I told my father I don't want or need a handmaid," she answered, yawning again and turning over and closing her eyes.

"I'm sorry, but I am only doing my job." Emma opened the shutter. Bright light filled the room. Even with her eyes closed, Raven could tell. "You missed the meal in the great hall and your mother is worried that you might be sick."

"I am," she said, with her eyes still closed. "Sick and tired of being told what to do."

"Cousin, ye are a lazy oaf—now get up and start yer day." The covers were ripped off of her and a chill traveled through her body. Raven's eyes popped open, a smile crossing her face.

"Lark? Lark! What are you doing here?" Raven bolted to an upright position, giving her Scottish cousin a big hug.

While Raven was the daughter of the English lord Corbett Blake, Lark was the daughter of Corbett's sister, Wren. Wren married a Highlander named Storm MacKeefe. The MacKeefes were known to be crazy at times, and even called madmen on occasion. Storm and his clan proved that was true by their actions.

"I traveled here to help ye prepare yerself for yer upcomin' weddin'." Lark scooted onto the bed next to Raven, leaning back next to her.

"How did you even know about it?" asked Raven.

"Yer father told mine a week ago."

"A week ago?" she gasped. "I only found out about it two days ago. Why am I not surprised I'm the last to know?" Raven flopped down on her back and threw her arm over her face. "Well, your trip was for naught because I'm not getting married."

"Ye dinna have a choice," Lark told her. "No lassie ever does."

"Don't remind me." Raven sat up, leaning her

back against the wall that was directly behind the bed.

Emma emerged from the wardrobe, carrying one of Raven's best gowns over her arm. Emma was young, probably a few years younger than Raven. She'd just married another servant last year. "I think this is a good gown for you to wear today, my lady." It was a purple velvet gown with gold buttons up the bodice. Long white tippets made from a sheer material hung down to the ground, almost dragging on the floor since Emma was very short.

"Nay, not that one," said Raven, with a quick shake of her head.

That's one of my best gowns, Emma. Put it back. There is no need for me to wear it. It's for special occasions only."

"Lord Corbett insists that you must look nice today, my lady," protested the handmaid.

"Whatever for?" Raven yawned without covering her mouth.

"There are two lords in the solar waiting to meet you," Emma informed her.

"What?" Raven's head snapped around to face her handmaid. "Well, who are they? Why are they here?"

"I'm not sure," Emma answered timidly. She always seemed to pull back and become shy when Raven got upset. "All I know is that I'm supposed to make sure you look your best when you meet them."

"I think they are potential suitors," said Lark. "Actually, when I arrived here this mornin' with my father, he recognized them."

"He did? Are they Scottish?" asked Raven, feeling her heart pounding rapidly in her chest.

"Nay, they are both English," said Lark. "I heard

34

yer father tellin' mine that they are both single and will be competin' for yer hand in marriage at the tournament. Mayhap they want to meet ye ahead of time."

"Hrmph," she sniffed. "To see what they're getting, I suppose." Raven's anger grew. She wouldn't be put on display for anyone.

"Please, Lady Raven, you really need to dress now," begged Emma. "If you don't, I might be blamed for it." A frown turned down the corners of her mouth. "I need this job. Especially now." The handmaid's gaze dropped to the ground.

"Emma? What is it?" Raven slid off the bed and hurried over to her handmaid. "Something is troubling you, I can tell. What's wrong?"

"It's nothing, my lady. Not really. It's just that, I'm not sure how long Lord Corbett will let me keep my job... in my condition and all."

"Condition? What condition?" Raven had no idea what the girl meant.

"I ken what she means," said Lark excitedly, running over to join them. "Emma, ye're bairned, are ye no'?"

"Oh! You're pregnant?" Raven asked the girl in surprise.

"I am, my lady." A glow colored the handmaid's round cheeks. Instantly, her frown turned back into a smile. "My husband and I are expecting a baby." She put her free hand on her belly.

"We're so happy for ye," Lark told her, smiling and reaching out to hold the girl's hand.

"Aye, we are," agreed Raven, even though having a baby wasn't anything that excited her. Raven didn't particularly want children. Then again, neither did she want a husband. All she wanted was to make her own choices and practice with her weapons. What she'd really love was to be able to use her skills in a competition someday. That was naught but a dream because women were not allowed to do so. "You don't even look pregnant, Emma. Not really." Raven's eyes traveled down to the girl's waist. "Well, mayhap just a little."

"I will look very pregnant soon," said the girl with a giggle, putting both her hands on her belly and curving them out in a large circle.

"Emma, we dinna want ye to get in trouble. Do we, Raven?" Lark took the gown from the girl. "I'll help Raven dress. Now that I'm here, it'll allow ye more time to rest, Emma."

"Nay!" Emma's eyes opened wide in fear. "This is my job. I am not supposed to be resting." She reached out for the gown, but Lark held onto it.

"Emma, it's fine." Raven put her hand on the girl's shoulder. "I'd like to spend time with my cousin during her visit, so you are not needed."

"I'm not?" The handmaid looked terrified, thinking she was being let go.

"What my daft cousin means is that she doesna need help dressin' since I am here." Lark explained, putting the gown down on the bed. "However, she missed the mornin' meal, so she will need ye to go to the kitchen and prepare her somethin' to eat."

"Nay, I'm fine. I'm not hungry," said Raven, getting a stern look from Lark in return. "I mean... yes, that is what I need. Now hurry along, Emma," she said, escorting the girl to the door. Lark followed. "We'll meet you in the kitchen shortly."

"If you're sure, my lady." The handmaid still seemed as if she didn't want to go.

Raven realized the girl wouldn't be in any hurry to leave until Raven put her mind at ease. "I'll be sure to speak to my father. Don't worry. I promise you won't be in any trouble and neither will you lose your job when you have the baby. You can help in the kitchen until my cousin goes back to Scotland."

"Thank you, Lady Raven." Emma curtsied, smiling from ear to ear before turning and running out the door. Raven slowly closed the door behind her.

"Now, see?" asked Lark with a knowing smile. "That wasna hard, to put the lass's mind at ease and make her stop worryin', was it?"

"Plus, it got rid of her so we can talk in private." Raven giggled, grabbing Lark's hand and running and plopping down on the bed, pulling Lark along with her. "Tell me everything that's been happening in Scotland. It's been so long since I've seen you."

"I've missed ye, Raven. Things have happened. Bad things," she said, her smile fading.

"Bad? Oh, nay. What? Tell me." She held Lark's hand in both of hers. "Florie isn't ill, is she?" asked Raven, speaking of Lark's four-year-old daughter. "Where is she? Did she travel here with you?"

"Nay, Florie is in Scotland with my parents and she is fine. It's... it's Gregoire, I'm talking about."

"Oh, your husband. I see. Oh my. Did he die fighting in France?"

Lark had become pregnant with the Frenchman's baby when the French aligned with the Scottish for a spell, when she was only sixteen. She had discovered she was pregnant only after the man returned to

France. They'd had correspondence, but he never came back. In respect to her cousin, Raven referred to the man as Lark's husband, even though she wasn't married and the child was a bastard.

"Nay, Gregoire didna die but I wish he had," spat Lark, tears filling her eyes.

"Lark? What is it?" asked Raven, feeling her heart go out to her cousin. Something awful must have happened to upset the girl like this. Lark had always been so cool and calm until now.

"He's... he's married, Raven," she said, sniffing and wiping a tear from her eye.

"He married someone else when he knew you had birthed his child? How awful."

"Nay," protested Lark. "Ye dinna understand." She did her best to hold back the tears. "He was always married, and never intended to return for me or his daughter. He used me, Raven. I hate the man and never want to see him again."

"Oh, I'm so sorry." Raven held the girl in a hug as Lark wept softly on her shoulder. "So, is that the reason you're here? You didn't want Florie to see you so upset?"

Lark pulled back and looked up to Raven with watery green eyes. Tears dripped down her cheeks. Such a kindhearted girl who wouldn't raise a finger to hurt anyone should never be treated so badly. She didn't deserve this awful twist life had handed her. Raven reached out and wiped a tear from Lark's cheek.

"Aye, that's part of it," said Lark. "I also heard of yer upcomin' weddin' and decided I had to be here for ye."

"It seems everyone knew about this but me," Raven answered with a sigh. "Well, even if I'm not really getting married, at least the time away from your clan will do you good." Raven got up and walked over to a trunk, pulling out an oversized tunic and a pair of trews. "This will do. I'll get dressed and we'll make our way to the kitchen to see if the cook has prepared any pie this morning. That should make us both feel better."

"Nay." Lark jumped off the bed. "Ye canna wear that, Raven! Those are the clothes of a boy."

Raven chuckled. "They most certainly are. They are some of Rook's old clothes. I saved them because it's easier for me to practice with my weapons if I'm wearing a tunic and trews and not encumbered by a long gown and tippets tangling around me with every swipe of my blade."

"Yer father is goin' to kill ye," gasped Lark.

Lark was usually an obedient girl, never doing a thing wrong. That is, except for her brief encounter with the lusty Frenchman. That one act of passion ruined Lark's reputation forever. Even if she wanted to be married now, no man would ever want her. She had spoiled herself and tied herself down with a bastard child.

"I don't care what my father thinks. I don't want these noblemen to want me. I have to scare them off somehow." Raven continued to dress, attaching her weapon belt that held her sword and dagger.

"Nay, Cousin. Dinna do it. Ye should be thankful of what ye have. I only wish I could catch the eye of a nobleman."

"I don't want those curs looking at me at all." Raven pulled on a pair of boots and stomped over to the mirror, dragging a brush through her long hair.

"I would give anythin' to have a respectful nobleman look at me in any way besides disgust. Dinna ruin this chance, Raven. Ye have the opportunity to marry well and be rich and respected. Ye have everythin' to look forward to, so dinna do somethin' that ye'll regret someday. Like I did." She frowned and looked at the floor.

"Oh, Lark. If I could, I'd change places with you in a minute. You are welcome to any of the noblemen who want me for their bride, because I don't want a one of them."

"If only it were that easy."

"Come." Raven placed the boar bristle brush down on the dressing table. "Let's go have some fun." She took her cousin's hand and dragged her toward the door.

"I'm no' sure I like the sound of this, Raven. What are ye goin' to do?"

"I'm not sure yet," said Raven with a smile. "However, I assure you it'll be whatever it takes to make every eligible nobleman run the other way."

CHAPTER 4

"Is it really necessary that I wear this?" Jonathon stood with Rook in the castle's guardhouse, staring down at the clothes that Rook insisted he wear. They were the clothes of a castle guard. The tunic depicted the Blake crest of a silvery-white eagle with wings and talons spread and ready for attack, emblazoned over an azure field. He wore a pair of breeches that came down just below the knee with hose underneath. His feet were clad in leather boots. Over his shoulders was a long cloak made of black silk. At least he was able to wear his own weapon belt that included his sword and dagger that he'd constructed himself. Still, it all felt too pretentious. He wasn't really a castle guard. He was naught but an armorer, and a mercenary at times.

"Aye, it's necessary," insisted Rook, handing him a metal helm.

"The helm too?" Jonathon shook his head, not wanting to put it on. "I'm not fighting the enemy here, I'm just guarding your sister. Is this really necessary?"

"All right, forget the helm." Rook took it back and

threw it down with a loud clank. "But you need to look the part of a respectable guard if my sister is going to treat you as anything but a mere commoner."

"I see." Jonathon fidgeted with his clothes, trying to make them fit better. They felt too tight and were uncomfortable. He was used to working in the forge wearing very little—sometimes even going bare-chested, if he knew he wouldn't have customers that day. This wasn't him at all. It was much too constrict-ing. "So, do you really believe she is going to let me close to her?" he asked.

There was one other guard in the armory. Rook waited until the man left before he answered. He cleared his throat. "Actually, I discussed this with my father because I felt it would create a problem calling you her personal guard. I suggested we only tell her that you're a new guard here and will be working as security for the tournament. She'll accept that easier."

"She'll still wonder why I'm following her around." Jonathon reached back, tugging at his tunic.

"I thought of that, too. I think I'll tell Raven that she's to show you around the castle so you can devise ways to make it safer during the tournament."

"Why would she believe that? I'm not one of your father's normal soldiers, and neither am I titled. Plus, I'm only temporary. It seems far-fetched for even me to believe."

"Aye." Rook nodded. "You're right. Raven is smart. She'd never fall for it." He let out a deep breath. "Well, I guess we're back to plan one. We're just going to have to tell her the truth."

"The truth?" asked Jonathon, thinking that was

the worst idea of all. "We're going to tell her that I'm reporting all her doings back to you and Lord Corbett?"

"Nay, not that much truth." Rook looked over his shoulder to make sure no one heard. "And keep your voice down. These walls have ears."

"Well, what is the story?" asked Jonathon, already regretting he'd agreed to this lame task. Certainly with all these plans flying around he was going to somehow get tripped up.

"I've got it," said Rook, snapping his fingers. "You've had inside information that there is a man planning on abducting my sister since he wants her for himself."

"What? That's absurd," said Jonathon. "Besides, don't you think Lady Raven could defend herself? I certainly do."

"She's going to get a personal guard, or should I say *chaperone*, whether she wants one or not," said Rook with a frown. "We can't have her acting so reckless. You need to make it seem like she needs you."

"Me? How?" he asked, shaking his head.

"I don't know." Rook shrugged. "Just make it sound as if you're keeping her from danger, even though you're not."

This didn't sit well with Jonathon. "I assure you, I can protect her, my lord—that is not the problem." Jonathon didn't like the insinuation that he couldn't protect a woman when he was more than capable. "I know how to fight and I'm damned proud of it. I assure you, I won't let anyone harm her, even though there is no danger of that."

"Good, good, you're starting to sound believable," said Rook with a chuckle, looking over his shoulder again as two knights entered the armory. "Now, let me introduce you to some of the knights of Blake Castle." He was about to do just that when Jonathon stepped in front of him and greeted the knights himself.

"Sir Henry, Sir Robert, how are you today?" he asked with a bow.

"Jonathon? Is that you under those clothes?" asked Sir Henry with a smile.

"It is him," said Sir Robert, taking a closer look. "Jonathon, I've been meaning to stop by your shop and tell you what a fine job you did on repairing my armor."

"Thank you," said Jonathon with a nod. "I am glad that you approve of my work."

"While you're here, mayhap you can fix the hilt on my dagger. It's come loose," said Sir Henry, handing it to him.

"Of course," said Jonathon, taking it, turning it in his hands to inspect it.

"Nay. Not now," said Rook, stepping in and taking the dagger from Jonathon, returning it to Sir Henry. "Jonathon has been hired as an extra guard for the tournament," said Rook. "If you want him to fix anything, you'll have to wait until nighttime. He's also our temporary blacksmith and will be living here for a while."

"If you've been hired for the tournament, why are you here so soon?" questioned Sir Henry.

"Aye. The tournament isn't for another few weeks yet," pointed out Sir Robert.

"I'm here because... because..." Jonathon looked over to Rook, not able to bring himself to tell the knights he was here to watch over a woman who obviously didn't need his protection.

"Besides being the castle smith, Jonathon is also here as Lady Raven's personal guard," Rook blurted out, causing Jonathon to cringe. Just hearing him say it aloud sounded ridiculous. It didn't sound true or even remotely believable.

The knights looked at each other and burst out laughing.

"Nay, really," said Sir Henry. "Why are you here so early?"

"What's so funny?" asked Rook.

Jonathon felt as if they were laughing at him.

"No disrespect, my lord," said Sir Robert. "But everyone knows that Lady Raven doesn't need a-a personal guard, and will probably kill him." They both laughed again.

"Aye, it's more likely that Jonathon will end up needing a personal guard to protect himself from her," added Henry.

"Is this the way knights usually talk about their overlord's daughter?" asked Jonathon, not liking the way the men were acting. Belittling him since he was a commoner was expected. Bad-mouthing a noblewoman was downright rude. Especially since she was the daughter of their overlord.

"Nay, it isn't if they want to keep their positions and titles," said Rook in a low warning voice to the men.

"We're sorry, my lord." Henry bowed and Robert followed suit.

"We didn't mean anything by it. Please forgive us," said Robert.

"You're forgiven and dismissed," said Rook with a wave of his hand, sending the men away.

When Jonathon realized that the knights weren't going to be reprimanded or punished, that told him that Rook most likely jested about his sister with the knights in private on more than one occasion now. The whole thing disgusted Jonathon.

"Here," said Rook, shoving a pouch of coins into Jonathon's hand.

"What's this?" asked Jonathon, feeling the weight of the pouch. "I thought I wouldn't be paid in full until the end of my assignment."

"Consider it a bonus." Rook looked off in the opposite direction.

"For keeping my mouth shut about what I've just witnessed?" Jonathon probably shouldn't have said that, but he still felt infuriated about the knights' conduct and the fact Rook did nothing to reprimand them and stick up for his sister.

Rook's head snapped around. "You have to understand that my sister isn't always the easiest person to get along with, and she's very rebellious. It's no secret. Everyone knows it," he said in a low voice. "She's not like other ladies. It's best that you keep your eyes open and your mouth shut if you want things to go smoothly while you're here."

"I understand." Jonathon tested the weight of the pouch in his hands, knowing it was at least a guard's salary for a month. "I'll respect your wishes, my lord, but I won't take money to keep quiet about anyone speaking ill of Lady Raven." He pushed the pouch back into Rook's hand. "No matter how different your sister is, she still deserves the respect of a lady. From everyone, not just the knights." He was referring to

Rook, but didn't think it was wise to come out and say it aloud. Instead, he turned and started to walk out the door. He was certain he'd made his point clear and just hoped Rook wouldn't have his head for saying it.

"Jonathon, you haven't been dismissed yet," said Rook, stopping Jonathon in his tracks.

"I'm sorry, my lord." He turned to face Rook. "By your leave, then?"

"Aye. Of course," said Rook with a nod. "But first, I want to say it's a damned shame."

"My lord?"

"You're the first man I've ever heard defend my sister. I'll admit, it's not always an easy thing to do. I'm afraid I've been caught up in the gossip for so long that I've been pulled into the abyss along with them, without even realizing it. Thank you for subtly pointing this out to me. It is admirable that you defend her, if only with your words."

"It's my job to protect her now. In every way," said Jonathon.

"I want you to take this." He tossed the pouch to Jonathon who caught it.

"Nay." Jonathon's eyes focused on the pouch of coins. It was enough to feed his family for months. Still, it felt rather like blood money. "I'd rather not, my lord."

"I insist. It's not for keeping quiet, if that's what you're thinking," said Rook. "It's to keep others in their place if you hear them speaking badly about my sister again. Like you did just now."

"Me?" This caused him more alarm than hearing knights slander a lady. There was no way he wanted to be put in this position. "Nay, I'm afraid I can't. I have no right to tell a noble anything, my lord. I'm only a commoner, in case you've forgotten."

"I haven't forgotten. But yes, you're right, that wouldn't be appropriate, I suppose. Instead, you will report illicit behavior of the knights and soldiers directly to me or to my father. In private, of course."

"Of course," he said, not liking that idea either. Most of the nobles were his customers, and some of them even his friends. "Is that everything, my lord?" Jonathon was eager to get out of here and into the fresh air. It didn't feel good being confined, and he was extremely uncomfortable wearing these clothes.

"That's it," Rook answered. "However, I will say, Jonathon Armstrong, that it's a damned shame you are just a commoner. Because, if you were a nobleman, I think you'd make a good husband for my sister."

~

Raven had just entered the kitchen with Lark when she saw her brother and a guard enter the room and head over toward them.

"Raven," called out Rook, with his hand raised in the air. "I need to talk to you, anon."

"Whatever for?" Raven snatched a hunk of bread off a platter that her handmaid held out to her. "I don't have anything to say to you, Rook, so please leave me alone." She ripped off some bread with her teeth and chewed.

"Raven, I—" Rook stopped in front of her, looking her up and down. "What in bloody hell are you wearing?"

"Clothes, Brother. Why?" She smiled and continued to chew.

Lark watched silently while Emma put the tray down on a table and poured wine into goblets.

"Hello, Lark," said Rook with a nod, as he acknowledged his Scottish cousin. "I saw your father earlier and he told me you are here to help Raven prepare for her wedding. That is nice of you to do so."

"I'm not getting married," interrupted Raven before Lark could even respond. She reached over and snatched up a goblet, downing all the wine at once. Over the rim of her cup she noticed the guard watching her intently. She didn't recognize him, nor did she like him staring at her that way.

"Hello, Rook," said Lark, moving closer. "Yes, I am here to assist Raven."

"Then why in God's name did you let her leave her chamber looking like a scullery boy?" growled Rook.

"Don't blame Lark, it's not her fault." Raven slammed down the empty goblet and plucked a sweetmeat off the tray next. She held it pinched in her fingers as she spoke. "Lark wanted me to wear one of my best gowns, but I didn't see the need for it."

"Didn't see the need?" asked Rook. He turned to the guard and spoke under his breath. "She didn't see the need to look like a lady instead of a beggar? And on the day when Father is introducing potential suitors to her. See what I mean?"

Raven glared at her brother, shocked he'd be consulting with a mere guard about her behavior. She didn't like it at all.

"My lord, forgive me for speaking so freely, but I don't think Lady Raven looks at all like a beggar," said the guard. Raven popped the whole sweetmeat into her mouth, wondering if the guard was only saying this because he feared her wrath. "Perhaps she has something else to do that requires more... conventional clothing than a cumbersome gown," suggested the man, seeming to be defending her choice of apparel for some odd reason. While she appreciated the man sticking out his neck for her, it was really not the proper way to be talking to a lord. Even if it was just her brother.

"Who are you? You're not one of the castle guards," said Raven, swallowing down the food and licking her lips. She noticed the guard's eyes flick down to her mouth. He shifted from foot to foot, while his hand played with his weapon belt.

"I-I'm Jonathon. Jonathon Armstrong, my lady," he answered. He looked away as soon as he'd told her his name, almost as if he wasn't proud of it.

"Armstrong, Armstrong," she repeated, thinking about it for a moment. Where had she heard that name before? "Oh, now I remember you," said Raven. "You're that armorer from town. Don't you sometimes hire out your sword to my father?"

He looked directly at her this time. "Aye, my lady. That's me," he said softly.

"You're a damn mercenary! You would sell your own mother for money, or slit anyone's throat if you were paid enough. Why are you dressed in the clothes of a castle guard and wearing my family's crest? You're not allowed to wear those things, so take them off. You are naught but a fake, a phony. A simpleminded commoner."

Jonathon's jaw dropped. He wasn't sure how to respond to that! He saw now what Rook was talking about, and already regretted defending the shrew earlier. He'd never had anyone say such horrible things about him, and even talking about his mother. Plus, she called him a fake and a phony. Even if he had been called a simple commoner by the nobles more times than he could count, none of them had ever referred to him as simple-minded. Jonathon was ready to turn around and leave. He didn't ask to be here, and it wasn't his idea to dress this way. He might just be a commoner dressed like a castle guard, but she had no right degrading him like this in front of everyone.

Or mayhap she did, since she was a noble.

"Raven, that was no' nice," scolded Lark under her breath. Even the Scottish girl knew this was inappropriate behavior.

This job was already souring his disposition. Jonathon would rather be sweating to death over a hot forge, pounding out his frustrations with a hammer on an anvil, than to be standing here silently right now taking this. He felt suffocated in this attire, and it was getting harder to hold in his true feelings, being verbally attacked. Biting his tongue to keep himself from responding to her was almost more than he could take.

"Raven, stop it," warned Rook, coming to his aid now. "That kind of talk to anyone will not be tolerated here."

"Brother, don't chastise me."

"Father has hired Jonathon," Rook explained. "He's here for security reasons, and knows how to fight. I thought it would be better if he dressed that way, so he has my permission to do so."

"Oh. He's here for the tournament then." She

crossed her arms over her chest and eyed him up and down. "That's not for another three weeks yet," she told Jonathon straight on. "I'd suggest you go home to your little shop, Mr. Armstrong, and come back when you're really needed."

"I was told I'm needed now, my lady," Jonathon answered, trying his best to keep from giving her a piece of his mind.

"Now?" She laughed and looked over toward her cousin Lark. "He must think the horses or goats are in danger and need protection." She chuckled. "Come, Lark. I'm going to the practice yard where I can do something productive instead of wasting my time with this nonsense."

She started to leave, but Rook reached out and stopped her by grabbing her arm. "Nay, Raven. Father and two noblemen are waiting for you in the great hall. You'll need to change quickly and go greet them as is expected of you."

"I will not," she retorted. "I don't care what is considered proper, I'm not going anywhere but to the practice yard, and that is final." Jonathon noticed her hand lower to the hilt of her sword as if she were wanting to thrust it at someone—probably him or her brother.

"Nay, you won't. Jonathon will escort you back to your chamber to change and then to the great hall for the meeting," said Rook. "Now, hurry."

"Jonathon will escort me?" Her forehead creased and her brows dipped. She chuckled as if she were completely amused. "Why on earth would I go anywhere with the likes of him? Besides, no guard, and especially not a commoner *pretending* to be a guard, is allowed anywhere near my chamber."

"Raven, he's been hired as more than security for the tournament," Rook told her with a sigh, looking suddenly uncomfortable.

"Really?" She glanced over at her brother in a quizzical manner. "Oh, I understand. You brought him here early to fix and clean all the knights' armor to prepare for the upcoming joust. Good idea."

"True, I am also the temporary castle blacksmith, but nay, that is not what your brother is referring to, my lady," Jonathon answered before Rook could reply.

"No? Then tell me what in the name of the devil you two are talking about, since none of this makes a bit of sense," she said in frustration.

Jonathon couldn't play this addled game any longer. He needed to come out and just tell her the truth. Or most of it, leaving out the part of him spying on her, of course.

"I'm your... I'm your... personal guard," explained Jonathon, holding his breath, waiting for the girl to explode.

"My... *personal guard*?" She looked back at Lark again and started laughing. Lark remained quiet and didn't even smile. "Surely you jest. I'm sure you wouldn't even know how to protect me if someone did this to me." In one motion, she drew her dagger from her side, bringing the sharp edge up toward his neck.

Jonathon's reactions were instinctive. He didn't need a weapon to stop her. He grabbed her hand and twisted her wrist, pulling her body backwards and up against his. Her dagger went clattering to the floor as he pried it from her fingers.

"Let go of me!" she yelled, struggling in his hold,

trying to elbow him in the ribs but Jonathon held her tightly, not giving her the chance.

"Watch your feet," mumbled Rook just as Raven's foot swept out, meaning to knock Jonathon to the ground.

Jonathon released her quickly, and took a step backwards. Her foot missed him. However, the action set her off balance.

"My lady," he cried, as she started to fall. He grabbed for her, and when he did, she reached back and pulled him along with her. Jonathon had been fooled. He tried to keep her from getting hurt, and because of it, they both fell prone on the floor. He landed on top of her, trapping her body beneath his. Rook burst out laughing, while Lark gasped and held a hand over her mouth.

"This isn't funny!" spat Raven. "Get off of me, you fool." She pushed her hands against his chest.

Jonathon looked down at Raven and lifted up his chest so he wouldn't smash her with his weight. His long hair made a tent around their faces. This close up he could see Lady Raven better than he ever had before. She had beautiful silver eyes that sparkled with tiny flecks of gold. They looked almost birdlike, and magical, even though she was angrier than hell. Her thick, long black lashes curled upward like a flower opening to the sun. She blinked twice in succession. Surprisingly, she stilled long enough to look directly at him. Their gazes interlocked. For Jonathon, time momentarily stood still. He felt as if he were looking into the eyes of an angel. That is, a rebellious, defiant angel.

The girl's cheeks were flushed and her mouth, even though it was pursed, looked like a little bow, and ever so beautiful to him. Her cute little turned-up nose made her seem more like a kitten than the fierce lion she was trying to portray.

"Did you h-hear me?" she asked, breathing heavily, which only made the swells of her breasts move up and down beneath him. The oversized tunic had fallen to one side and he couldn't help but notice her cleavage showing. As his eyes roamed over to it, he breathed in her sweet, exotic scent. She smelled like lilacs or wildflowers on a warm summer's day.

Her long ebony tresses were loose instead of braided or hidden beneath a wimple. A few curly ringlets framed her heart-shaped face, while the rest fell around her shoulders like water cascading down a mountain. She was very enticing this close up, and not frightening in the least. The wench was actually alluring. When she wasn't fighting or chastising him, she almost seemed like a real lady. His eyes went to her lips that were so close to his that all he had to do was lean forward and he'd be able to kiss her.

Jonathon shook his head trying to clear away these crazy thoughts or they would only get him in trouble. Right now he was tempted to kiss the wench, when a moment ago he hated her. What sort of witchery did this girl hold over his thoughts and desires? A commoner just thinking of kissing a noble-woman could land them in the dungeon.

"Raven, are you all right?" Lark ran to her aid, followed by Rook.

"Get up, Sister. The game is over," spat Rook. "Father is waiting for you."

"I would move if my so-called personal guard would get off of me and stop hovering over me and staring at me like a wolf in sheep's clothing about ready to eat me," she ground out.

Jonathon sprang to his feet, feeling embarrassed and as if he'd voiced his desire aloud to kiss her. God, he hoped no one had noticed the way he was staring at her. His unspoken actions just violated a titled lady! It wasn't right. He did feel a little like a wolf on the prowl, and it disgusted him. Now this is the way she saw him, when it is not at all what he'd intended. This job just became so much harder.

"Come, Raven." Rook reached down and pulled his sister to her feet. "Whether or not you're going to change your clothes before you go to the great hall, I no longer care. Just go and meet with the nobles. You'll make a spectacle of yourself in front of them, and you'll have to live with the gossip as well as deal with Father's wrath, but that is your choice."

"I'm sorry, my lady," Jonathon apologized. "I didn't mean to... to hurt you."

"Hurt me?" she asked in confusion, and then smiled. "Ha! You can't hurt me," she told him, brushing off her clothes.

"Please, allow me to escort you to the great hall." Jonathon fixed his clothing and ran a hand through his tangled hair. "I'm sure your father is eager to find a suitable man for you to marry."

Raven looked up at him and their eyes interlocked once more. It was only for a brief moment, but damned if he didn't see desire in those enchanting silver orbs. Could she be looking at him with intent, the same way he'd been looking at her just moments ago? Was it too bold of him to even imagine it was so?

"Stop staring at me," she retorted, her brash words wiping any fool thought from his head.

It might be desire he saw in her eyes, but it certainly wasn't desire to kiss him. Nay, he was sure what she wanted was probably to punch him instead.

"I'm sorry, my lady," he apologized once more. "I didn't realize I was staring." He lowered his head in respect and held out his arm to escort her. She looked at him and made a face as if she'd smelled something foul.

"Nay. I'll meet you in great hall. Let's go, Lark," she said to her cousin as she headed for the door.

"Raven, you can't leave Jonathon," Rook called out. "He was hired to be at your side every minute of the day."

She stopped in the doorway and turned around. "Every minute? Nay! I'm going to my chamber to change my clothes, and he is not coming with me."

"I thought you didn't care about how you looked," said Rook. "Why bother changing?"

"Well, mayhap I've changed my mind. After all, it is no one's decision but mine what I wear." She stormed out the door with Lark on her heels.

Rook let out a sigh and shook his head. "This isn't going to be easy, Jonathon, and I don't envy you in the least. Watching over my sister is not unlike trying to catch and tame a wildcat without having a trap or even a proper cage."

"Aye, in many ways she is much like a wildcat, I suppose." Jonathon's gaze traveled to where Raven had just been standing. He found himself wondering once again what it would feel like to kiss her. "I'm not worried about it," he told Rook. "Not really."

"You're not? How can you say that?"

"I happen to like wildcats," he answered with a smile, realizing his job would now include taming a shrew. "Now, if you had compared her to a badger, then I'd be concerned. I cornered one of those in the woods once, and it wasn't a pretty outcome at all."

Rook chuckled. "Either way, you are going to earn every coin we pay you, and I can't say it'll be enough."

"It's not a problem, my lord. I like a challenge," Jonathon answered with a nod, not able to stop thinking how Raven's body felt beneath his. It had been a while since he'd taken a wench to his bed. And even though he'd never attempt bedding a lady, catching one's interest was going to be enough to satisfy him for a long time.

He now wanted that desire he saw in Lady Raven's eyes to change, and he'd do anything to make it happen. Then, the next time he looked into her eyes, he would hopefully see her desire turn from loathe to lust. If he could do that with a woman like Raven, he would feel like he'd accomplished the impossible.

And *impossible* was not a word that had any place in Jonathon's life.

CHAPTER 5

"Och, Raven, I'm so glad ye decided to dress like a lady after all." Lark followed Raven into the bedchamber and closed the door behind her. "Ye always need to look yer best and to act like a proper lady if ye're goin' to catch a nobleman's eye."

"I assure you, I don't care about catching any nobleman's eye." Raven walked over to the bed where they'd left her fancy purple gown. She pulled off her tunic, up over her head, throwing it on the bed. Then she kicked off her boots and removed her trews.

"If no', then why are you changin' yer clothes as if ye do care?" Lark helped her to don her gown.

"I just feel like it, that's all." Raven pulled the gown down and laced up the bodice. "Lark, will you help me to plait my hair really quick?" she asked, thinking about the way Jonathon's hair had felt brushing against her cheek. It was soft and smooth. In a way, it felt exciting.

"Of course I can. But I still think there's a reason ye've changed yer mind."

Raven sat down in silence. Lark ran a brush over her hair.

59

"No reason," Raven finally said, picking up a bottle of rose water from the dressing table. She usually only used this after bathing or washing her hair. She uncorked the bottle and sniffed it. Unless she was mistaken, when Jonathon was atop her, she saw him actually sniff her. He seemed to like her scent.

"That personal guard of yers is very handsome." Lark started to plait Raven's hair. "What was his name?"

"Jonathon. Jonathon Armstrong, but he's not my personal guard. Not really." Raven put a dab of rose water behind each ear.

"Yer brother said he was."

"I know what Rook said, but that is ridiculous. Anyone can see that I don't need a personal guard," she said with a roll of her eyes. "Besides, he's only the town's armorer who hires out his sword on occasion for extra coin. I swear, some men will do anything for money." She continued to splash a little rose water between her breasts.

"By the way ye're bathin' in that rose water, I'd think ye fancy the man. That is why ye suddenly care about how ye look and smell, right?" Lark giggled as she continued fixing Raven's hair.

"That's absurd!" Raven corked up the bottle and put it back on her dressing table with a huff. "I'm a lady. A noble. A titled woman. He is nothing at all. He's just a commoner. Why would I even care about him?" She tried to sound and look as if she weren't interested in the man, but damn, if his body pressed up against hers didn't have her mind reeling right now. She'd liked it. She'd *really* liked it. Raven had said some nasty things to the man, but honestly, it was only because she was so angry with her brother and father. Now, she almost felt bad talking to the man that way.

"Hmmm," said Lark in a playful manner. "I hear armorers make good money. She continued fixing Raven's hair. "Plus, he obviously kens how to wield a sword if he's a mercenary, so he's got to be a good protector. Dinna ye agree?"

Raven's head jerked upward and she glared at her cousin.

"What are you trying to say?"

"I mean, even if ye dinna need to be protected, who cares if he's with ye?" continued Lark, turning Raven's head and continuing to plait her hair.

"I care. I'm not going to be followed around all day by anyone."

"Ye realize that yer father and brother must trust him completely to make him yer personal guard. That should tell ye that they like the man. Do ye like him as well?"

There was no way Raven was going to answer that. It was absurd to be attracted to a man below her status. While she didn't want any of the noblemen as her husband, she also didn't want to be longing for anyone below the salt.

"We're finished here," said Raven, having had enough of this ridiculous conversation. She stood up, not wanting to waste her time talking about a mere commoner.

"Wait. Ye need a flower in yer hair." Lark reached over to a vase of flowers on the table and plucked off the end of a narcissus. She stuck the golden flower into Raven's plaited hair. "There, that makes ye look bonnie and also more like a lady."

"Hrmph," grunted Raven, thinking she shouldn't

have bothered. Mayhap a moment of infatuation with Jonathon had made her want to look good, but she was starting to change her mind quickly. She never should have acted so impulsively. It would be best to just wipe the thought of that handsome man right out of her mind.

"This flower is also said to ensure happiness and good fortune." Lark reached up and fussed with the flower.

"I am already happy, and I have good fortune," said Raven, pushing her cousin's hand away. She didn't want to hear what Lark told her of what the flower promised to bring. Wearing a nice gown and rose water was already making her uncomfortable. The last thing she needed was to be doting over flowers that were supposed to bring good luck. "I don't need a flower for anything. I make my own good fortune," Raven told her.

Lark's smile faded, as if she didn't understand. "It's also said this flower symbolizes new beginnin's," explained Lark as Raven strapped on her weapon belt right over her gown. "Mayhap this means ye'll find a man ye want to marry?"

"Never," said Raven with a pout, heading for the door. "I don't ever want to marry, and there is no man who could possibly take my interest since they are all dolts." She swung open the door, surprised to see Jonathon standing there. His sudden presence made her jerk backward and hold a hand over her heart.

"Hello," said Jonathon with a wide smile, showing off his straight, white teeth. He reached up and brushed a stray lock of hair from his eyes. God's toes, why was her heart beating so fast around him? It must only be because he surprised her, that's all.

"How long have you been out here?" snapped Raven, suddenly worried that he may have heard them talking about him. She hoped not. All she needed was this commoner to think she fancied him. If so, he would never leave her alone.

"I've been hired to guard you, my lady, so I'll escort you to the great hall now," said Jonathon, holding out his arm, not answering her question in the least.

"I'm afraid not. I'm with my cousin," she told him. "It would prove rather rude if I took your arm while she followed behind us. She's a lady too, you know." Raven hoped she'd put an end to all this nonsense now.

Jonathon lowered his arm and looked over at Lark who was standing right behind Raven. "Oh nay. I would never want someone as fine as Lady Lark to have to follow behind us." He lifted his arm, holding it up to Lark now. "It would be an honor to escort you as well, Lady Lark," he said with a slight bow.

Damn, thought Raven, this man was so polite. He knew his position around the nobles, and must be trying to win points by acting this way.

"Don't bother," said Raven, throwing her nose in the air. "Lady Lark won't-"

Her words were cut off by her cousin's answer.

"Och, I'd love that. Thank ye, Jonathon," said Lark with a giggle, taking his proffered arm.

Raven looked over at Lark and shook her head, silently warning her not to do it. She wasn't watching her, or mayhap she just didn't care. Lark smiled at Jonathon and laid her hand atop his arm with no qualms whatsoever.

"Hurry, Raven. Take his other arm," said Lark. "If

we dinna move quickly, Uncle Corbett is goin' to be furious with us."

"I'm certain no man could possibly be angry with you, Lady Lark," said Jonathon, giving all his attention to Lark and ignoring Raven completely. "You are so kind, and pretty, if you don't mind me speaking so freely."

"Not at all," answered Lark, beaming with excitement.

"Your accent makes you unique as well," Jonathon continued. "You–"

"Enough! Let's go," said Raven, taking Jonathon's other arm and all but pulling him down the corridor. If she had to stand there and listen to his silly, shallow compliments any longer, it would bore her to tears.

"Excuse me, Lady Raven?" asked Jonathon as they walked.

"Yes?" She paid him a sideways glance from the corners of her eyes, not wanting to look directly at him. She'd seen his bright blue eyes with tones of indigo near the edges when he was atop her on the floor of the kitchen. They were truly spellbinding eyes, and she didn't want to be drawn into them again. Or did she? Sadly, after hearing what he said to Lark, part of her wanted him to say kind things about her, too. Then again, what did any of it matter? He was only here temporarily. After the tournament she'd probably never see him again.

"That flower in your hair," he said, cocking his head and stretching his neck to see it. His sudden perusal of her made her feel warm inside. She wondered if he'd notice she was wearing rose water as well.

"What about the flower?" she asked, thinking he

liked it. Mayhap it was a good idea that Lark suggested she wear it after all.

"There is a big ant crawling on it. May I kill it for you?" He reached up for it, but Lark pushed his hand away.

"Never mind. I'll do it myself." She ripped the flower from her hair and threw it to the ground, proceeding to stomp on it, crushing not only the ant but also the delicate petals. When she looked back up, both Lark and Jonathon were staring at the ground with their mouths hanging open. "I didn't want to wear the stupid thing in the first place," she said, with a sardonic smile.

Raven hurried off to the great hall, no longer wanting to be holding on to Jonathon's arm when she entered the room. She didn't need a man's assistance, and she certainly didn't need a personal guard. That became even more clear to her when she stepped into the great hall to see her father talking with two of the ugliest men she'd ever seen in her life.

"Raven! Where have you been?" growled her father. "Come and meet Lord Belmouth from Manchester and Lord Whitehead from Liverpool. They will be competing in the tournament to win your hand in marriage and they requested to make your acquaintance ahead of time."

Raven's heart dropped in her chest. Just like his name, Lord Belmouth had a wide mouth on him that reminded her of a bell or possibly a frog. He was also probably closer to her father's age than he was to hers. Lord Whitehead, on the other hand, didn't have white hair like his name implied. As a matter of fact, the man didn't have any hair at all. His round, shiny head gleamed in the firelight of the candles and torches lining the great hall. His ears stuck out like a donkey, and drooped down a little on both sides, reminding her of the ears of her hounds.

It sickened her to even imagine being married to either of these men. After Jonathon's soft hair had brushed across her cheek and encompassed them like being in a tent, thinking of Lord Whitehead atop her with no hair at all made her want to retch. She couldn't stop thinking of Jonathon's mouth so close to hers as well. His lips looked strong and enticing. Not too wide, not too small. Just perfect for kissing. Looking back at Lord Belmouth, his lips looked more like a fish now than a frog. She could only imagine the feel of him slobbering all over her body. It sent a shiver of disgust right through her.

Something cold and wet touched her hand at exactly the same moment that she had the thought. It made her jump. She gasped, pulling back her hand to see that it was only her hound.

"Brindy, you scared me," she said, hunkering down to pet the dog and kiss it on the head.

Her other dog, Copper, jumped up on Lord Whitehead, wagging its tail.

"Nay! Get that slobbery mongrel away from me." Lord Whitehead pushed it away and stepped back, holding up his palms.

"So sorry, my lord." It was Jonathon who came forward. He stepped in front of Raven, grabbing the dog by Lord Whitehead, and hunkering down to hold it. Copper licked his face, making him chuckle. It was as if he didn't even mind being slobbered upon. "You need to stop being so friendly."

Raven stood up. "I don't think Lord Whitehead was acting friendly at all toward my dog."

Jonathon looked up at Raven, then over to Lord Whitehead, and back again before he spoke softly. "I was speaking to the dog."

"Raven, how many times do I need to tell you that your hounds aren't welcome in the great hall when we have guests?" Corbett raised his chin, looking out into the room. "Where is the kennelgroom? He needs to take these dogs outside anon."

"I'm not sure, my lord," answered one of his men from nearby.

"I'll take them," offered Jonathon, starting to walk away, and then stopping and turning back to Raven. "What are their names?" he asked.

"Copper and Brindy," Raven told him.

"Come on, Copper. Let's go, Brindy." Jonathon bent over and motioned the dogs to him.

"They won't go with you. They don't know you." Raven's mouth fell open as both dogs eagerly ran over to Jonathon, wagging their tails. He reached down and petted them behind the ears. "I'll return momentarily," he told the others, starting out of the great hall with both the dogs at his heels.

"Raven, yer hounds sure seem to like Jonathon," said Lark with a smile, watching the man leave.

"Aye. I suppose they do," she answered, wondering what it was about the armorer that made her dogs so fond of him.

"Who is that man?" asked Lord Belmouth.

"He's no one," Raven quickly answered.

"He's my cousin's personal guard," Lark spoke up, making Raven cringe. She was starting to wish that Lark hadn't accompanied her here after all.

"Personal guard?" asked Belmouth with a

chuckle. "I doubt that man even knows how to use a weapon."

"Who is he?" asked Whitehead. "He's dressed like a castle guard, but certainly doesn't act like one. He almost seems familiar."

"Jonathon is here by my request," explained Corbett. "He's here temporarily to help out for the tournament."

"Doing what?" chuckled Whitehead. "Tending to the hounds?"

"I think I know who he is," said Belmouth. "Isn't he that armorer from town? I'm sure of it. I've used his services once, long ago."

"He's also a mercenary," Raven informed them, wanting the men to stop belittling Jonathon. For some reason it bothered her.

"Mercenary?" Whitehead looked over to Corbett. "You've got a mercenary guarding your daughter?"

"How can you even trust someone like that?" asked Belmouth. "Mayhap you should hire someone to keep an eye on the likes of him instead."

"Gentlemen, I think this meeting is over," said Corbett in a dismissing manner.

Raven looked over at her father who seemed as if he were trying to bite his tongue rather than to reply to their comments. "I'll see you to the door."

"Nay, wait," said Belmouth, looking over at Raven. "I wanted to get to know my possible bride-to-be."

"Me too," complained Whitehead. "Let me take her on a ride through the country."

"Nay," said Raven, her eyes flashing over to Lark who looked just as terrified as she by the thought of being alone with either one of them. "I have another appointment. Good day." She picked up her skirts and all but ran to the door of the great hall with Lark keeping up with her pace. Thankfully, Raven's father didn't command her to stay.

Raven didn't stop until she made it out into the courtyard and into the fresh air.

"Raven?" Her mother was conversing with some of the noblewomen over by the well. She excused herself and came over to join them. "How did the meeting with the lords go?" asked Lady Devon with a smile.

"They are horrible, Mother. They are true monsters. I don't want anything to do with either of them."

"What?" Devon's smile faded.

"I agree, they were rather nasty," added Lark, in Raven's defense.

"Not to mention old and ugly," added Raven under her breath.

"I'm sorry to hear that," said Devon. "Well, there will be many other suitors, so hopefully you'll find someone you like."

"Suitors? I wouldn't call any of them that. More like hungry competitors out for the dowry, is all. What does it matter, anyway?" snapped Raven. "I don't seem to have a choice in whom I marry. If Lord Whitehead or Lord Belmouth wins the tournament, I'll have to marry one of them! My life is over." Raven's emotions raged within her. She needed to hit something before she exploded.

Raven ran off, leaving her mother and Lark behind. She wanted to get away and think. As she raced for the stable to get her horse, she passed by the kennels. Jonathon stepped out and she barreled right into him.

"Whoa, there," said Jonathon, catching her by the shoulders and righting her so she wouldn't fall. "We need to stop colliding like this, my lady."

"I'm not a horse, so don't tell me *whoa* and speak to me as if I were," she snapped, still upset about what had just transpired inside the great hall.

"I'm sorry. I didn't mean to offend you." As his hands slipped from her shoulders, Raven felt his warmth go with them. After meeting those two awful noblemen, being in Jonathon's presence felt so much nicer, and actually calming.

"Nay. I'm sorry," she told him with a shake of her head, regaining her composure. "I didn't mean to sound so shrewd with you here, or in the kitchen earlier either. I'm just upset, that's all." She stepped back and looked the other way.

"I see," he answered, sounding as if he knew the problem. "Well, the lords are leaving so I am guessing your meeting is over?"

"I-I suppose so." She bit her bottom lip, still not looking at him.

"Were you going somewhere, my lady?"

"I usually go to the practice yard when I'm upset, but today I was planning on going for a ride to clear my head."

"I'll saddle your horse for you, and go with you. Let me accompany you to the stable."

Raven looked over to see the lords approaching the stable to get their horses. She quickly changed her mind, wrapping her arms around her. "I don't think I'll go for a ride after all. Not now."

Jonathon's head turned to see the reason. "Perhaps you could show me the blacksmith's shop then," he suggested. "I will be living there until after the tournament, and I haven't seen it in years."

"Oh." Her arms fell to her sides. "Of course. It's right over there. I can show it to you."

"I'd like that," he said, holding out his arm to accompany her.

Raven wasn't used to this. It felt awkward and much too intimate to be taking the arm of a commoner. "I'll just walk next to you."

He looked surprised, not to mention disappointed. Slowly, he lowered his arm. "Of course. Whatever you desire, my lady."

They walked in silence to the building that contained the forge.

Jonathon opened the door to the forge and stopped in his tracks. It took a moment for his eyes to get accustomed to the dark. The bright sun spilled into the room, slowly revealing the place to him.

"This is the forge and where our last blacksmith lived," said Raven from behind him.

"I barely remember it, since it has been so long since I've been here." Jonathon took a few steps into the room and Raven followed.

"It smells so smoky in here." Raven wrinkled her nose. "I don't know how anyone could work here, let alone live here."

Jonathon turned to look at her. "It's the life of a blacksmith, and takes a while to get used to," he told her. "Before too long you'll not even notice the smell anymore."

"Oh," she said, looking around the darkened room. "I've only been in here a few times, since I try to avoid it. I don't really know much about it, so I'm not sure what to tell you."

"You don't need to tell me anything about it. I will manage." Jonathon walked over to a window and threw open the shutters, letting in the fresh breeze.

"Is this similar to your shop?" she asked, curiously. "I don't think I've ever been to your place in town."

"In some ways, yes, but in others, no." He walked over and opened a second window. With the sunlight now filling the room, he had his first real view of the castle forge. He had only been here once or twice as a child, accompanying his father to visit the castle's blacksmith.

Housed in a building made of brick was a small forge at the far end of the room. It was a stone hearth that vented out a hole in the roof. In front of the hearth were two small bellows, attached to ropes that were pulled to work them, to blow air on the fire and make it hotter. There was, of course, an anvil, and blacksmith tools hanging on the walls, but not much else. The floor was wood and very dusty.

It seemed as if the entire place was covered in filth. True, blacksmith shops were always filled with smoke and covered with soot, but he kept their shop in town clean. His family prided themselves on keeping their work area presentable for their customers, and especially the nobles. The condition of the castle's forge surprised him. He could see now why the nobles came to him instead of using their own castle's smith for what they needed at times. The conditions here were severely lacking.

"How is it different?" she asked, seeming genuinely interested.

"Well, for one, this is a very small shop. Mine is much bigger."

"Really?" she asked with a grin. "How much bigger is yours?"

Jonathon could have kicked himself for saying that. Her smirk told him that she was being flirty and not talking about his shop anymore. Or at least, he hoped not. He smiled inwardly, liking this playful side of Raven that he had never seen. From all the stories he'd heard of her, and from what he'd experienced so far, he didn't think the woman knew how to jest, or even how to smile.

"Did you want to see it for yourself so you can compare?" Now it was his turn to grin. Her cheeks became rosy and her face was flushed. Since there was no fire in the forge, he knew it wasn't from the heat.

"I suppose this one is small because it is right here in the castle courtyard, and there isn't much room to expand," explained Raven, picking up a punch to inspect it. "There are so many outbuildings, that none of them can be too large."

"Oh, put that down. You don't want to play with that. It's dirty," he said, taking the metal punch from her. His hand brushed against hers and he couldn't help noticing how soft her skin felt. It surprised him since she worked with weapons. He half-expected her hands to be rough or even callused. He quickly put the punch down and turned away.

"Wow, this is big," she said, causing him to look over his shoulder. She reached out and picked up one of the blacksmith's hammers.

"Those are heavy. Be careful," he said, rushing over to take it from her, but stopped. She held it in one hand and didn't drop it. It was truly impressive since most females could barely even lift it with both hands. "You're quite strong. For a lady, I mean."

"Yes, I suppose I am," she said, almost gloating. "I wield a full-sized sword one-handed, you realize. I hardly think a mere blacksmith's hammer is going to break me."

"I can see that," he said with a nod.

"This isn't much of a place to live," she remarked, putting down the hammer.

"It'll do," he replied, walking over and peeking into the attached room that was the bedroom. A small bed with a torn mattress filled most of the room. A small, dirty pallet lay on the floor in the corner with straw sticking out of it. "I see two places to sleep. Did someone live here with the blacksmith?"

"He was an old widower, but he did have a son named Gerold. He's the one who lived here with him. Gerold was his apprentice."

"Oh, that's right. I think your father mentioned that to me."

"Gerold stayed here at the castle after his father's death, so I'm sure he'll be assigned to help you."

"Didn't he go to live with other family members after his father's death? I mean, your father said he was just an apprentice so I'm surprised that he stayed."

"Nay. He has no one else. His father was the only family he had."

"Oh. So, he is going to become a journeyman and take his father's place someday soon?"

"I hardly think so," she said, finding his words funny, though he didn't know why.

"Hello?" came a voice from the door.

"It's my father," said Raven in a hushed whisper.

"Lord Corbett?" Jonathon walked out of the adjoining room to find Corbett Blake standing in the doorway, blocking the light. He was tall, like Jonathon, and had to duck to enter the forge.

"What's going on here?" asked Corbett in a low voice.

Jonathon now realized it probably hadn't been a good idea to bring the lord's daughter here. It was a dark, dirty place, and not fit for a noblewoman. Besides, he shouldn't be in here alone with her, and especially not in the bedroom. He was sure that wasn't going to sit right with Lord Corbett. It wasn't proper. Especially since he was a commoner.

"Father, I was just showing Jonathon his temporary home," said Raven, approaching her father and giving him a quick kiss on the cheek. "I hope you don't mind. I had to get away from Lords Whitehead and Belmouth. I didn't like them."

"I'm afraid to say I have to agree with you, Daughter," said Corbett. "They weren't the most amicable men I've ever met." He turned his attention to Jonathon. "How do you find the forge?"

"He finds it smaller than his," Raven answered for him, looking over and grinning.

"It's fine, my lord," said Jonathon, not wanting to anger Lord Corbett, and a little embarrassed by Raven saying his was bigger.

"He also said it is very dirty in here," continued Raven, making Jonathon want to hide under a chair now. Why did she have to say these things and not let him speak for himself?

"I realize the place is lacking," said Corbett. "That is why I brought Gerold with me. He'll be your apprentice during the duration of your stay, so just let him know what needs to be done to tidy things up."

"Gerold is here?" Jonathon peered out the door over Corbett's shoulder, but didn't see anyone else. "Where is he?"

"I'm right here," came a little voice from behind Corbett. Out stepped a young lad who was skinny and small and looked too frail to even lift a punch, let alone a hammer.

"You? You're going to be my apprentice?" asked Jonathon in surprise.

"He's young, but is a good worker," said Corbett.

"Gerold, how old are you?" Jonathon could see this was not going to work. He needed someone who was strong and who could aid him. Not a lad that he'd have to watch over closer than tending to the hounds.

"I just turned nine," said the boy proudly. He might be nine, but honestly, he was so small and skinny that he looked more like he was only six or seven.

"So, then you've just started your apprenticeship," said Jonathon.

"He's lived here with his father all his life. His mother died when he was born," explained Corbett.

"I know everything about the forge," bragged the boy, but Jonathon didn't believe it.

"I'm sure you do," he said, looking from the boy back up to Corbett. "You did say my brother Avery could assist me?" Jonathon checked. "I mean, he is twenty years of age and has also just completed his apprenticeship. He is a journeyman now and will be a great asset."

"Are you a journeyman too?" Raven asked Jonathon.

"I am," he answered. "Actually, I am only one masterpiece away from being a master at my trade. Your father assured me I would have time to work on my presentation for the guild masters who are to judge it sometime soon."

"Yes, I did say that, and of course your brother is welcome here to assist you, as well," said Corbett. "However, there isn't much room for all three of you to live here."

"Lord Corbett, will I have to give up my pallet in the bedroom?" asked the boy looking up to the lord of the castle with sad eyes.

"Well, that will be up to Jonathon," answered Corbett, looking over to him, putting him in a terrible position.

Jonathon didn't want the child living there with him and his brother. He would only be in the way. He certainly didn't want the lad sleeping in the same room, either. But how could he turn the child away? This was his home. He didn't have anyone now, and was an orphan. He'd lost everything he'd ever had. Jonathon's heart broke for him. He wasn't going to be the one to take away the boy's home as well.

"He's welcome to stay," answered Jonathon, realizing how long his time here was going to feel, now that he answered in this manner.

"Thank you," said the little boy, wiping his nose with his sleeve. Dirt streaked across his face. His clothes were worn thin and covered in ash. He wasn't even wearing shoes, although at first Jonathon thought he was since his feet looked almost black. "What's my first job?" asked Gerold excitedly.

"Grab a broom and start sweeping," Jonathon told the boy. "I want this place to shine."

"Right away, my lord." Gerold ran barefooted to grab the broom.

"I'm not a lord," he told the boy. "Just call me Jonathon."

"Aye, Jonathon." The boy sniffled and once more wiped his nose with his sleeve.

"Do you have other clothes? And a pair of shoes, Gerold?" asked Jonathon. "The forge is too dangerous to be working here barefooted. Besides, everything and everyone in the forge needs to stay as clean as possible. I insist upon it."

"I had shoes but they fell apart last week," said the boy, sweeping quickly, causing a big cloud of dust to rise up into the air. "These are my only clothes."

"I'll get him some shoes," offered Corbett. "I had no idea of his condition."

"I'll get him clothes," said Jonathon. "I have a younger brother just a little older than you, Gerold. You can have his clothes that he's outgrown."

"Fine," said Corbett, turning to go.

"Father," said Raven, making Corbett stop and turn around. "Can I go to town with Jonathon to see his shop?"

"Why?" Corbett's eyes drifted over to Jonathon.

"I will need to bring some of my tools here. This shop is small and lacking. There are some things I will require to do my job," explained Jonathon.

"Plus, he has to get my new clothes," little Gerold reminded him, sounding excited to be getting something new. Or new to him, at least, even if they were hand-me-downs.

"I suppose that would be all right. Just stay with

Jonathon at all times, Raven," warned her father. "Remember, when the castle gates close at nightfall, leave him alone, since he'll have work to do in the forge."

"Why?" she asked.

"Why what?" asked Corbett.

"Why are you making me stay with him? What are you and Rook up to, Father?"

"I'll watch over her, my lord," said Jonathon, knowing that Corbett wasn't going to want to answer that question. They never explained to her why they felt she needed a personal guard, and hell if Jonathon was going to be the one to do it. "Gerold, slow down and sweep gently or we're all going to choke to death on the dust."

"Sorry," answered the boy.

"I suggest we go out in the fresh air, my lady." Jonathon stretched out his arm, motioning Raven out the door after her father.

Once outside, he looked back at the boy again, shaking his head. Now, he would have two to watch over instead of just one. How in heaven's name was he ever going to find time to construct a piece worthy enough to be accepted into the guild as a master of his trade when he had so many other duties that would be taking his attention?

CHAPTER 6

Jonathon reached up to help Raven from her horse once they'd stopped in front of his shop in town a little while later. She didn't need or want his help, but something made her accept it. Perhaps it was because she wanted to feel his hands on her waist again. Or mayhap it was because she was hoping he'd realize she was wearing rose water and comment on it. He didn't.

"Watch out for the puddles," Jonathon told her, releasing her quickly and not taking an extra moment to sniff her which made her a bit disappointed. "The streets in town are full of ruts and mud. They are not fit for a lady." He tied up the horses to the hitching post in front of the shop. Hanging out from over the door to the shop was a metal shield with two swords crossed behind it. This symbolized that an armorer worked here.

Only the nobles, clergy, and a small number of the tradesmen or merchants could read and write. Most of the commoners, the servants, and serfs didn't have these skills. Therefore, in front of each shop hung a sign depicting what service was offered inside. The butcher had a wooden sign with a cleaver and a pig painted on it. The tavern's sign was a wine cask and a tankard, stating that this place had both wine and ale. The chandler had a sign with a candle on it, and the cordwainer's sign was cut into the shape of a shoe.

There were wooden walkways in front of the stores, which were connected all in a row. The streets of the town were in horrendous condition. Besides mud and ruts, people threw their scraps and waste right into the road. They even emptied their chamber pots out the second story windows. It paid to look up while walking past the buildings, or one might get a terrible surprise.

The stench of the town was even worse than the smell of the gongpit at the castle on a hot summer's day. This is one of the reasons that Raven never came here. The worst stench by far had to be by the tanners. Also, the fishmonger's place where guts from their catches were flung outside for the stray cats and pigs to feast on.

She didn't want Jonathon to know how she really felt about coming here. Raven was still feeling bad for the way she'd talked to him earlier, so instead she said nothing about the stench. Now she was glad she dabbed on extra rose water before leaving the castle.

"I'm not afraid of a little mud." She took one step and stopped as her foot sank into a mixture of mud and clay, mixed with who-knows-what. "God's feet!" she exclaimed, no longer able to stay silent. She'd just ruined her favorite pair of shoes.

"It's not God's feet that are in trouble," he said, looking down. "I did warn you. Hold on tightly, my lady," he told her from behind. Before she had a chance to ask what he meant, he swept her up into his arms and trudged through the mud, carrying her to the door.

Raven's arms clasped around his neck since she didn't want to fall. It was embarrassing to say the least, but still, part of her really didn't mind. Instead, she was entranced by the scent of woodsmoke on Jonathon's clothes and the way his arms felt wrapped around her. She let one of her hands slide down to his upper arm, surprised to feel his big muscles that were rock hard. Swinging a hammer at the forge all day long seemed to have given him a very toned body.

Thankfully, he no longer wore the clothes of a guard. He'd changed back into his own clothes before leaving the castle, telling her he couldn't be dressed like that in his own town, and she agreed.

Jonathon carried her up a few stairs to a wooden walkway that attached his family's shop to the others all in a row. She liked the feel of being in his arms and might have taken a moment to enjoy it if she hadn't looked over his shoulder and saw all the townspeople staring at them. Suddenly, she felt on edge again.

"Put me down," she commanded, trying to squirm out of his hold.

"Easy, my lady," he said in a low voice, gently putting her feet on the wooden walkway. She felt the warmth of his hold dissipate quickly.

"Well, what do you think? Do you like it? Are you ready for more?"

"What?" she gasped, thinking he was speaking of being in his arms. She felt her face redden. How did he know? Raven did like it, and secretly wanted him to carry her again, but without everyone watching. She was now under the perusal of every commoner in town, and she didn't like it. "How can you think a titled woman is going to like being in a commoner's arms? And how can you have the audacity of asking a noblewoman if she likes it and wants more?"

He looked at her oddly and slowly shook his head. One side of his mouth flipped upward into a cocky grin. "I was speaking about the shop," he told her. "However, I can see that is not where your mind is at the moment."

"Oh," she said, suddenly feeling very foolish. She looked down and busied herself brushing off her gown, rather than have to look directly at him at a time like this. She could feel the eyes of all the townsfolk drilling into her and felt the need to get indoors quickly. "Yes, I'd like to see more. Of the shop, that is." She led the way, not waiting for him to invite her inside. Pushing open the door, she barged in, only to stop in her tracks. Seven people inside the building all looked up and stopped what they were doing. Once again everyone stared at her. Would this ever end? One of the men was inside an adjoining room that had the forge in it, but he put down his hammer when he saw them.

"Lady Raven, I'd like to introduce you to my family," said Jonathon, entering the shop and walking up next to her. She didn't move. He put his hand on her elbow, directing her forward.

"Jonathon, what's this all about?" asked the older man, stepping out from behind the counter. He limped over to them, nodding.

"Lady Raven, this is my father, Crispin Armstrong, and my mother, Avice," he said, introducing her to an older woman standing across the room as well. A young girl and a young boy were with her. They put down their things and hurried over to join them.

"Hello," Raven squeaked out, feeling very uncomfortable meeting Jonathon's family. Or all of them at once, anyway.

"Are you a noble from the castle?" asked the young boy.

"Yes, she is," Jonathon answered for her. "Raven, this is my youngest brother, Heathcliff. He's twelve."

"Do you have any brothers my age?" asked Heathcliff.

"Heathcliff, that's not an appropriate thing to ask her," said Jonathon in a low voice.

"Nay, it's fine," Raven answered. "I have two younger brothers, but they are sixteen and eighteen," she told him. "They don't live at the castle because they are being fostered by other lords. My twin brother, Rook, lives at the castle though."

"I've met him," said Heathcliff. "Did you know my friends call me Cliff?" asked the boy, staring at her.

"I do now," she answered. "Are you an apprentice? Because there is a boy about your age at the castle who was apprentice to the former blacksmith. His name is Gerold, and he's nine."

"Really? Mayhap I can meet him someday. Can I, Jonathon?" asked the boy eagerly.

"We'll talk about that later," said Jonathon, introducing her to his fourteen-year-old sister, Estrilda, and then his eighteen-year-old sister, Hildeth.

"Hello," said Raven with a nod, not sure she wasn't going to swoon. It was very hot in the forge and she found it hard to breathe, let alone meet Jonathon's entire family at once.

"This is my sister Hildeth's new husband, Leith,"

Jonathon said, introducing her to the man in the main part of the shop. "Leith is the town's baker, so they live at his place now."

"Hildeth has been a big help at the bakery," said Leith. "She can bake things that I've never even imagined trying. Because of her, my business has grown just since we've married."

"Thank you, Leith," said Hildeth, and the two lovingly smiled at each other like no one else was in the room.

"That's nice," said Raven, not knowing what else to say. It wasn't as if hearing about baking bread and pastries interested her in the least.

"Don't forget about me, Brother." Another man walked out of the forge area wiping his hands with a cloth. He was bare-chested but wore a leather apron that covered most of the front of him.

"Oh, my." Raven turned away, feeling embarrassed since the man was without a shirt.

"God's eyes, Avery, cover up," spat Jonathon, taking a cloak from a hook and tossing it to him. "You are in the presence of a lady." Jonathon turned to speak to Raven. "This is my brother Avery. He'll be living at the castle forge with me."

"What?" Avery looked up as he hurriedly donned the cloak. "I will?" he asked.

"Aye," said Jonathon. "Did I forget to mention that? While I'm at the castle, I am the temporary smith, as well as Lady Raven's personal guard."

"Can I be her personal guard too?" asked Avery, with a chuckle and a big smile.

"I don't need a personal guard, and although your brother thinks he's mine, he's really not," said Raven with a stiff upper lip. "Now, I think we should be getting back to the castle."

"We just got here, my lady," said Jonathon. "I thought you wanted to compare the size of my shop to the one at the castle."

"Did she, now," mumbled Avery. "Well, I hope you're not disappointed, at the size of Jonathon's... shop."

"Avery, get back to work," said Jonathon's father. "We have orders to fill."

"My lady, I notice mud on your shoe," said Jonathon's mother. "Please, let me and my daughters clean it for you. I have a nice chair for you to use, right over here while we do it."

"Well, I don't know." Raven looked over to Jonathon.

"It'll take me a little while to get some things together that I need at the castle," Jonathon told her.

"I'm sure you must be parched from your ride here," said his mother. "Estrilda, quickly, get Lady Raven some wine."

"I was just dropping off some fig hand pies I made this morning," Hildeth told her. "Would you like to try one?" Hildeth hurried over with a basket over her arm.

"Oh, I don't know," said Raven, suddenly getting a whiff of the delectable scent of the fruit pies. Since she missed the meal this morning, she was feeling famished. "Well, mayhap just a taste."

Jonathon watched his family escort Lady Raven to the other side of the shop and do their best to make her comfortable. He then turned around and spoke in a low tone to his brother.

"I managed to secure you a spot at the castle

forge, but if you're going to be saying things to embarrass me and constantly walking around half-undressed, you're not coming with me."

"Nay, I won't," he said. "I'll do whatever you say." Avery grabbed Jonathon by the arm. "You know how much I want this."

"All right then, go pack a few things. I'll need you to help me load up some of my tools as well."

"Right away, Brother." Avery ran to get ready.

"Father, Lord Corbett said he'd pay for another man or two to help out here at the shop until our return," Jonathon told him, gathering up a few things he would need.

"Fine, fine," said Crispin, his eyes still on Lady Raven. "She's a real looker, that one," he said.

"Yes, she is pretty, I agree." Jonathon opened up a leather bag and started to load his personal files, stones, and punches. He then looked around for his favorite hammer.

"She'd make a good wife for you, son."

"Stop it," Jonathon grumbled, his eyes flashing over to Raven, hoping to hell she hadn't heard his father. Thankfully, Jonathon's mother and the rest of his family were busy seeing to the lady's needs. None of them were paying any attention to him. "She's a titled lady and I am just a common man. How could you even suggest such a thing?" He found his hammer and loaded that into the bag as well.

"I've heard this one also has a mind of her own. I know Lord Corbett has a hard time handling her. That's why he's assigned you to watch over her, isn't it?"

"I'm her personal guard, Father. And only until

the tournament, when the winner will take her as his wife."

"I have a feeling there is more to this story than you are letting on."

"That is all I can tell you." He yanked the ties closed on the bag. "I'll need to borrow a few more tools if you don't mind. The smithy at the castle is pretty primitive, and I need to get started on my masterpiece to present to the guild masters."

"Sure, take what you need," said Crispin, his eyes still on the girl. "What did you decide on? For your presentation piece, I mean. It needs to be something different and unique and of the highest quality if you want to be awarded the title of master craftsman."

"I don't know yet. I haven't had time to think about it."

"Well, it is getting harder and harder to be accepted as a master of the trade. If you can't impress the guild judges, you might have to wait another year, Jon. After all, it seems like you're not going to have any real time to construct it, now that you have another job to tend to."

"I'll do it, Father. If I have to stop sleeping for the next month to get it done, I will. I want to become a master craftsman more than anything, and you know it. I want my own shop."

"I know, Son." He slowly looked back to Jonathon. "But mayhap life has other opportunities for you." His eyes traveled back to Raven again.

"I know what you're thinking, and stop it. You know as well as I that nobles and commoners don't belong together. It's not allowed. It'll never happen."

"You like the girl, don't you?"

"What are you saying?" Jonathon busied himself, not wanting to answer his father truthfully.

"I'm saying, the girl has eyes for you."

"You're imagining things. She does not and never will. Besides, even if she did, nothing could ever come of it. In three weeks' time, she'll be married to a noble."

"Mayhap," said his father, sounding as if he knew some secret.

"Is there something you're not telling me?" asked Jonathon.

"Nay, son. You know I'd never keep things from you. I suppose I was only hoping that someday one of my children could really make something of themselves."

"I am. I'm going to be a master at my craft and follow in your footsteps."

"Mayhap my footsteps aren't the best ones to follow."

"Why would you say that?"

"Go where your heart leads you. Don't settle on something just because you think it is what you're supposed to do."

"I can't believe you are talking this way," said Jonathon, knowing every father's goal is to have their sons follow in their footsteps.

"Jonathon, you are getting older now and still don't have a woman in your life. If someone takes an interest in you or what you do, don't push them away just because you don't believe you belong together."

"Lady Raven takes no interest in me or my life, I assure you. So you can stop with all the addled dreaming right now, Father. This isn't like you."

"With age comes change and wisdom. You never

know what might happen. Just think about it, that's all I ask."

"Jonathon, I'm almost ready to leave," stated Raven, approaching them with a smile on her face. "But first, I think I'd like to see the rest of your place just as you've promised, while I finish my hand pie and wine." She held a wooden cup in one hand and a cloth wrapped around a small pie with the other. All Jonathon could think of was how she should be drinking from an ornate goblet and using a silver plate and spoon for that pie. Those were things that he would never be able to provide.

"Of course," said Jonathon, leading her to the forge area of his shop. He glanced back over his shoulder to see his father grinning from ear to ear. Was Lady Raven really interested in him and his life, just like his father said? Was his father suddenly filled with some prophetic wisdom now that he was getting older? Nay, he decided. Raven was only asking to see his shop to be polite. Then again, Lady Raven was known for being rude. Especially when it had to do with commoners.

CHAPTER 7

"Here is the forge and where we will live," Jonathon told his brother as soon as they'd returned to the castle. They had been gone all day since Jonathon and Avery had to finish up a few projects at the shop before they left. It also took a while to load up the horses with tools and supplies and their personal belongings.

Raven had spent the time talking to his sisters and mother, and seemed to enjoy watching them prepare a meal. It surprised Jonathon that she changed her mind and wanted to stay longer with his family. After all, he saw how the stench in town disgusted her, and also how upset she became when she stepped in the mud. Perhaps carrying her to the shop was a good idea after all, since it seemed to calm her.

It also shocked Jonathon that Raven wanted to eat a meal at his house when his mother offered. This noblewoman either liked change, or was trying to avoid going back to the castle, he decided. Or more likely, she was just downright crazy. If Jonathon was noble, the last place he'd want to be spending time was with a common family in town.

"Ah, it is a small place, just like you said." Avery stopped the horse and jumped down from the wagon bench. "However, the castle is mighty large." He smiled and turned a full circle looking over the keep and courtyard, taking it all in. "You said we can eat in the great hall, right?" he asked. Jonathon swore he saw his brother already salivating. Avery was a few years younger, but had the same build as Jonathon. His appetite was twice as large.

"Yes, Avery, that's correct," answered Raven. "You both are invited to do so for every meal." She reached out for Jonathon to help her from her horse. He didn't expect this, but didn't object. He rather liked the feel of her body beneath his hands.

When he put her down, she looked up with her bright silver eyes and actually smiled. Miracles would never cease today. This woman didn't even seem to be the same one he'd met earlier. Her dogs came running to greet her, and she bent over to pet them.

"Why are you smiling?" he asked, not sure if she was happy because he'd touched her, or if it was only because she saw her dogs approaching. After all, it wasn't in her disposition to smile or be pleasant. Or at least from all the gossip he heard, he didn't think so. He bent over and petted the dogs as well.

"I always smile when my dogs greet me because they make me happy," she answered.

"Oh. Of course," he said, feeling a little disappointed. Part of him wished she had been smiling because of him.

"I enjoyed seeing your shop and spending time with your family today," she said sweetly, hunkering down and giggling as Copper licked her face.

"You did?"

"Aye. It was very interesting."

He wasn't sure what she meant by *interesting*, but since she sounded pleased, he didn't want to risk it by asking. "I'm glad," he answered, not quite sure how to respond. He didn't think it was a good idea to point out that it was far below her status to even be at his home in the first place. He wondered if his life really interested her or if she was just pretending to like it for some odd reason. He decided to say nothing.

"Lord Jonathon, look at my new shoes." Gerold ran up and held out his foot. He wore shoes that looked a little too big for him, but they were clean and in good condition. He'd grow into them in time.

"I'm not a lord," he reminded the boy. "But I do like your shoes. Now try to keep them clean. I brought some of my little brother's clothes he outgrew for you to wear as well."

"Yay!" said Gerold, kneeling down petting the dogs, laughing when they knocked him to the ground.

"Who's this?" asked Avery, eyeing up the boy.

"This is Gerold. Your new apprentice," said Raven, brushing the wrinkles out of her gown.

"You? You're just a child and so skinny. I'm sure you can't even lift one of our hammers." Avery chuckled, perusing the young and frail-looking boy. Gerold frowned, knowing he was being laughed at.

"Excuse my brother and his rudeness, Gerold," apologized Jonathon, reaching between the two giant dogs and helping the boy to his feet. "He's not used to such young apprentices, that's all."

Gerold's eyes turned to slits and he made a pouty face. "I thought you said you had a brother who is an apprentice that is about my age."

"He's right," Jonathon told Avery with a shrug. "It's no different than working with Heathcliff, I'm sure."

"Well I... well I..." Avery tried to find the right words but couldn't.

"Gerold, I have a job for you," said Jonathon, to break the tension.

"I'm ready!" The boy perked up immediately. "What do you want me to do?"

"I want you to assist my brother Avery with unloading the horses. Show him the shop and where he'll be sleeping as well."

"I will, but I'm not giving him my pallet to sleep on." The boy crossed his arms over his chest.

"You won't have to," said Corbett, walking up with Rook to join them, overhearing what Gerold said.

"My lords," said Jonathon, with a nod and half-bow to greet them.

"My lords, I am Avery," said his brother, bowing deeply, thrilled by being in the nobles' presence.

"We wondered if you were ever returning," said Rook. "You were gone most of the day."

"Jonathon and his brother had some things to take care of in town," said Raven. "I stayed, as well as ate with them. Were you worried?"

"You did what?" asked Rook, looking as surprised as Jonathon had felt when Raven decided she wanted to stay with his family longer.

"We weren't worried," said Corbett. "I knew you were with your personal guard, so you were in no danger."

Avery stifled a chuckle, causing Jonathon to throw him a nasty look to shut him up. Avery got the message, covering up his laugh with a forced cough.

"Lord Corbett, what did you mean about the pallet?" asked Jonathon curiously.

"I've had three new pallets brought to the forge for you, Gerold, and your brother," said Corbett. "I also had the servants bring over more blankets and pillows for you to use. I'm sorry the living area is so small, but it is all I have for now. Plus, it's only temporary."

"Aye, of course. Thank you, my lord," said Jonathon. "We are very grateful."

"I get to choose the pallet I want, so you two get what's left," said Gerold, taking off at a run in his new shoes to get a look at the new things.

"We came to tell you the main meal is about to be served," said Rook. "Since it sounds as if you've already eaten, I'm sure none of you will be interested in joining us."

"I will," said Avery, his head popping up. "I'm still hungry."

"I wouldn't mind another bite to eat, either. Thank you—we'll be there as soon as we unpack," Jonathon told the lords with a quick nod.

"Good," said Corbett. "Armstrong, since you are my daughter's personal guard, I'm granting you permission to sit next to her up on the dais. However, your brother will have to sit below the salt."

"What?" both Jonathon and Raven said together. Jonathon was pleasantly surprised by this, but Raven was scowling as if she didn't approve.

"I'm honored, my lord, but I wouldn't feel comfortable, since it's not my place," said Jonathon shaking his head.

"Yes, I agree. The dais is only for nobles and everyone knows it," said Raven, her kind disposition suddenly turning dark again. "Everyone else sits below the salt, and that includes armorers." She looked directly at Jonathon. This time, there was nothing in her eyes saying she was interested in him in the least.

"That may be true—however, I think I'll allow Jonathon to join us atop the dais as our special guest while he's here," said Corbett, confident in his decision.

"You will?" both Jonathon and Rook said at the same time.

"Father, I have to agree with Raven on this one. I mean, think of what you're saying," said Rook in a low voice, but Corbett didn't change his mind.

"I've already thought about it and I believe it'll be a good way to introduce Jonathon as Raven's personal guard. Everyone will know I value him, since he'll be up at the dais with us. I want everyone to see him. Oh, and be sure to wear the clothes of one of my guards, since you need to look like more than just a commoner to sit at my table."

"Aye, my lord." Jonathon's eyes closed and he groaned inwardly. He already felt like a fool being in this position, and now he was going to be stared at by the entire castle and have to wear those stupid clothes again. He felt like such a fake.

"Father, he's a commoner, and I will not allow it," complained Raven, her true personality showing again.

"Daughter, I'll warn you to watch your sharp tongue," Corbett told Raven. "You have nothing to say

96

about what goes on at the castle. It is my decision and I'll not hear another word about it."

"But–"

"Nay!" said Corbett, raising his gloved hand in the air. "Now, it's a temporary thing, so it doesn't really matter. I am only doing it so the rest of the castle will accept him in this new position." Corbett turned and walked away, looking back over his shoulder. "Let the others unload your things, Armstrong. If you're sitting up at the dais you can't be arriving late, so make sure you are there before the meal begins."

"Aye, my lord," said Jonathon with a nod. When he looked over to Avery, his brother's jaw dropped open in surprise. Then he looked over to Rook who was smirking at his sister. When his gaze met Raven's, a shiver went up his spine. She honestly looked as if she wanted to kill him.

"Can I accompany you to the great hall, my lady?" Jonathon held out his arm.

"Get out of my way, you cur!" She pushed away his arm and stormed past him. "You're going to make me look like the castle fool."

When she walked away, Rook looked over to Jonathon and shrugged. "Mayhap my father has a reason for his madness, I don't really know. But even if he doesn't, it will be amusing to watch my sister's reactions with you at her side at the dais. I wouldn't miss this for the world." Rook chuckled and walked away.

"Are you really going to sit up at the dais with the nobles?" asked Avery. "Above the salt?" He sounded very jealous.

"I have no choice. It is what Lord Corbett wants."

"I wish it were me instead. I'd love to eat the food of the nobles and have white bread instead of brown."

The nobles ate food that the others didn't. One of the prime things being white bread, and another being that they had ornate cellars filled with salt on the table with which to season their food. These things were expensive and not given to the commoners or anyone who didn't sit at the dais.

"I wish it were you as well," mumbled Jonathon, handing his brother a travel bag with tools that he'd removed from his horse. He slipped another bag over his shoulder. A groom ran out from the stables to take care of their horses.

Jonathon headed to the smithy to change back into the uncomfortable clothes of a castle guard, hating every minute of this charade. Since Raven's disposition changed so quickly, he had the feeling that everything was about to go downhill from here and there was nothing he could do to stop it.

~

By the time Raven washed up and made her way back to the great hall with Lark, Jonathon was already in the great hall dressed like a guard again, standing at the end of the dais waiting for her. She stopped in her tracks, her hands balling into fists, and with her teeth clenched. This wasn't right. Her father and brother were only doing this to make a fool out of her, and she didn't like it.

"Cousin, why are ye so upset?" asked Lark.

"That man has got to go."

"Oh, ye mean Jonathon? What's the matter with

him? Didna ye have a good time at his family's home in town today?"

She let out a deep sigh, her eyes still fastened to Jonathon. Even though he shouldn't be wearing the castle's crest, he did look handsome with it on his chest.

"Actually, I enjoyed that part very much," Raven admitted. "His family was so nice to me. Their food was naught but simple pottage and brown bread, but it was comforting eating with them, for some reason. They all seemed so... happy."

"Then why are ye so angry?" asked Lark.

She turned her eyes away from Jonathon and looked directly at her cousin. "It's fine for me to socialize with a commoner when I'm in town and none of the nobles or castle occupants can see it. But to flaunt the fact he's supposedly my personal guard and now is going to be sitting at my side atop the dais is preposterous. Everyone will be staring. What will they think?"

"What difference does it make what anyone thinks?" she asked Raven. Lark's smiled faded. "I've had my entire clan starin' at me for years since I am unwed and have a bastard child. I've learned to accept it."

"This is different," said Raven, feeling a knot growing in her stomach.

"How so?"

"You did something to deserve those stares. I didn't."

"You didn't what?" asked Jonathon, walking up and hearing the end of her conversation.

"Nothing. Never mind." Raven looked the other way.

"May I escort you, my lady?" His damned arm was out again, and part of her wanted to take it. Yet, another part of her knew that this whole thing was most likely some kind of punishment for her since she'd been caught jousting. Well, her brother and father were not going to get the last laugh as far as she was concerned.

"Out of my way," spat Raven, pushing past him and climbing the stairs to the dais herself. She plopped down in her chair, feeling like screaming. "Can you believe him, Lark? He's pretending he's a noble now. Lark?" She thought her cousin had been right behind her, but she wasn't. When Raven looked up, she saw Lark sashaying up to the dais, smiling and laughing and holding onto Jonathon's arm.

"Ugh," she grunted, holding out her goblet, nodding for the cupbearer to fill it. When the boy did, she chugged it down.

Jonathon started to seat Lark next to Raven, but her father stopped that quickly.

"Nay. You sit next to my daughter, Jonathon," called out Corbett from the center of the table. Once Jonathon was seated, Raven's father stood up and made an announcement to everyone that only twisted the knife he'd already embedded in her back.

"I'd like to make a toast to my daughter, Lady Raven," said Corbett, holding up the goblet in the air. "In a few weeks from now she'll be married to the lucky winner of the tournament. Until then, she will practice having a man at her side at the dais, since I have invited Jonathon Armstrong to join us. Jonathon is my daughter's personal guard and also the temporary castle smith."

"Personal guard?" someone called out. "Who is going to protect him from her?"

Everyone laughed.

"Enough!" shouted Corbett. "Mr. Armstrong will also be reporting directly to me, anyone who so much as disrespects or says an unkind word about my daughter."

"What?" Raven's head snapped around and her eyes opened wide as she looked at Jonathon. "Is this true?"

"Well," said Jonathon clearing his throat. "Not exactly. It was your brother who came up with that idea, although I can't say I agree with it in the least."

"You are ruining my life and I wish I never met you." Raven sprang out of her chair and ran from the dais. Jonathon got up to go after her.

"Nay," said Rook, grabbing his arm as Jonathon passed him. "Let her go. When she gets this way, it is best to let her calm down before anyone approaches her. If you go after her now, it'll only make things worse."

"But it's my job, I have to go," said Jonathon, looking back at Corbett. Corbett slowly sat down, shaking his head, not agreeing with what Jonathon wanted to do.

"Sit down and have something to eat," said Rook, taking Raven's empty spot. The servants started placing platters of delicious-looking food in front of him on the table. He spied an entire roasted pig on a platter with an apple in its mouth. Around it was a variety of root vegetables and even roasted chestnuts. Platters of fresh fruit were stacked so high he could barely see over the tops of them. There were baskets of bread and rolls covered with seeds, all of them looking like they were made from white flour, which was considered rare and only for nobles, since it took so long to sift.

"What's that?" asked Jonathon, as a servant put a huge steaming hot pie in front of him.

"That's venison pie. My mother's favorite is venison, so we eat a lot of it," said Rook.

"That aroma," he said, sniffing the air, always aware of different scents. "I've never smelled that before. What is it?"

"The pie is heavily spiced with cardamom and saffron and other exotic spices. I personally don't like all the spices, but my father favors them."

"Can I fill your goblet, my lords?" asked a cup-bearer, coming up behind them with a decanter in each hand.

"He's not a lord," said Rook, holding out his goblet, letting the boy fill it. "Have you ever tasted Elder-flower Summer Ale?" asked Rook. "It's one of my favorite drinks."

"Nay, I haven't." Jonathon noticed the fruity, floral scent coming from the ale and it intrigued him.

"Or the cupbearer also has pear cider. Your choice," said Rook, taking a drink of the ale.

"Pear cider?" he asked, never having had that either.

"It's all right, but it's not even as strong as wine. I prefer the ale," said Rook.

Jonathon really wanted to eat, but he couldn't stay. Not now. Not after what just happened with Raven. He looked down at the rest of the trestle tables below the salt. The food the others were being served seemed to consist of very little meat, but lots of cabbage, brown bread and vegetables. Avery sat next to

Gerold, conversing with the others. His brother looked up, holding a hunk of brown bread in his hand. His eyes devoured the fancier food sitting in front of Jonathon, especially the white bread. He knew how much Avery wanted to try the nobles' food, and that only made Jonathon feel worse about sitting up here. He didn't belong at the dais. He felt like a fraud, and as if sitting up here dressed like this was only making a mockery of him as well. He started regretting accepting this job after all.

"No, thank you. I'm fine," he told the cupbearer. The boy looked puzzled.

With a shake of Rook's head, the cupbearer moved on to fill Lark's goblet instead.

"You seem uncomfortable up here," said Rook.

"I am. I don't belong here and you know it."

"I agree," said Rook, taking another drink of ale. "However, it is my father's decision and I have nothing to say about it."

"If you don't mind, I'd like to set up the forge so I think I'll skip the meal. Unless you'd like me to wait for Lady Raven to return."

"You can go, Armstrong," said Corbett walking over to talk with them. "My daughter will most likely be spending the rest of the night in her chamber sulking like she usually does when she doesn't get her way. I'm sorry for her outburst. The sun has set now, so you are free to work in the forge for the rest of the night. Your service to my daughter is not needed again until the morning."

"Thank you, my lord," said Jonathon, hurrying off the dais, not able to wait to get out of there. As he left the great hall, he could not only hear everyone talking about him, but he could feel their eyes burning into his back as well. He wanted to run from the room, just like Raven had, but he wouldn't. Instead, he held his head high and left the great hall with the poise and grace of a noble, even if he was naught but a common man. Jonathon headed across the courtyard, making a beeline for the blacksmith's shop, pulling off the surcoat with the Blake crest on it as he walked.

He entered the smithy, thinking he heard someone sniffle from within. His bet would be on Gerold, if he hadn't just seen the boy sitting next to his brother in the great hall, so it couldn't be him. Slowly, he entered the room, having just enough light from outside to see a candle and flint on a table. He put down the surcoat and lit the candle with his back to the rest of the room, slowly closing the door. Then, without bothering to turn around, he spoke.

"I know you're here, so you might as well show yourself." When he turned around, Raven walked out from behind a cupboard, but said nothing to him.

"Why are you here and what are you doing?" he asked in a low voice, using the candle to light the logs on the hearth. After getting the fire going, he got up and turned to see Raven sitting quietly at the small table.

"I'm only here because I need something from you and I'm running out of time," she said, staring off into nothingness instead of even looking at him at all.

"Really." He found that interesting yet confusing at the same time. He approached her, pulling off the gloves he wore, holding them in one hand. "Now, what could a woman like you possibly need from a man like me?" He took a step closer, his legs brushing against her knees. When she didn't answer, he reached out and tilted her chin upward until she was looking directly at him. Something told him that what she really needed was a kiss. That must be it, he decided. This woman was complicated, but why else would she be here in secret, waiting for him to return? Throwing caution aside, Jonathon leaned in to her for a kiss, but it never happened. Instead, Raven pushed him hard, sending him falling back, hitting the cupboard. The gloves he'd been holding fell to the ground.

"Stop it!" she warned him.

"Stop it? I don't understand." He slowly righted himself. "One minute you act as if you like me and the next as if you hate my guts. I don't like this addled game at all."

"Is that what you think?" she asked, slowly standing and walking over to him. "You thought I wanted you to kiss me, didn't you?"

"Why the hell else would you come here in secret and wait in the dark if you didn't?" He bent down to pick up his gloves, but she did so at the same time, taking one while he picked up the other.

"What are you doing?" he asked, knowing it wasn't proper for a noble to pick up something for a commoner. Hunkered down, they faced each other. The firelight from the hearth splashed across her face, making her eyes seem to glow. Her raven-colored hair glistened in tones of blue-black, looking soft and silky. The woman's skin was smooth, and she smelled intoxicating. Like roses, if he wasn't mistaken. God's eyes, the wench was beautiful. Why was she playing these games with him? Was she purposely trying to make him go crazy?

"I'm picking up the gauntlet," she said, standing, slapping the leather glove against her palm.

"Huh?" He stood as well, still holding the matching glove.

"When I am faced with a challenge, I embrace it."

"I don't understand what you mean."

"You're an armorer, aren't you?"

"You know I am." He started to wonder if the girl was addled.

"Then I want you to make me a set of armor."

"I see." He nodded, thinking she really meant it. "For whom shall I make this armor?" he asked, bewildered why she would be asking him, instead of the man who needed it.

"It's for me, you fool. I want armor that is lightweight and proportioned appropriately for a lady."

"For *you*?" He made a face and chuckled. "Nay," he said, shaking his head. "Women don't wear armor."

"But they could if they wanted to, couldn't they?" She seemed flustered, and sounded like she wasn't going to give up this crazy idea. She really wanted this armor for herself. God's eyes, the woman was an anomaly. He'd never met any female in his life who thought the way she did.

"I-I suppose a woman could wear armor. That is, if she had some to fit her."

"Good. That's what I thought."

"However, I have no idea how to do it, so I have to object to your request."

"I see." She paced back and forth, still slapping the glove against her palm. The sound of it hitting her skin oddly made his loins tighten. "It's not a request, it's an order."

"I'm sorry, my lady, but I have to object. It's not proper for a lady to wear armor. Besides, your father and brother would kill me if I did what you ask."

"Nay, that's not true," she said, looking sly all of a sudden. "They won't know about it, so there is no harm in it."

"I won't lie to them, if that's what you're asking me to do."

"You'll do what's best for both of us, and I'll hear nothing more about it."

"What in the world does that mean?"

"I mean, if you don't make the armor for me, then I will—I will tell them that you cornered me here in the forge and kissed me."

"That's ridiculous. I never kissed–" His words were cut off as Raven reached out and pulled him to her by the shoulders, forcing her lips up against his in one hell of a kiss. That took him by surprise, and left him speechless. All he could think about was that her lush lips tasted like honeyed mead, and he wanted a second helping. His arms encircled her waist and he pulled her closer, never breaking their connection. He hungrily kissed her back, letting his tongue slip into her mouth, getting carried away and feeling as if he were enchanted. Bid the devil, he was excited!

She didn't push him away at all. Instead, her head fell back and she moaned aloud, sounding ever so sexy. When he broke the kiss, he noticed her eyes were closed and she looked like she was in ecstasy. Her long, smooth neck was so enticing, that he needed to touch her. Running his fingers down her neck, his hand stopped at the neckline of her bodice. Not able to stop himself, he brought his mouth to the small hollow at the base of her neck, kissing her gently. She moaned again and pressed up against him. His mind went crazy with want. His groin tightened with an erection. Damn, he wanted this siren of a woman, and it was taking all his control not to throw her down on the table and push up her skirts and thrust into her right now.

The door to the forge opened, bringing Jonathon back to his senses. He released her so fast that she lost her balance and ended up falling and sitting on the floor.

"Brother?" asked Avery, walking in with a plate of food in his hand. "Did I interrupt something?" His eyes shot down to Raven.

"Nay, not at all," said Jonathon, reaching out and pulling Raven to her feet. She didn't look at all happy. However, her cheeks looked rosy and her lips swollen. Her chest moved in and out with each deep breath she took. Damn, it wasn't helping matters any. He quickly looked the other way.

"Your brother just kissed me and started to fondle me too," said Raven. "Thank goodness you walked in when you did, or who knows what he would have tried next."

"What?" Jonathon's head snapped around and his mouth fell open. It was a bold-faced lie since *she* was the one who kissed *him*, and he hadn't fondled her at all. It was a simple grazing of his fingers down her neck and a couple of harmless kisses. What the hell was she doing?

"Y-you did that, Jonathon?" Avery looked over to Jonathon and his mouth hung open in surprise.

"That's not what happened. I mean, not exactly." He adjusted his tunic, hoping no one noticed the bulge beneath his trews. When he looked back at Raven, she had a smirk on her face. Then she reached out, handing him the glove.

"I'll expect that little project finished before the

tournament begins," she said, turning and walking to the door. It was now clear what was going on. She used her wily ways to make sure he couldn't deny her stupid request. There was no way of getting out of this now.

"Wait. Don't do this to me," said Jonathon, causing her to stop in the doorway and look back over her shoulder.

"You will always address me as 'my lady' or Lady Raven when speaking to me," she corrected him. "Don't make that mistake again. Remember, I am a titled woman. Now, if you don't do what I want, I'll tell my brother and father you cornered me and kissed me." She looked over at Avery next. "I have a witness to strengthen my claim."

"Don't try to blackmail me, because it won't work," snapped Jonathon, losing his patience with the wench and becoming madder than hell. "My lady," he added as an afterthought. "Avery didn't see anything, so dragging him into this isn't going to help matters any."

"That's right. I didn't see a thing," said Avery nervously, still holding his plate of food that he'd brought with him from the meal.

"Besides, we both know your father and Rook like me and will think you are lying." Jonathon kept trying to change her mind.

"Mayhap you're right," she said with a shrug. "But even if you and your brother stay quiet, it doesn't matter. I have a witness that will prove my claim and won't be able to keep quiet about what just happened here."

"What does she mean?" asked Avery.

"Nothing," said Jonathon. "Her threats have nothing to back them up, don't worry."

"Oh, I would worry if I were you." She reached out the open door and yanked Gerold into the room. The little boy looked up with frightened eyes. "What did you see, Gerold?" asked Raven. "Don't lie to me or I swear you'll be punished severely."

"Nay," shouted Jonathon, not wanting the boy to agree to having seen something, and not wanting Raven to use a child in this manner. It just wasn't right.

"I-I saw you kissing Jonathon," said the little boy, causing Raven to smile.

"You mean, you saw Jonathon kissing me, don't you?" she corrected him. She let go and crossed her arms over her chest as she waited for Gerold's answer.

"Aye, that's what I mean, my lady." The little boys eyes were wide as he looked over to Jonathon and then back to Raven. "He kissed you. I saw it."

"Well?" said Raven, glaring at Jonathon. "What do you have to say now?"

Jonathon knew he had no choice. He'd been lured into the vixen's trap and taken the bait. Now he would have no choice but to do her bidding. He couldn't risk it when the child was involved. Gerold was frightened of Raven, there was no doubt about it. Most of the castle's occupants were scared of the wench. If Raven forced the boy to confess to her father and brother that he saw them kissing, Jonathon could lose his head over this. Commoners weren't allowed to kiss nobles and get away with it. He was hired to guard the girl, and with her silly story, it was going to ruin everything for him, since Corbett and

Rook trusted him. He didn't want them to think he betrayed them, because none of this was really his fault.

"I'll get started on the armor right away, my lady," said Jonathon, throwing down both gloves on the table. He was always up for a challenge, but didn't like being blackmailed or having a woman throwing down the gauntlet at his feet.

At least, not when there were conditions added.

CHAPTER 8

"I can't believe we're really staying here in this dirt pit instead of inside the castle in a nice warm chamber with curtains around a bed." Avery sat up on the pallet the next morning and yawned. His and Gerold's pallets were right on the floor. Jonathon had the only bed, even though it was small and uncomfortable. Avery proceeded to rub his back. "We'd be better off sleeping in a trench somewhere. At least then we'd have fresh air."

"Well, I can't believe you're still sleeping when the sun is already up," was Jonathon's reply. He held a list in his hand that he'd just finished making, checking it over once more. "Be grateful you're here within the castle's walls at all. It's an opportunity of a lifetime that most commoners never get."

"Right," said Avery, releasing a deep breath. "What's that in your hand?" Avery got up and walked over to join him, rubbing his eyes.

"It is a list I made of supplies I'll need to make a suit of armor for Lady Raven."

"Nay." Avery shook his head. "You're not really thinking of doing it, are you? That's absurd."

"You heard her. She'll tell her father I abducted and kissed her if I don't."

"Nay, she's just trying to scare you. She wouldn't do that. Would she?"

"I don't know, but with Lady Raven, I wouldn't doubt it and can't take the risk. "She involved a child in her daft deception, and I won't let little Gerold get hurt. He's already lost his family and everything he has."

"Gerold," repeated Avery looking back at the boy's sleeping pallet. "Where is he?"

"He's already up and about for the day, like you should be."

"I'm up now, so stop your whining," said Avery, with another yawn.

"The Lords Blake have hired me to do a job," Jonathon reminded his brother. "They are trusting in me. I am supposed to report any man who bad-mouths Lady Raven or does anything improper toward her. I don't want them thinking I took advantage of this position when I don't report myself. Here." Jonathon shoved the list into Avery's hand and turned back to finish dressing. He wore his own clothes today, not wanting to don the garments of a guard ever again. He just didn't feel comfortable wearing them. Hopefully, he could convince the Lords Blake not to make him wear them again.

"Here, what?" Avery made a face and held up the parchment and surveyed it. "Why are you giving this to me?"

"I need you to collect the supplies I'll need."

"Me? Nay," he said, trying to give the parchment back to Jonathon. "I'm not your lackey. I'm a journey-man, not an errand boy. Do it yourself."

"I can't." Jonathon didn't take the parchment. Instead, he donned his weapon belt with sword and dagger. "I've got somewhere I need to be."

"Oh." Avery surveyed him and lowered his hand. "Then get the boy to do this menial task. He's the apprentice."

Jonathon took out his sword and used his sleeve to shine it. "Gerold looked hungry so I sent him to the kitchen, hoping the cooks would take pity on him and feed him. Besides, he's just a child. If he tries to purchase these things by himself, he'll most likely be robbed before he returns. But take him with you, because I think he'd like that."

"What about me? Don't you ever worry about what I might like?"

"Avery, now who's whining? I got you the position inside the castle walls, so just hush up and do as I ask. We've got a lot of the supplies that I need already at our shop, but you'll have to buy the rest. You can introduce Gerold to Heathcliff, since they're about the same age. The boy needs friends."

Avery looked at the list and shook his head. "I think I know where I can pick up the steel you want, but it's going to be expensive. Where am I supposed to come up with that kind of money?"

"Aye. I see your point." Jonathon remembered the coin pouch that Rook had given him, and pulled it out of his bag. He had hoped to give this money to his family since they were struggling lately, but he didn't have a choice now. He needed those supplies, and he needed them fast. "Use this. It should be more than enough to pay for everything. Give whatever is left over to Father." He tossed the pouch of coins to his brother. Avery caught it and looked inside, releasing a slow whistle.

"Where did you get this kind of money, Brother?"

"Let's just say it's a bonus for a job I'm expected to do."

Avery nodded, closing up the pouch and looking back at Jonathon. "Where are you going, dressed like that? I hardly think you need to carry a full weapon belt around just to protect Lady Raven. We're not at war here. It is a little too much, don't you think?"

"Actually, not really." Jonathon grabbed his cloak and put it over his shoulders. He wore the clothes of a mercenary today, but it was who he was. "I might need to take a mace and axe just to keep her in line, but honestly, I'm headed to the practice yard to spar with the knights before the main meal."

"Spar? With the knights?" This got Avery's attention. "What about me? I want to go to the practice yard, too."

"You're no good with a sword in your hand unless you're heating it in the forge and we both know it. It's not for you, Brother."

"I don't have to fight the knights. I just want to watch."

"Not today. Now, get going right away. It'll take you some time to find and collect everything on that list."

"Right away? Oh, so now you want me to miss the meal as well?" complained Avery, throwing the list down on his pallet. "I thought when you brought me here it was because I always wanted to experience life in a castle, and you were being nice to your younger brother."

"You're experiencing it, aren't you?" asked

Jonathon, heading for the door. "It might be from inside the forge, but at least you have your foot in the door."

"What about all the work that needs to be done here?" asked Avery from behind him. "Besides cleaning up this pit, I'll need to set up shop. It's only a matter of time before the nobles show up wanting something fixed. Who's going to do that?"

"I've got a job during the day, so it's up to you for now. Gerold will help you. I'll pitch in when I can. Once the sun sets."

"How will you do that?" Avery demanded to know. "You'll be spending all your blasted free time on that stupid armor now. Father will be short-handed at the shop, now that both of us are gone, so we'll need to pick up the overflow there as well."

"Then you'd better hurry up and get going." Jonathon left the forge, hightailing it over to the practice field, anxious to spar against the knights and nobles. When he got to the practice yard, none of the men would even acknowledge him. Rook and Corbett weren't there yet, and he felt very uncomfortable.

"Good morning," he said, trying to start up conversations with several of the men he knew who had commissioned him to do jobs for them in the past. "I'm looking for a partner for some swordplay." No one volunteered or even looked at him. He figured after yesterday's announcement that he was going to report them to Corbett or Rook if they badmouthed Raven, they were all on edge being around him. "I assure you, Lords Corbett and Rook invited me here. Plus, most of you know me from my shop in town, or because I've hired out my sword to Blake Castle on several occasions now."

Still nothing. The men practiced with each other, but none of them wanted anything to do with Jonathon.

"I'll fight you," he heard from behind him, turning to see Raven standing there with her sword in hand, wearing the clothes of a man again, instead of donning her gown. Her cousin Lark was hovering a little ways behind her in the shadows.

"Lady Raven," said Jonathon with a slight chuckle. "I thought you'd still be sleeping this early."

"I'm usually in the practice yard before the sun even rises, so this is normal for me. However, I am surprised to even see you here at all."

"Your father and brother invited me."

"I know that. I was speaking of your special job that you need to complete, and in a timely manner. I thought you'd be working on that."

Raven walked up to Jonathon, gripping her sword. He knew exactly what she meant but was playing dumb. He had her armor to make. If he didn't start soon, he'd never get it completed by the tournament.

"Don't worry about my doings," he said, slowly walking a circle around her. She kept turning, acting like a warrior, never putting her back to anyone she didn't trust. "Why don't you head back to the great hall and wait for me there, my lady?" he suggested. "I'll join you there soon for the meal to break the fast. That is, as soon as I get in a little practice."

"Isn't it a little hard to practice when no one will partner with you?" she answered snidely.

"I suppose you'd know about that." His eyes darted over to the rest of the men who ignored her as much as they had him. "I don't see anyone beating down the door to practice with you, either. My lady."

"All the more reason for you to spar with me, then."

"I'm afraid not," he answered. "I will not raise a sword to a lady, or any female, for that matter." As soon as he looked away, she used it to her advantage. She swung her blade at him, bringing it close to his face.

It impressed her how fast Jonathon's reflexes were. He yanked out his sword and defended himself, lifting his blade, as if it were second nature. His sword clashed with hers as he stopped her blow, even though she wasn't really intending to hit him. She just decided to urge him on a little, that's all.

"You are a stubborn wench," he said through gritted teeth, his sword still crossed with hers.

"And you are now getting the attention of every man here," she answered. "Congratulations."

His back was toward the other soldiers, but she knew his pride would make him look. Sure enough, he gave the other men a sideways glance. When he did so, she put her plan to action.

With one fast swipe, she twisted her sword, un-arming Jonathon completely. His sword skidded across the ground. She chuckled. "Never be distracted or you'll regret it," she told him. "It's the first rule of being a good warrior."

"Well, you can tell your father that, since here he comes now." He nodded, quickly glancing over her shoulder.

She turned to look, not wanting to have to deal with the wrath of her father so early in the day. As soon as she did, Jonathon dove to the ground and sprang back up to a standing position, with his sword in two hands, aimed directly at her. She attacked and he defended. Metal rang out loudly, causing the men in the practice yard to start wandering over in curiosity.

"Don't tell me how to fight," Jonathon told her. "Mayhap instead, you should heed your own warning."

"You are naught but a liar. You played me for a fool. My father isn't even here. You'll pay for that, armorer."

"Please, stop. I don't want to fight you, my lady," said Jonathon, but she kept coming at him and he had no choice but to defend himself or get hit. He was fast, she'd give him that. He managed to parry every time she thrust. However, he only defended himself and never attacked like she wanted him to do.

"Fight with me like you mean it. The way you would with a man," she commanded.

"Nay. I don't want to hurt you. After all, I've been hired to protect you, my lady, so to do so would be breaking my contract with your father."

"Then we won't tell him, will we? Now fight me! Act like a man, not a mouse." She kept attacking, and he kept defending, but he was holding back and she didn't like that.

"I'd think you'd know by now that there are no secrets from the lord of the castle," he told her. "You'd better stop this nonsense because Lord Corbett is heading this way and he doesn't look happy."

"I'm not falling for that ploy again," she spat, not bothering to turn around this time since he was obviously lying, just trying to distract her. "At least try to come up with something different and more believable. For a man who creates things in a forge all day, I'm surprised that you really lack imagination."

"Raven, listen to him," called out Lark.

"I'll not take orders from a mere commoner, Lark." Raven continued to spar with him, becoming angry that he wasn't treating her like a true opponent.

"Raven, put down the sword and act like a lady," came her father's growl directly from behind her. She groaned inwardly, her eyes snapping up to meet Jonathon's.

"I told you so," he said, lowering his sword and bowing as Corbett approached. "Good morning, my lord. My lady," he added.

"What? Mother is here too?" Raven spun around on her heel to see not only her parents, but also her brother standing next to Lark, glaring at her.

"What is going on here?" asked Lady Devon. "Raven, you know we don't like you down here at the practice yard. We told you to stop doing this. You'll be married soon and need to start acting like a proper lady."

"I've been sparring with Jonathon," she told them. Her eyes flashed over to her personal guard who was slowly shaking his head.

"I've only been defending myself against your daughter's attacks," replied Jonathon. "I would never do anything to hurt her and was very careful that she wouldn't get nicked."

"I thank you for that, Armstrong," said Corbett. He looked up at the rest of the men, who had stopped their practice and were all watching this drama unfold. Then he spoke to her softly. "Raven, go change out of those ridiculous clothes right now, and wash up for the meal."

"I'll go with her," said Lark, coming over and putting her hand on Raven's arm.

"Fine," she said, sheathing her sword. She started to leave, then stopped and looked back at Jonathon. "What about him?" she asked. "Father, he doesn't belong here."

"My lord, I only came to practice with my blade as you suggested," Jonathon told Corbett.

"Then stay for now," said Corbett. "Who is going to spar with the armorer?" Corbett looked up, speaking to his men.

When none of the men came forward, but instead looked in the opposite direction, Raven smiled. This would put the arrogant armorer in his place. He'd have to go back to the smithy now, and that is where he belonged.

"I'd actually like to spar with him," said Rook, pulling his sword from the sheath.

"What?" gasped Raven. "Brother, nay!"

"I would like to fight him too," said Corbett. "He's worked for me many times, but I'm curious to see how good he really is."

"Mother, tell them it's time for the meal," Raven said to Devon in a panic. She didn't want Jonathon to get his way when she was being sent to her room like a scorned child.

"I'll not tell your father a thing, and neither will you," said her mother. "Now, let's go back to the castle and wait in the great hall for them to finish their practice so we can have our meal." Devon took her arm and led her away.

Raven looked over her shoulder seeing Rook sparring with Jonathon. Jonathon was good. Damned good with a blade. Suddenly, the rest of the men lined up, as they all wanted their turn to fight against the armorer.

Raven let out a frustrated sigh. Sometimes, it was so unfair to be a woman. Even a commoner like Jonathon Armstrong was now getting more attention and respect than she did.

~

An hour and a half later, Raven still sat at the dais, waiting for the return of the men from the practice yard so the meal could begin. The servants all stood patiently at the door to the kitchen, trying to keep the food warm. Even the minstrels had stopped playing, and everyone in the great hall had become quite bored.

Raven shot to her feet. "This is preposterous! I am not going to sit here another minute waiting on the men to join us. Come, Lark, let's go back to my chamber."

"Nay," said Devon. "Here come your father and brother now. Sit down. Both of you. And don't say a word about it." Devon took a sip of wine and smiled pleasantly at her husband as he took his seat next to her. When Rook walked by, Raven grabbed him by the arm.

"What was going on out there? Why did it take so long?" she demanded to know. "We were waiting for you for nearly two hours."

"I can't help it," said Rook with a shrug. "Once Father and I sparred with Jonathon, the rest of the men wanted to do so, too. He's got one hell of a sword arm and his endurance is incredible. It's probably from him swinging all those heavy hammers in the forge all day long," said Rook. "The man never seems to get winded or tired. I've never seen such stamina in my life, even from the knights."

"Well, where is he now?" she asked through gritted teeth, not liking that the man was getting so much attention.

"Where is who?" Jonathon walked up behind her. She quickly let go of her brother. Both men took a seat. Jonathon, of course, sat right next to her. Raven looked over to see that his hair was dripping wet. He also smelled like lye soap.

"That's not what you were wearing earlier," she said, noticing him dressed in a plain brown tunic.

"Nay. I became soaked with sweat after sparring with a dozen men, so I had to change and wash. After all, I wouldn't want to show up at the dais dirty, sweaty, and disrespectful." He held out his goblet for the cupbearer to fill. "I'll try some of that Elderflower Ale. Thank you," he said to the boy in a sincere and pleasant tone.

"We don't thank servants for doing their job," she sniffed.

"Really." Jonathon looked at her over the rim of his cup at he drank. "Why not?"

"Because, we're nobles and they are mere servants, that's why. It is expected of them to serve us. It's their job. It's not like they're doing us a favor."

He slowly put down his cup. "Like me doing my job, you mean?"

"Yes, that's right," she said, thinking he finally understood.

"Well, since I'm not a noble, I realize how hard

these 'mere servants' work. Therefore, I find it appropriate to thank them. A little kindness goes a long way, my lady. You really should try it sometime." He turned and started talking to Lark before she could even answer.

The meal started and they ate in silence at first. But before long, every few minutes it seemed that another knight or soldier approached the dais to talk to Jonathon over the edge of the table.

"Jonathon, I've got a crack in the hilt of my sword," said Sir Lionel, showing him his sword over the edge of the table. "Do you think you can fix it?"

"Of course," answered Jonathon. "I'd be happy to. Just drop it off at the castle's forge and I'll take a look at it later tonight."

"My brother is building a barn and needs a barrel or two of nails," said Randolph, the falconer. "I've been waiting for another blacksmith to arrive at the castle, but since you're our temporary smith, can you do it?"

"I don't see why not. I'll get to it right away." Jonathon didn't turn anyone away.

Before the meal was over, another six men approached Jonathon and he promised them all he'd fix or make something for them. It was outrageous that he could even think he'd have time for all this work when he had her armor to construct.

Finally, Raven cleared her throat and Jonathon looked up.

"Did you want to say something, my lady? Please, go ahead. My attention is all yours." He popped a sweetmeat into his mouth and her eyes followed. Just the way he chewed and swallowed made her remember the kiss in the forge. God's eyes, she was starting to feel warm just watching the man eat.

And why did he have to always be so polite? That only made everyone like him more.

She leaned over and whispered to him, when no one else seemed to be listening. "How are you going to make my armor when you're taking on so much other side work? My armor is more important and that is what you should be focusing on, not horse-shoes and nails. Turn away these requests," she demanded. "Tell everyone you are too busy."

"I-I can't. I'm the castle's smith now, and it's my job," he said in a low voice. "I've made them promises that I refuse to break."

"Well, what about your promise to me? To make my armor?" she whispered.

"Promise?" His eyebrows raised. "Is that what we're calling it now?"

"Of course. Why? What would you call it?"

"Oh, I don't know. He shrugged, most likely for effect. "Words like blackmail, trickery, and deceit are the first to come to mind."

"Shhhh," she said, her eyes scanning the table.

"You never told me why you want the armor." He looked at her and waited for an answer.

"That's right, I didn't.

His craggy brows raised in question, only making him seem even more handsome. "Well?"

"It's... it's... none of your business. Now, when will you be able to start on it? I want it finished before the tournament, remember."

"Why?"

She realized he was becoming suspicious and she didn't want him to figure out what she planned to do.

"It's because I know you'll be gone after the tournament, that's why."

"I don't like this game you're playing," he growled.

"Then don't make the armor, that's fine with me. I don't care." Her eyes darted over to her father and back to him. "I'm sure my father and Rook will understand why you were kissing me, unchaperoned in the forge."

"That's not what happened and you know it. And don't you dare say a word to either of them about it. It won't bode well for me."

"Then, you'll make it?" she asked, raising her chin and looking down her nose at him.

"I said I would, didn't I?"

"Not really, but it'll do. When will you start?"

"I can't start until I know your measurements. Armor is constructed to fit like a glove on its owner. Each set of armor is different."

"Oh. All right. So... how do we do that?"

"I'll need you to come to the smithy after dark. After everyone has gone to sleep for the night."

"Really?" she asked, feeling her heart speed up. She was excited and a little scared by this request. Still, it did intrigue her. She glanced over the edge of the table and saw Avery and Gerold coming to the meal late. They would both be there at the smithy when she arrived, she realized. Therefore, she wouldn't have to be alone with Jonathon, so she had nothing to fear. "All right, I'll do it," she said, feeling smug but liking the way it felt. She was finally going to have her own armor.

"Excuse me, my lady, but I see my brother is here now and I need to speak with him about the supplies for making our secret little project." Jonathon left the dais, going down to talk to his brother.

"Raven?" asked Lark, moving over to Jonathon's vacated seat. "What were ye two whisperin' about?"

Raven leaned over and whispered back to Lark. "Jonathon's going to measure me for my armor tonight."

"What? Really?" Lark's cheeks became a little rosier. "Do you really think he should do that?"

"He has to, because he needs to know what size to make it."

"B-but, I mean, do ye think... do ye think that ye should go?"

"If I want armor, I need to be measured for it," she told her cousin. "After all, I am going to have to joust and win the tournament." She'd already told Lark all about her plan of competing in the tournament in secret, and winning. "If I don't win, I'll end up marrying whichever disgusting man does, no matter how he looks, smells, or how old he might be. Like hell if I'm going to do that!"

She glanced back at Jonathon who was talking to the stablemaster now. It sounded as if the man was asking him to make a set of horseshoes. Even with Jonathon's hair wet and slicked back, she thought he looked extremely handsome. He was also skilled with a sword, and she liked that about him. He wasn't a mouse after all, but a man. Too bad he was the wrong man. He reached out to shake the stablemaster's hand and when he did, she got a good view of his muscular forearms. Damn, he was strong. She could tell it just by the way he'd blocked her blows with the sword, not to mention she'd felt those muscles when he'd carried her through the mud. Jonathon could probably hold a two-handed claymore one-fisted and not get tired fighting an army of Scots.

Suddenly, she couldn't stop herself from thinking about how it had felt to have his hands around her waist as he'd helped her from her horse. She liked it for some reason, even though she knew she shouldn't. Raven had also liked the way the man kissed. He had been gentle yet aggressive at the same time, slipping his tongue into her mouth. Just the thought of part of him having entered her, made her squirm.

His lips were strong but soft. He had tasted so... so *manly*. Just thinking about this made her feel hot down to her inner core. Why was she always attracted to what she shouldn't be doing or couldn't have? He was no exception.

Jonathon looked over at her just then and smiled. Straight white teeth and sparkling blue eyes drew her in. He had no right looking so good. After all, he was just a simple commoner. A glorified blacksmith. An armorer.

And probably a terrific lover.

"Nay," she said aloud, turning and trying to shake the illicit thoughts from her head. Even though she wouldn't be alone with him tonight, part of her wished she would be. Her curiosity about him was strong. Raven couldn't stop wondering exactly how this man planned on taking her measurements for her armor. Even though she had no idea how it was done, one thing was for certain. In order to get her measurements, the man was going to have to touch her, and that was something she looked forward to right now, more than anything else.

CHAPTER 9

"More air," Jonathon told the boy. "I need more air to fan the flames."

Gerold pulled the rope to work the bellows, causing the fire of the forge to surge up and become brighter. With his gloved hand, Jonathon held a long pair of tongs. Clasped in the tongs was a metal rod. As soon as the rod was glowing, he moved it over to the anvil, using a hammer to make it square on all four sides, and to shape it into a point at the end.

He cut the end off to make a nail. Then he put the end through a hole in the bench, letting part of it stick out, using the tongs to hold it steady. As he banged the end with a hammer, it flattened out to make the head of the nail. Pulling it out with the tongs, he then dropped it into a barrel with the rest of the nails that he and his brother had made that day.

"Hello? Jonathon?" came a voice from the door. He turned to see Raven peeking inside. It was night-time and dark. Most everyone had already gone to bed.

"That's enough for the night," Jonathon told

Gerold and Avery. "You two can go to bed now. Come in, Lady Raven."

"Go to bed? Already?" asked Avery. Gerold yawned and wiped one eye.

"Don't we need to clean up first?" asked Gerold.

"I'll take care of it as well as shutting down the forge. We'll start early in the morning, so get some shut-eye," Jonathon told them, wanting to be alone with Raven.

"My lady," said Avery, nodding, then glowering at Jonathon before turning and taking the boy with him to the adjoining room that was used for sleeping.

"Close the door behind you," Jonathon called out to his brother, wanting privacy. Avery grumbled but did as he was told.

"You didn't need to send them away," said Raven, feeling a little uncomfortable to be alone with Jonathon.

"This doesn't concern them and it is best if they're not involved."

Raven watched as Jonathon used the long tongs to spread out the hot coals on the forge, preparing to shut it down. He then picked up a bottle of water and sprinkled it over the flames, causing smoke to rise up in thin tendrils.

"What were you making?" asked Raven, curiously walking over to where he'd been hitting his hammer against an anvil. She reached out for a rod lying there.

"Don't touch that! It might still be hot." He reached out and took her hand and led her across the room. "We were making nails," he mumbled, releasing her hand and digging for something in a drawer.

Raven coughed since it was still smoky in there,

even though a hole in the roof vented the air. Her eyes traveled down Jonathon's body as he bent over now, digging through a leather bag.

"I know it's here somewhere."

"What are you looking for?" she asked, walking closer to him. His skin glistened from sweat, but it only made him more enticing. Soot covered his bare forearms, the hairs looking black even though the hair on his head was brown and tied back, trailing down the nape of his neck. He wore breeches that hugged the muscles of his hips. The tunic under his long leather apron was open at the neck, showing off part of his chest. "It's hot in here," she said, feeling suddenly warmer than before as she drank in his manly physique.

"I can open the front door if you'd like." He took a step toward it, but she reached out and touched his arm to stop him.

"Nay," she said. "I wouldn't want anyone to see me in here so late at night."

"Aye," he agreed, with a slight nod. "I suppose that would only cause trouble. Oh, there it is." He walked over to a hook on the wall and removed a long piece of twine that seemed to have markings down it. He held it up, and walked back to her.

"What is that?" she asked.

"It's my measuring string. To measure you for your armor."

"Oh. I see."

He stood there holding the string and looking at her, seeming not to know where to start.

"What do you need to measure first?"

"I-I suppose your arms," he told her.

131

She stood straight and held her arms out to her sides. "Go ahead."

"Nay, my lady. Not like that."

"Then how?" She slowly lowered her arms.

"Well, first I need to know the length of both your upper arm and your forearm." He gently reached out, lifting one of her arms forward instead of out to the side. He used the string to measure the distance, looking at the marks on it. Then he bent her arm upward from her elbow so her hand was against her chest, and measured it that way, too.

"All right. Now I need to know the size of your legs." He looked down and stopped. She was wearing a gown and her legs were covered.

"Oh. I suppose I should have worn trews?"

"Aye, this would have been a good time to dress like a man." He cleared his throat and got down on one knee. He reached out for the hem of her gown but pulled his hands back and shook his head. "Nay. I can't do this."

"Would this help?" She hoisted up the gown, showing the bottoms of her legs. She wore hose that extended halfway up her legs and were tied around the bottom of her knees with garters to keep them from falling.

He gently measured her legs to the knees, and then looked up at her. She saw something in his eyes she couldn't describe. To her, it seemed like a mixture of lust and terror.

"Forgive me, my lady, but I'll need to put my hands under your gown to measure the length of your upper legs. All the way up to your waist and... and groin."

"I see," she said in a breathy whisper. "I didn't re-alize you had to do that."

He shook his head again. "This can wait until to-morrow. Come back dressed in trews and we'll con-tinue then."

"Nay!" She raised her voice as he started to get up, her hand on his shoulder stopping him. "Please, continue. I don't want to waste any more time. This is important."

"If you insist, my lady." He nervously cleared his throat again. A click sounded like the door to the bed-chamber opening. He glanced back over his shoulder. "Good night," he called out, and the door to the ad-joining room slowly closed with a thud. Again.

"I'm ready," she said, still holding up her gown to her knees.

"I'll be quick about it," he told her, looking up with bright blue eyes.

"Take your time." She felt her breath hitch when his fingers touched her knee with the measuring string. Then ever so slowly, with his other hand he slid the rest of the string up the bare skin of her thigh, rounding the outside curve of her hip. A warmth coursed through her. His hand was on her bare skin and very close to her most private parts.

"Almost done," he said, his voice sounding husky again. "I'm going to measure the-the inside of your upper leg now.

"Of course," she said, watching him with his hands under her skirt. She felt him pressing the string against the inside of her leg, slowly sliding it against her bare skin higher… and higher… and higher.

Her undergarment consisted of only a thin chemise. She wore no braies, as most women didn't unless they had their menses. The top part of her legs were bare, as well as all her womanly parts. The feel of his hand sliding up her leg toward her groin sent a tingle of desire rushing through her.

"I'm sorry, my lady," he whispered, clearing his throat once again. He seemed more nervous about this than she felt. "I'll need you to spread... I mean, open... I mean, can you move your legs apart slightly?"

"Certainly." She took a wider stance, feeling his fingers pressing the string up where her leg ended and her most private part started. The back of his hand actually brushed against her womanly folds. When it did, she felt herself contract, and a strong vibration go through her. This intimate action made her feel so alive. So wanton, and hot and lusty. "Oooooh," she moaned softly, not able to tamp her desire.

It must have alarmed him, because he quickly removed his hand from under her gown and bolted to an upright position.

"Let me... let me just record the numbers." He headed back to a table to write down the measurements. She noticed him running his hand through his hair and adjusting the waist of his tied apron before he turned back around.

"Are you finished?" she asked, hoping not.

"I assure you, I have only just begun." He came back holding his string, standing right in front of her, so close that she swore she felt heat emanating off his body. Or was it hers? "I need to measure your upper body now."

"I understand." Her tongue shot out to lick her dry lips. She could hear the spitting of the coals on the forge, not wanting to be extinguished. It felt as if she had a fire within her and she was trying to contain it before it raged up out of control. "Go on, then."

"Hold up your arms slightly. I need to measure your chest."

She did as he instructed. He took the string and put it around the back of her, bringing it forward over her breasts, holding the string together in front. She could feel the pressure of the measuring string right through her clothes, pressing against her nipples.

His fingers had brushed slightly against her breasts this time. The action excited her and made her breathe heavily, which only made her chest expand and contract, causing the string to get tighter and then looser.

"My lady, perhaps you need to hold your breath?" Jonathon seemed suddenly different. His eyes were fastened to her chest. If she wasn't mistaken, his hands were shaking. "If you really insist on wearing armor, you'll have to bind your breasts, you realize."

"Bind my breasts?" she asked, thinking it ridiculous since she was well endowed. Never had she ever imagined having to do something like that. "Will it hurt?"

"I don't know," he said, his eyes meeting hers now. "I've never had... breasts." They stared into each other's eyes.

Raven felt parched and could barely swallow. She swore she felt her nipples harden just from his eyes on her chest. The light throbbing between her thighs became stronger, and all she could think about was being naked and pressed up next to Jonathon's naked body.

Her lips felt dry, so she licked them. That's when

his eyes fastened to her mouth. His body was close to hers, his hands still holding the string around her breasts. He leaned in closer. So did she. Then, before she had a chance to even think this through, their lips touched and their mouths pressed together in a kiss.

Her eyes closed and her hands slid up his arms and to his shoulders. The kiss deepened and the passion she felt inside alarmed her. His lips started to pull away but she did not want it to end. Instead, she went back for another kiss, craving the taste of this man on her tongue.

Jonathon hungrily took what she offered. Raven's body tingled and a heat rose inside her belly that had nothing to do with the fire from the forge. And when his palms gently settled over her breasts and he gave them a light squeeze, she lost all her morals and almost her mind as well.

She pushed up against him, lifting her face for another kiss. A bulge protruded from under his apron, pressing up against her belly. He was hard and it made her feel wanton. Raven didn't care if she wasn't acting like a lady. She liked it and wanted more. Then she felt his hands slip down her thighs and snake around to cup her buttocks. When he pulled her hard against his evident desire for her, she gasped in excitement. She cupped his face in her hands and hurriedly removed the tie holding back his hair, causing his hair to fall around his shoulders. God's eyes, this man looked handsome. Dark and dangerous, just the way she liked it.

"Yes," she whispered in a breathy voice, ready to pull up her gown and wrap her bare legs around his waist. His erection pressed up against her, feeling so big. So hard. So ready. She was ready too. All she could think about at this moment was that she wanted him inside her. If she didn't find her release soon, she thought she might burst with lust.

To her disappointment, instead of continuing, he pushed away, breaking their intimate connection.

Raven's heart dropped in her chest. She wanted to shout at him to keep going, but she didn't say a thing. Instead, she just watched Jonathon turn away and drag a weary hand through his hair, cursing under his breath. Then he stared into the dying flames of the forge. "I-I'm sorry," he said in a gruff whisper. "I didn't mean to do that."

"Well, mayhap I did," she answered boldly, not wanting him to walk away from her right now. She had felt as if she were coming to life beneath his touch. No one had ever made her feel this way before.

"It's wrong." He turned to face her. "For a moment I forgot exactly who you were, my lady."

The use of her title at this moment brought her back to her senses.

"Mayhap you're right," she said, feeling disappointment fill her, as well as a tinge of shame. "I got carried away as well, forgetting that I'm a noble and you're a commoner. Being intimate together is not allowed."

"Please, don't say anything about this to anyone," he all but begged her.

"Of course not," she answered, wanting to yell from the battlements that she kissed Jonathon Armstrong and almost shattered in his arms from just his touch. "It wouldn't be proper."

"You'd better leave now before someone discovers you're here." He turned and walked back to the forge, pumping the bellows to bring the fire back to life.

Why couldn't she get the thought out of her head of him pumping into her, to bring her to life as well?

Raven felt like that forge, being fanned to a full flame by the touch of the armorer named Jonathon Armstrong. He didn't look at her again. Instead, he picked up the iron rod with the long tongs and shoved it into the fire. It was as if nothing had just happened between them. Or perhaps he really didn't care.

"Don't you need more measurements?" she asked.

"Nay!" he said, almost too quickly. "I mean, aye, but just for the helm. I'll get it later. That will be the last piece I make so it's not important right now."

"I see." She stood there for a moment, but he still didn't turn to face her. "How long will it take to complete my armor? I'd like it as soon as possible."

"I don't know," he said, starting to sound now as if he were getting irritated by her questions, or perhaps just from her presence here in the forge. "An entire suit of plate armor usually takes months to make," he told her.

"Months?" she gasped. "Nay. That's too long. I need it in a few weeks' time."

"That's impossible. Unless I just make the necessary plates and not everything."

"It needs to cover my identity."

He stopped and glanced over his shoulder. "Did you say your identity? What does that mean?"

"Nay, that's not what I meant. Never mind. Just please make it quickly."

"These things can't be rushed. Now, I'll let you know when I need something from you again. Goodnight."

Raven had never been dismissed like this in her

life. Or at least, not from someone below her status. The man's arrogance bothered her. This time, he didn't even use her title. Did he think a little intimacy between them granted him permission to be so casual with her now? If so, he was wrong. Thinking about what just happened between them, Raven felt used and wanton at the same time. It wasn't a good feeling in the least.

"Next time you need something from me, I might not be so obliged to give it," she spat.

"Pardon me?" He finally turned and looked at her fully, but any special connection between them was gone. Her anger rose and she felt like hitting something. Or someone.

"You heard me," she said through gritted teeth. "I suggest from now on you remember just who you are, Mr. Armstrong. You are a commoner and have no right to touch me, speak to me in such a familiar way, or in such a dismissive manner."

"What did I do?" he asked, honestly looking bewildered.

"Good night. Don't bother seeing me to the door." She turned on her heel and ran out of the forge, holding back the tears, not wanting him to know how much he'd truly upset her.

～

The door to the bedchamber opened and Avery poked his head out. "Jonathon? What's all the yelling about?" he asked.

"I wasn't the one raising my voice, and neither did I deserve the chastising tongue-lashing I just received."

"What do you mean? What's going on?" He closed the door so Gerold wouldn't wake up, and walked over to talk to Jonathon. "What are you doing? I thought we were done working for the night."

"I need something to hit," snarled Jonathon, picking up a hammer and banging it down against the hot metal, over and over again, filling the air with a loud clinking noise.

"It didn't go well between you, then?" asked Avery.

"Actually, it went a little too well," he answered. "However, I won't make that mistake again."

"What the hell does that mean?"

"It means that tomorrow I am going to tell Lord Corbett that I no longer wish to stay here at Blake Castle."

"You're going to quit your job? Lord Corbett won't like that. You made a deal with him and need to honor that."

"I know you are right. Honestly, I don't know if I can get out of my commitment without losing too many customers, anyway. However, all I know is that I cannot continue to be around Lady Raven anymore. If I am, I'll lose my mind."

"I'm confused," said Avery, looking at Jonathon as if he thought he was already out of his mind. "So, do you like the girl or hate her?"

"A little of both at the moment, but it doesn't matter."

"It doesn't? Why not?"

Jonathon threw the hammer onto the table, picked up a cloth, and wiped his brow and then his hands. "I kissed her, Brother. And I damn well liked it."

"Well, who wouldn't?" asked Avery with a wide smile. "So, why did she leave? Oh God, did she slap you?"

"Nay. She seemed to like the kiss and even encouraged more to happen."

"Really? Nice," said Avery, nodding his head. "Then, I don't understand. Why did I hear yelling?"

"I sent her away."

"Are you mad?"

"I'm beginning to think so. Mad for a woman I can never have. I made a mistake, but it won't happen again."

"Oh, you think she'll mention it to her father, don't you?"

"Nay. I'm sure she won't." Jonathon sadly stared into the glowing fire, thinking of the way she'd moaned. It was something that he had never expected. She sounded so full of passion from just a kiss and a touch. "The wench liked what happened between us just as much as I did. That's the part that scares me."

"It sounds to me like you're a lucky dog, Brother. Don't knock it. I'd give anything to kiss a beautiful woman like her."

"Avery, think about it. I'm supposed to be watching and protecting her and reporting back to Lord Corbett. It's not like I can I tell her father that I want to bed his daughter."

"Nay. I'm sure that wouldn't go over well," said Avery, finally catching on. "So, what are you going to do?"

"What can I do? I'm committed to this, just as much as I am to making armor for a lady who doesn't need it and will never wear it. I'm in too deep to ever get out. I won't be able to change anything until after the tournament. Once the wench is married, my job is over and I'm out of here. I guess I'll just have to put up with it until then." Jonathon plopped down on a chair and rubbed his hands over his face.

"Is it going to be hard seeing Lady Raven marry a noble?" asked Avery.

"Yes," he answered, his eyes closing. In his mind he saw the beautiful face of a woman he craved but could never have. Just thinking of touching and kissing her made him feel hot all over again. "Harder than you think, Brother. Much harder than you think."

CHAPTER 10

"Raven, why were ye gone so long?" asked Lark, as soon as Raven had returned to her room. "I was afraid yer handmaid would come to check on ye and realize ye werena here." She ran over and looked up and down the corridor, checking for anyone who might have seen her. When she realized no one had, she hurriedly closed the door.

"I kissed Jonathon. Again," said Raven, letting out a sigh. She removed her cloak and fell atop her bed fully clothed.

"Ye did? How excitin'." Lark climbed up on the bed next to her. "Tell me all about it."

"He was taking measurements for my armor," Raven explained. "If I had known he'd be putting his hands under my gown, I would have worn my trews. I was trying to look pretty for him by donning the gown."

"Wait. He did what?" Lark's eyes opened wide.

"He touched my breasts as well, while we kissed."

"Raven, ye should no' have been doin' that! What were ye thinkin'?" gasped Lark, putting her hand to her mouth.

"Look who's talking," said Raven flippantly. She flopped over onto her back, grabbing her pillow and hugging it tightly.

"I ken I am no angel, Cousin, but at least the man who bedded me was a noble. And he promised to marry me. Or at least that is what he told me."

"Men are all liars," Raven said, holding back the tears. "I don't ever want to get married."

"I think ye like the armorer but are upset since he's just a commoner. Ye ken yer father will never allow ye to be together."

"I don't care what my father says." She bolted up to a sitting position. "Mayhap I should just lure Jonathon to bed. Yes, that's what I'll do. Then I'll tell everyone about it. No man will want to marry me after that."

"Och, nay. Dinna say that!" Lark made a face. "What do ye think would happen to Jonathon if ye did such a daft thing? He'd be imprisoned and sent to the gallows, that's what would happen. If he was lucky. It's more likely he'd be drawn and quartered for even thinkin' about touchin' a titled lady."

"You're right, Lark," said Raven, realizing how foolish she sounded right now. "I can't do that to Jonathon. Even if he did dismiss me tonight, I don't want to see him imprisoned or killed. He doesn't deserve that."

"He probably dismissed ye because he came to his senses in time. That is more than I can say for ye, Cousin. What are ye goin' to do?"

"The only thing I can do. I'm going to learn to joust, and enter the contest and win the tournament. Then I won't have to marry anyone. All my problems will be over."

"Ye dinna really think yer father is goin' to let ye do that, do ye?"

"He won't know it's me under the armor. I'll give a fictitious name of some noble and enter the competition that way. Hopefully, no one will notice until it's too late and after I've won the contest."

"Ye will never win the tournament against a trained knight. That kind of clishmaclaver is only goin' to get ye killed. It's the stupidest plan I've ever heard. It will never work."

"Well, do you have a better one?"

"If ye're askin' me for advice with men, all I can say is, dinna let a man bed ye unless ye are wearin' his ring on yer finger." She held up her ringless finger to prove her point. "That is what I learned."

"I'm sorry. I didn't mean to be so insensitive, Lark." Raven reached out and held her cousin's hand. This poor girl was a single mother raising a bastard child, and everyone knew it. No man would ever want Lark now, because she'd ruined her reputation over one night of unbridled passion.

Why the hell couldn't Raven be so lucky?

"I suggest ye get some sleep, Raven. I'm sure things will look better on the morrow."

"Aye. I'm sure you're right," said Raven, turning on her side and hugging the pillow, wishing she were hugging Jonathon instead. What was happening to her? And why in heaven's name was a simple, common man exciting her and controlling her thoughts? She needed to forget all about him. Her best bet would be to get far away from him. Nay, that would be impossible since her father hired him to supposedly protect her.

Raven needed to take matters into her own hands.

She also needed to learn how to joust, or she was never going to have a chance to win the tournament and be saved from marrying men like Frogmouth or Baldhead.

She squeezed her eyes closed and tried to think of anything but Jonathon, but couldn't. It was going to be a lot harder to forget him than she thought. Lark was right, she never should have kissed Jonathon or let down her guard around him. She and Jonathon were from two different walks of life. They didn't belong together. It was times like this that being a noble was more troublesome, in her opinion, than it was worth.

"Jonathon, get up! Jonathon, did you hear me?"

Jonathon awoke the next morning to his brother shaking him by one shoulder. He lifted his head and looked around the room, taking a moment to realize he had fallen asleep at his bench last night. The embers from the forge glowed, and thin wisps of smoke lazily curled up to the ceiling from the nearly extinguished fire. The smoke drifted off through a vent hole in the roof of the blacksmith's shop, where sun was shining through.

"What time is it?" asked Jonathon, rubbing his eyes.

"We all overslept. I'm sure by now we've missed most of the morning meal," said Avery, not sounding at all happy about it. "I sent Gerold ahead to see if everyone is still in the great hall."

"Mmph," mumbled Jonathon, still half-asleep. He had worked out his frustration with Raven, spending most of the night filling the orders from the castle's nobles.

"Why did you sleep out here in the shop instead of coming to bed?" Avery looked down in surprise to see two full barrels of nails as well as a set of horseshoes. "My, you got a lot done."

"I needed to hit something after Raven left." He stood up and stretched and yawned.

"They're still there yet," announced Gerold excitedly, running into the shop. "The meal is almost over, but we can sneak in and still get some food if we hurry."

"Good. Let's go." Avery led the way out the door.

Jonathon followed, still trying to wake up. When he got to the great hall, his brother and the boy sat at a back table near the entrance to the kitchen. Jonathon made his way over to the dais but was stopped by a guard.

"I'm sorry but you're not allowed up there," said the guard.

"Of course I am," Jonathon answered. "I'm supposed to sit by Lady Raven."

"You are late for the meal and it is not tolerated," explained the guard. "Besides, Lady Raven is not here."

"She's not?" He looked up to the dais to see that what the guard said was true. "Where is she?"

"She is ill today, so you won't be needed."

"Really," said Jonathon, side-stepping the guard and making his way to the front of the dais, stopping in front of Lord Corbett's seat. "My lord, I'm sorry I am late. I was up all night working on the orders for your men. Your guard told me I'm not allowed on the dais."

"Jonathon." Corbett looked up and then leaned forward and spoke in a hushed voice over the edge of the table. "I'm sorry, but you'll have to eat with your brother below the salt from now on."

"I don't understand. Why?"

"My daughter told me that there are a lot of nobles thinking I am giving you special treatment. They are upset about it, so I think it is best you stay off the dais for now."

"I see." Jonathon was sure this had nothing to do with the other men and everything to do with Raven. She was angry with him about last night, and now she was making him pay. "That's fine," he told Corbett. "Your guard also said Lady Raven was ill and that I wasn't needed to protect her today."

"She was here earlier," said Rook, getting in on the conversation. "She barely ate. Then she and Lark left. Raven said she had a headache and wanted to stay in her chamber today."

"You can tend to things in the shop," said Corbett. "I know you have a lot to do."

"Would you mind if I checked in on Lady Raven?" he asked.

"You'd better not," said Rook. "Raven is right about this. Gossip is also starting since you've been seen outside her bedchamber more than once now. Mayhap you shouldn't do that."

"Yes, I was, but only to escort her to the great hall. I didn't step a foot inside her room, I swear."

"It wouldn't usually be a problem for a guard to meet her at her bedchamber to escort her. I mean, if you weren't a commoner," said Corbett. "That is starting to create a small stir."

"It might be best if you stayed away from the

practice yard for a few days too," suggested Rook. "Just until things calm down. We don't want any problems."

Jonathon wanted to go up to Raven's room to talk to her, but now he realized it would have to wait. He didn't know why Corbett or Rook suddenly cared what anyone thought. They were the ones who invited Jonathon to practice with them and to sit at the dais in the first place. No one seemed to really be upset with him, or at least not that he'd heard of. He was sure this was all Raven's doing. Still, it wasn't his place to object.

"Of course, my lords," said Jonathon with a nod. "If you'll give your permission, I'd like to go back to town today. I have a special project I am working on, and I need to use the equipment at my father's shop."

"Oh, this must have something to do with that masterpiece you're making to present to the guild," said Rook. "So what did you decide to make?"

"I-I'm working with plate armor," he said, not lying to them but not exactly telling them either that is wasn't for his presentation to the guild. Still, he didn't think saying he was making armor for Lord Corbett's daughter would be a good idea, so he kept that part to himself.

"By all means, work there whenever you need to," said Corbett. "When Raven is feeling better, you can take her along with you on your trips to town. I'm sure she'd like to know what goes on at a forge."

"I think she already does, but I will do so next time I see her," he answered, not able to stop thinking about his intimate time with Raven last night at the forge. "By your leave, my lords?"

"Godspeed," said Corbett, sending Jonathon on his way.

"Brother, where are you off to, and why are you not sitting at the dais?" asked Avery, meeting him at the door.

"I'm not welcome there anymore," said Jonathon. "I think Lady Raven is up to her tricks, and I don't like it."

"Where is she?" Avery scanned the room. "I don't see her."

"She's supposedly in her chamber with a headache, but I have a feeling that's not where she is at all."

"What do you mean?"

"Just keep an eye open for her. I'm going home for a while but will be back later today."

Jonathon made his way out to the stable to get his horse. The stablemaster greeted him.

"Jonathon? Did you want me to saddle your horse?" he asked.

"I'll get it, Jacob, but thank you." Jonathon started saddling his horse, looking over to the stall where Raven's horse was kept. He wasn't surprised to see it missing.

"Where is Lady Raven's horse?" he asked.

"The page took it earlier," answered the man. "He said Lady Raven wanted him to exercise the horse since she wasn't feeling well today."

"Did she, now." Jonathon hoisted himself into the saddle.

"The odd part is, he also took a horse and cart out right afterwards."

"Yes, that's strange." Jonathon turned back. "Jacob, have you heard any of the nobles complaining about me at all?"

"Nay," answered the man, with a shake of his head. "Not really. Everyone seems to like you."

"So, there's no gossip stirring around me?" he asked.

"Not as far as I know, but I'm usually stuck in here and I don't hear everything that is going on."

"I don't want to cause trouble."

"Well, the nobles might not have been happy about a commoner like you getting such special attention at first. But once Lords Corbett and Blake accepted you and even sparred with you, they realized you're not so bad. I really don't think you need to worry."

"Thank you," he said, turning and riding out the gate. Jonathon was on his way back home when he decided to make a stop before heading to town. He liked to sit and think by the creek in the woods. It helped him to clear his mind. Mayhap a few minutes by himself out in the fresh air would help him get his head on straight about everything that had happened.

He made his way to the creek, hearing voices up ahead. Veering off the path, he followed the sound, stopping his horse when he saw Raven atop her horse, holding a lance. There was a horse and cart there as well. Lark and the squire named Albert were with her.

Raven kicked her heels into her horse, heading right for a quintain that was set up in the woods. She managed to hit the arm on the quintain and it spun around, but she was too slow. The sandbag on the other end hit her in the back, knocking her from her horse and to the ground.

"Ooomph," she mumbled as she hit the dirt.

"Not a bad attempt, but you need to be faster," Jonathon called out, riding to the group.

"Jonathon?" Raven's head came up, but she was still lying on the ground.

"Raven, are ye all right?" Lark hurried over to her while the page ran after the horse.

"Your father said you were in your chamber, not feeling well. You don't look ill to me," he said, dismounting and hurrying over to help her up. "Was that just a story you concocted to throw me off your trail?"

Without asking, he put his hands under her shoulders and pulled her to her feet.

"I don't need your help," she told him. "And everything isn't always about you, Jonathon Armstrong."

"Actually, I think you do need me." He started to brush the dirt off her clothes. She wore trews and a tunic today instead of a gown.

"Don't touch me." She pushed his hand away and stepped back.

Jonathon held his palms up in the air. "Excuse me, my lady. I was just trying to help."

"Raven, I told ye we shouldna have come here," said Lark, looking over at Jonathon from the sides of her eyes. "He's goin' to tell yer brother or yer father now."

"Nay, he won't," said Raven.

"So sure of yourself, are you?" asked Jonathon.

"You won't say anything, because if you do, I'll tell my father about–" she stopped for a moment, looking over to the page to make sure he was out of earshot. "I'll tell him about the kiss."

"Go ahead," he challenged her, more or less throwing down the gauntlet. "I doubt you'll tell him, because once he hears you lied about being ill and instead sneaked off to the woods, he'll never believe a word you say."

"He already doesn't," she said, sounding so sad. "Well, I guess I'll never learn to joust now."

"Why do you even want to learn? It makes no sense," said Jonathon.

"She wants to do it so she can–"

"Lark, that's enough," Raven stopped her cousin from telling him more, making him very curious now.

"We should go back to the castle, Raven," said Lark, looking very nervous.

"I'm not going back yet. I still need to practice," said Raven.

"I know how to joust," said Jonathon, surprising her.

"You?" She laughed. "What do you know about the joust?"

"More than you, my lady."

"I doubt it."

"Let me show you." He picked up the lance that she dropped and quickly mounted his horse. "You've got to give it a quick jab. Don't let the contact linger. And keep moving until you are out of reach of the swivel arm. Like this," he said, riding fast toward the quintain.

Raven watched in awe as Jonathon hit the quintain and rode on past so quickly that the sandbag on the opposite side of the swivel arm missed him completely.

"That was great," said Lark.

"It was perfect," agreed Albert, bringing Raven's horse back to her. "He's really good at it, my lady. For a commoner, I mean."

"Yes. He is, isn't he?" Her eyes were fastened to him. She also had an idea of how she could use this to her advantage.

"That's how you do it, my lady." Jonathon rode back to her with the lance in his hand.

"Can you teach me to joust?" she blurted out, not even taking the time to compliment him.

"You are serious about learning to do this, aren't you?"

"I am."

"Now, why would you want to take up such a dangerous sport? One that is only for men?"

"Don't ask questions. Answer mine instead. Can you teach me?"

Jonathon looked over to Lark and Albert. "I'll help you load the equipment back into the cart. You'd better get these things back to the castle before they're missed."

"Nay," protested Raven. "I brought those things here so I can practice."

"Not now," he told her, taking apart the quintain while Lark and Albert collected the lances.

"Put that back, right now," she commanded.

"Raven, I think Jonathon is right," said Lark. "We should get these things back to the castle before anyone notices them missing."

"Nay. I planned on practicing the quintain today."

Jonathon ignored her and loaded the quintain into the back of the wagon with Albert helping.

"Lady Lark, if anyone is looking for your cousin,

please tell them she is with me today," said Jonathon, helping Lark to the wagon seat. "I'm going to be spending the day in town back at my father's forge. Lord Corbett already knows that. Just let him know Lady Raven is safe with me and under my protection. We will return later."

"Aye, I'll tell them," said Lark. "Albert, can we go now?"

"I'm ready." Albert joined Lark, taking the reins of the horse to drive the wagon.

"My father won't like that I'm in town," stated Raven.

"It was his idea for me to take you with me."

"Goodbye, Raven," said Lark, waving as they rode away.

Once they left, Raven asked Jonathon a question. "How do you know how to joust?"

"I learned a long time ago and have been doing it for years. As a bonus of hiring out my sword to so many different lords, I was allowed to practice with weapons against the knights and other soldiers on occasion."

He helped her mount her horse.

"Swordplay I can see, but only knights or nobles are allowed to joust, so how could you have learned to do it?" asked Raven.

"It doesn't matter." He rode with Raven as they headed for town.

"I had no idea you were skilled in so many different things," said Raven. "Now, tell me. Can you teach me to joust or not?"

"I could, but I won't."

"Why not?" she asked. "I really want to learn."

"I don't think your father or your brother would agree with it."

"They don't agree to anything I want to do." Totally frustrated, she rode in silence for a short time before Jonathon started to question her.

"Tell me the real reason you want to joust, and just mayhap I'll reconsider."

"Really?" she turned to face him, suddenly feeling hope again. Mayhap her plan would work after all. However, she didn't want to tell him why she really wanted to learn to joust. If he knew the truth, he'd try to stop her from doing it. She would have to answer in a roundabout way.

"I know once I'm married, I'll have to lay down my sword and I will never be allowed to try the things that interest me in life again."

"So, you're saying you want to get your wild ways out of your system before you are forced to act like a lady?"

"I'm saying, no man would ever let his wife try the joust, let alone use a sword, even though I am highly skilled in using weapons."

"So I've found out," he said with a nod, looking over at her and smiling.

"I told you why I want to learn, so will you teach me then?"

"Well... all right. I'll teach you the joust, even though I know I'm going to end up regretting it."

"Oh, thank you!" she shouted, so excited by this that she felt like throwing herself into his arms and kissing him, even though she was on a horse.

"All I ask is that you don't play games with me, my lady. If so, we both know it will only end badly."

"Games? What do you mean?"

"I think you know exactly what I mean."

There was no doubt he was talking about their intimate time together in the forge, and not the joust. He thought she was playing with him, but actually, it was so much more than that. Raven wanted to tell him he was wrong. She wanted him to know the kisses between them were real. She also wanted to tell him how good it felt to be pressed up against him and to be held in his strong arms. Sadly, she realized it would do no good to mention this to him. It would only make things between them more awkward.

He was already taking a huge risk by agreeing to teach her to joust. If he knew why she really wanted to learn, he would most likely try to talk her out of her plan. And if he knew how infatuated she was with him, he would probably run the other way. Mayhap it was better to leave her feelings out of this and keep the truth between them unsaid.

Her heart about broke as she rode with him to town, because she knew he was right in calling it a game. After all, people like her weren't allowed to have feelings for someone like him. If there was a way to change that, she would, but there wasn't. Jonathon Armstrong was the first man she ever actually had romantic feelings for, but it would end right there.

Unfortunately, these feelings were all wrong between them, and certainly not allowed.

CHAPTER 11

"**T**his is unbelievable," said Raven, once they'd arrived in town and Jonathon took her out back. There, in an empty field behind the shop, was what looked to her like a tiltyard. "Why is this here?"

"I built it myself," Jonathon told her, pride showing in his voice. "I constructed not only a quintain, but a place to joust with the knights when they come to pick up their armor."

"You can't do that, can you?"

"I assure the knights quality in my work. Each set of armor is constructed for each of them specifically. It has to fit like a glove. This is a way that they can test out their armor before actually paying me for it. I've been doing it for years and no one has complained about it yet."

"But if they are wearing the armor you made especially for them, what do you wear?"

"I made myself a set of armor, as well as lances and a quintain."

"Don't you get hurt? I mean, jousting against knights?"

"Of course, I did. At first. But with testing all that armor, through the years I became good at the sport."

"Do my father and brother know this is here?" She walked over to inspect the quintain. It looked sturdier than the ones at the castle.

"Nay, I don't believe so. I've only repaired their armor, not made them new suits of armor, so there was no need to point this out."

"It's quite a risk for a commoner to be jousting, let alone have a tiltyard behind his shop, don't you think?"

"I suppose so. However, it isn't as if I'm posing a threat to any of the nobles. I am doing this only to help them."

"You like to live dangerously, I see."

He shrugged. "I suppose you aren't the only one who takes risks, my lady."

"Well, I have to say I agree, and believe it is a risk worth taking. Now, teach me to joust. I want to start right now." She was so excited that she could barely stand it. This was the perfect place to practice without her father or brother discovering what she was doing. If they didn't know about this tiltyard, when she came to town and used it, they couldn't object to it. This would work out perfectly.

"You need armor to joust, my lady. Remember, I haven't made yours yet," he explained.

"I can at least start with mastering the quintain, can't I? I don't need armor for that, do I?"

"I suppose not. You can also practice with the rings."

"Let's do it," she said. "I'll get my horse and we'll start."

"Not so fast," said Jonathon with a chuckle, liking

Raven's enthusiasm, but still being a little leery to give her what she wanted. "I have some other things to take care of in the shop first. Besides, if you want me to make your armor, you're going to have to give me time to do it."

"All right, I'll wait," she said, her eyes fastened on the equipment as she tried to hold in her bubbling enthusiasm. "How long will it take you? To finish up things in the shop, I mean. Mayhap I could start by myself."

"Lady Raven, slow down," he said, taking hold of her arm. She looked up to him with those beautiful eyes, causing his heart to about burst in his chest. "We need to take it slow." He wasn't talking about the joust anymore. He meant them, and she knew it.

"*Slow* isn't a word I use often, and neither do I like it."

"Then I'll teach you to accept it," he said, reaching out and brushing back a stray strand of her hair behind her ear. "I know we don't belong together and that it could never be between us. Still, I can't help wanting to enjoy every minute I spend with you."

"R-really?" she asked, her eyes flashing down to his mouth and then back up to his eyes again. "Jonathon, I have to admit that I-I like you, too. Even though I know it's wrong and against the rules."

"Funny, but somehow I thought you lived to break the rules."

"Who said I didn't?" She grinned and stood on her tiptoes and kissed him on the mouth, right out there in the open.

"Slowly," he said, looking around to make sure no one saw them. "Perhaps we could start the training now," he told her, when he realized that they both needed to get their minds on something else. Too bad that the 'something else' he wanted to do with her had nothing at all to do with jousting.

∼

"Now try it again, and this time keep your eye on the rings. Every one of them," said Jonathon a week later, impressed by how quickly Raven was progressing with her training.

The space where he'd set up the practice field once housed the bakery and several other shops before they burned down years ago. The shops were moved to a different part of town afterwards, leaving the land empty.

Jonathon had brought Raven here every day since he'd found her in the woods after sneaking away to try to learn this sport on her own. His family liked her a lot, and that made him happy. After practicing all morning, today Raven actually had been helping his mother and sisters preparing the meals. That was something he never thought he'd see. Jonathon worked with his father on orders that had been coming in, while Avery and Gerold tended to things back at the castle's forge. Everything seemed to be going smoothly.

Jonathon had also started on Raven's armor, and it was coming along nicely. He sometimes worked on it here, and other times back at the castle at the end of the day. His family's home was only a simple building. They didn't have a lot of anything, even though they were well paid for completing jobs for the nobles.

Raven didn't seem to mind the close quarters or

even the smoky smell from the forge anymore. Yesterday, she had even picked up a broom and swept the floor on her own. He tried to stop her, since nobles shouldn't be doing such menial tasks. She told him she wanted to do it—she was tired of being told how to act and what to do. This had been her own decision.

Jonathon's mother had been making Heathcliff's old clothes smaller for Gerold. Not realizing that Raven even knew how to sew, Jonathon was shocked to find her helping with that as well.

His mother and sisters lovingly accepted Raven into their family. Jonathon noticed a lot of laughing coming from the kitchen when the girls were all together. He didn't even realize that Raven knew how to laugh. Back at the castle, she always seemed angry or serious. He decided bringing her here each day was a good idea after all.

He let her act as if she belonged here, always watching her from the corners of his eyes when she didn't know it. Damn, it felt nice to have a woman in his life. Nay, it felt good to have *Raven* in his life. Sadly, her lifestyle and his would never coincide. Having her spend time here with his family was only making it harder on both of them. Raven kept telling him how much she liked being around him and his family, and that concerned him. This would be over in a few weeks, and then what would happen to them? He didn't really want to know.

"I can do this," said Raven, riding her horse back to the start while Jonathon's young brother, Heathcliff, placed metal rings with ribbons attached, hanging from poles stuck into the ground.

"All right, go," said Jonathon, slapping Raven's

horse, sending it off at a run. Raven had been having trouble getting all five rings, usually missing the last one. This time, however, she surprised him, spearing each ring onto her lance and riding back to him with the lance held high in the air.

"I did it!" she exclaimed, handing her lance to Heathcliff and getting off the horse. She excitedly ran over to Jonathon, and hugged him. "Thanks to you and all your help, I did it."

Jonathon liked the feel of her arms around him, but realized how risky this was since they were out in the open. He didn't want any of the townspeople or his family to think anything was going on between them. That would only mean trouble for them both.

"Aye, that wasn't bad," he said, stepping away from her and turning away. "For a girl," he added softly, teasing her and meaning for her to hear it.

"Not bad?" Her smile faded. "It was very good, and you know it. Even for a girl," she added, narrowing her eyes at him when he stopped to look back over his shoulder.

"Oh, you heard that?" he playfully asked.

"Of course, I did." Then she saw him smiling.

"You are teasing me, aren't you?" She ran over and pretended to hit him. Jonathon laughed and grabbed her arms. They lost balance and both fell to the ground. Having her atop him made his mind race in many directions. Prone on the ground, she looked deeply into his eyes. Jonathon had the feeling she wanted to kiss him again. That scared him a little since someone might see. He hurriedly stood up, pulling her to her feet.

"Just admit that you think I could learn the joust," she told him. "Say it, because you know it's true."

"Mayhap in time you could learn the basics," he agreed. "But remember, it takes six months to a year for a trained knight to be able to joust. It's not like you can learn it in a few weeks. That's a crazy thought and you know it. Especially for a girl."

"Well, you know how to joust, so practice with me. I am running out of time."

"Running out of time? What do you mean by that?" He turned around fully to face her.

"I-I just mean I'm in a hurry. To learn it before I'm married and my husband forbids me to ever do it again."

"Yes. So you've said. However, I'm starting to get the feeling there is something you aren't telling me."

"Whatever do you mean? I'm easy enough to understand."

"Hardly. Between you wanting me to teach you to joust and also make you armor, if I didn't know better, I'd say you were planning on competing in the tournament yourself."

"Me?" Raven forced a laugh and tried to sound flippant. "I'm a girl. I could never do that."

"Nay, you couldn't. However, if there was a way to enter, I'm sure you'd be the one to figure out just how to do it." Jonathon turned and walked back to the shop.

"Just admit it. I'm better at it than you thought," said Raven, fishing for a compliment from him. She knew Jonathon liked her, but ever since the night he measured her for her armor, he seemed to be trying to distance himself from her and that bothered her.

"Raven, you're only hooking rings onto a lance. It is not the same as jousting. Far from it."

"I don't care. Teach me more. I want to learn." She ran to keep up with him.

"Nay. You'll hurt yourself."

"No, I won't. Please, won't you practice with me? I want to know how it feels to actually joust with a person."

Jonathon thought about it for a second, and almost considered doing so, but knew he shouldn't. He'd been enjoying tutoring her in this manner. The only thing was, the more time they spent together, the harder it was for him to accept that she'd be married in a few weeks' time. Then he'd never be able to spend time alone with her again. Mayhap it was better if he just stopped this right now. It couldn't go any further.

"I don't have time for this." He continued on to the shop and she followed at his heels. "I have work to do."

"Your job during the day is to be with me," she reminded him. "That is what my father is paying you to do, so don't forget it."

"If your father knew what I've been teaching you to do every time we make a trip to town, he would have my head. I'm sorry, my lady, but I can no longer take the risk." He made his way into the shop where his father was working. His mother and sisters helped clean the shop and also to fan the forge with the bellows.

"Where is Heathcliff? I need his help," grumbled Jonathon's father. "The business has been picking up again with the upcoming tournament so near and I am too old to do all this work by myself."

"I'm here, Father," said Jonathon. "I'll help you."

"Son, you spend too much time out back. Even

when you are here, you are not helping me much. You are working on that armor." His father seemed agitated today for some reason. "With you and Avery gone, I'm overwhelmed and can't catch up."

"I'm sorry, Father. Heathcliff was assisting me outside. Is there something I can do for you now?"

"Jonathon?" His mother emerged from the kitchen with his sister, Hildeth, who stopped by with fresh baked bread from her husband's bakery.

"Hello, Hildeth," said Jonathon.

"Hello," she responded, seeming as if something was bothering her.

"Your sister has something to tell you," said his mother.

"What is it, Hildeth?" he asked.

His sister looked over to Raven who had sat down on a chair to fix her shoe. She seemed hesitant to speak freely.

"You can talk in front of Raven. It's fine."

"If you insist. Brother, the townspeople had a meeting at the bakery this morning. They don't like the fact that you are bringing Lady Raven here so often. It makes them uncomfortable."

"It does? Why?" he asked, seeing Raven look up in surprise and listen. "She's not causing any problems. I thought you all liked her."

"Of course we do," said his mother. "She is a joy to be around but, she doesn't belong here."

"That's right," said Hildeth. "This is our home and town, not hers. The townspeople believe that she should be back at the castle. They feel on edge knowing there is a noble here so often watching their every move."

"Really?" asked Raven, standing up, looking hurt. "They feel that way about me?"

"Nay, I'm sure they don't really," said Jonathon, but his words fell on deaf ears.

"My lady, it's just that the townspeople live a different life than you," said Jonathon's mother. "With you always here, they feel nervous that they might do something wrong and you'll report it to your father."

"Nay, she wouldn't do that," Jonathon told them. "They are worrying for nothing."

"Nay. They're right," Raven softly answered. "I don't belong here anymore than you belong sitting at the dais back at the castle."

"Jonathon, I'm sorry, but I'm afraid you bringing Lady Raven here might be putting us all in danger," said his mother, wringing her hands together.

"Aye, Jonathon," agreed his sister Estrilda. "If the nobles find out you're teaching Lady Raven to joust, we will all be punished because of it."

"I might even lose the business," said his father. "I'm sorry, son, but I agree with the others. You need to stop bringing Lady Raven here and end this nonsense of training a lady to joust. It isn't right, and neither is it allowed."

"We are only commoners and live simply," said Hildeth. "My lady, no disrespect, but you live a much different life than we do."

"Lady Raven, we all like you, we really do," said his mother. "Please, don't take it the wrong way. You need to understand the position you are putting us in by being here. It is too risky for us. We live under the shadow of those with royal blood, and will be punished severely if word gets out about what you've been doing here."

"You're right," said Raven softly. "It's not good, and it's all my fault. I'm the one who asked Jonathon to teach me the joust and put him in a bad situation. Please, don't worry. I'll make sure you're all protected, I promise I will. I'll talk to my father if need be. You won't be in trouble because of it."

"That is kind of you, but you can't guarantee that," said Jonathon. "You don't know how your father will react."

"Here comes Avery," announced Hildeth, looking out the front window. "He has a boy with him."

"That's Gerold, the son of the late castle smith," said Estrilda. "We've already met him, Sister."

Jonathon looked up. "Yes. He's the one who we've been giving the clothes to and who is my apprentice at the castle. "I wonder what they want." He met them at the door.

"Jonathon, you need to get back to the castle with Lady Raven, anon," said Avery, looking rather worried.

"Why? What's wrong?" asked Raven.

"My lady, you shouldn't be coming here so often," said Avery. "The gossip is starting to grow back at the castle about... about..."

"About what?" asked Raven.

"I think he means about us," said Jonathon with a sigh. "You are noble and shouldn't be spending so much time in town or with me and my family. Of course there is going to be talk about it—what did we expect?"

"Nay. That's nonsense." Raven waved away the thought. "You're my personal guard, Jonathon. No one is talking about us, and my father knows I'm here. I'm supposed to be with you. You are only doing what you were hired to do."

"Everyone is wondering where you two go when you come to town," said little Gerold.

"Hi, Gerold," said Heathcliff, having entered the shop through the back door with the lances and rings in his arms.

"Why do you have Lord Corbett's lances here?" asked Gerold.

"These aren't his," explained Heathcliff. "My brother made them. They're ours. Jonathon is teaching Lady Raven how to joust."

"Really?" asked Gerold. "But you're commoners and not allowed to joust. And Lady Raven is a girl so she shouldn't be doing it either."

"Avery" growled Jonathon in a low voice. "Why the hell did you have to bring the boy here right now?" This was all he needed. It was bad enough that the townspeople knew Raven was coming here, but if the boy went back to the castle and told Raven's father what he saw, there was probably going to be trouble.

"He saw me leaving and followed," Avery whispered back. "What was I supposed to do?"

"Gerold, you can't say anything about this," Raven told Gerold. "Do you understand?"

"Why not?" he asked, innocently. "Do you want me to lie?"

"No one is asking anyone to lie," said Jonathon. "We're not doing anything wrong, we just want to keep it a secret."

"Lady Raven thinks she's a knight or something, and doesn't want anyone to know it," Heathcliff whispered to Gerold behind his hand.

"Jonathon, do something about this," mumbled Avery. "I don't believe the boy will stay quiet."

"Gerold, do you like this shop?" asked Jonathon.

"Do I!" said the boy with a big smile.

"Father, Gerold has grown up as an apprentice to his late father who was the castle blacksmith," said Jonathon. "I think he would be a good addition to this shop, don't you?"

"What?" asked his father in surprise. "Nay, he's too young to be of any help."

"He's not that much younger than Heathcliff," Jonathon pointed out. "Besides, he knows a lot about the forge. He's already been a big help to me at the castle's smithy."

"Jonathon, your father is getting older and he needs a man here to help him," said his mother. "Not another boy."

"I'll stay," offered Avery. "At least until Father gets caught up with the work."

"Can I stay with you too?" asked Gerold excitedly.

"I'd like Gerold to stay since we're now friends," said Heathcliff, excited to meet someone close to his age. He didn't have many friends in town since he was required to work at the shop all day long.

"What about the work back at the castle?" asked Raven. "Who will do that?"

"We're pretty much caught up for now," Jonathon told her. "I think it's a good idea for Avery and Gerold to help out here for a while. At least until the knights start arriving for the tournament. Then they can re-turn to the castle. I can handle things by myself until then. My lady, we should be going now."

"What about my training?" asked Raven.

"We will talk about that later," said Jonathon.

"Let's get back to the castle before your father or brother come looking for us." Jonathon packed up the armor he'd been working on for Raven, sticking the pieces into a large leather bag with a strap and slipping it over his shoulder.

Jonathon's family had been nothing but kind to her, and Raven felt bad to have put them in this position. "I'm sorry," she said, not knowing what else to say.

None of them responded.

"This was a mistake," mumbled Jonathon, heading for the door and she followed. Just as they were about to leave, two men walked in, causing Raven to gasp.

"Lord Whitehead. Lord Belmouth," said Jonathon. "How can we help you?"

"Lady Raven?" Whitehead looked over to Raven, his eyes drinking her in. "What are you doing here, in town?"

"This is no place for a lady." Belmouth walked in, making Jonathon step backward. "Does your father know you're here?"

"Lord Corbett has made me Lady Raven's guardian," said Jonathon. "I assure you, he knows she is with me and perfectly safe."

"Hmph," sniffed Whitehead. "I still don't see why Lord Corbett would make a commoner the girl's guardian. This whole thing is odd if you ask me."

"My lords, how can I help you?" Jonathon's father ran over to greet them.

"We stopped by to drop off our armor before the tournament begins," said Whitehead. "It needs a few repairs and also polishing."

"Yes, of course," said Crispin. "I'd be happy to take care of that for you."

Whitehead spotted the jousting lances lying on the floor. "What are those doing here?" He pointed to them. "Don't they belong at the castle?"

Gerold spoke up before anyone could answer. "Those are Jonathon's, and he's teaching Lady Raven to—"

Avery clasped his hand over the boy's mouth. "My brother uses them to test out the new armor with our noble customers to make sure it is up to their standards before they pay for it."

"We only do quality work at this shop," added Jonathon, sounding as if he were wishing these men would leave. She certainly did.

"My lords, can I see your armor that needs repairing?" asked Jonathon's father.

"I'll carry it in for you," offered Avery rushing forward, glancing over at Jonathon. "Jonathon, I'm sure you are in a hurry to bring Lady Raven back to the castle. You really shouldn't tarry any longer."

"Aye," said Jonathon with a nod, looking very disturbed by this whole situation. He held the door for Raven and they made their way to their horses. Jonathon didn't say a word.

"I'm sure everything will be fine," said Raven, trying to make conversation and to lighten the mood. She accepted his help in mounting her steed.

"It will be, because we will no longer be coming here for you to learn the joust. It was a foolish thing for me to agree to it in the first place. I put my friends and family in danger because I didn't consider how it would affect them."

"But I need you to teach me. Please. It's important."

"I find it odd that you are so adamant about learning the joust, even after what just transpired. Is there more to this that you are telling me?"

"I don't know what you mean."

"Aye, I'm sure you don't," he said in a sarcastic tone, leading the way out of town and back to the castle.

CHAPTER 12

Jonathon headed to the great hall the next morning, being stopped by Rook in the courtyard.

"My lord," said Jonathon with a nod to greet him.

"Jonathon, how has my sister been doing?" he asked.

"Just fine," he answered, not adding more.

"You haven't reported a thing to us about her, and we find that puzzling since she is always getting into trouble. Is there something you're not telling us?"

"In what manner do you mean?"

Rook looked around and then leaned in closer. "I ran across Lords Whitehead and Belmouth late yesterday while I was out. They told me they saw you and Raven at your shop in town earlier that day."

"Yes," said Jonathon, knowing this couldn't end well. "Your father gave me permission to help out my family, as well as to take your sister with me. It's no secret that we were there."

"They also said they saw jousting lances there."

"Yes. They're mine."

"I took a walk over to your father's shop to discover not only a quintain but also a makeshift tiltyard behind the building that I never knew was there. After talking to some of the knights, I discovered they knew about it and told me it has been there for years."

Jonathon groaned inwardly. He didn't like where this was heading. If he asked if Raven had been involved in jousting, he wasn't going to be able to lie. "Aye," he answered. "I constructed the tiltyard myself. I'm sure the knights told you it is used for them to test out their armor against me before they pay. To make sure it is to their liking. I want them to be satisfied with my work since my family prides itself with quality work and perfection."

"I see," said Rook with a nod. "I suppose that is expected, since your father is a master craftsman. That's an admirable thing to do. For some reason, I had the feeling Raven was trying to joust again in secret."

Jonathon could no longer hide the truth. He needed to be upfront with Rook since the subject was brought up, and he'd been hired to report Raven's doings to Rook and his father. "Lord Rook, I'm sorry I didn't say something sooner. I found Lady Raven in the woods practicing the joust about a week ago."

"You did? And you didn't tell us?"

"I realize I should have said something, and I am sorry that I didn't."

"Why wouldn't you report this to us? That is why you were hired." Rook scowled at him.

"I didn't think it important enough to bother you, with how busy you have been preparing for the upcoming tournament."

"Aye, it has been a lot of work," agreed Rook.

"Your sister begged me to teach her how to joust. When she saw my tilt yard, she was very excited."

"I'm sure she was. Egads, you didn't teach her, did you?"

"My lord, I knew if I said no, she'd only keep sneaking away to practice on her own in the woods. If so, it was only a matter of time before she got hurt."

"You do make a good point."

"I figured, at least if she was with me, I could guarantee her safety."

"Oh. I see your point." Rook put his hand to his chin in thought. "I suppose you did the right thing," said Rook as they started to walk to the great hall together.

"I'm glad you agree." This was not at all what Jonathon expected Rook to say.

"Yes. My father will agree with it, once I tell him."

"You're going to mention it to Lord Corbett?" This bothered Jonathon more than anything. Everything was coming to a head, and it wasn't looking good for him or his family now. Even if Rook thought it was a good idea to teach his sister the joust, Lord Corbett, he was sure, wouldn't be so forgiving.

"Don't sound so worried. My father is happy you stopped Raven from sneaking off to places, and that you have been chaperoning her. It takes the burden off of him. It was driving him mad."

"I was supposed to stop her from doing those type of things and I only assisted her instead. I am sorry, my lord. It won't happen again, I promise. I even told her I wouldn't train her anymore, so you needn't worry."

"Nay, you have to train her."

"My lord?"

"I want you to do it."

"I don't understand." This confused Jonathon more than anything. "You do?"

"Aye. You see, we know that until my sister marries, she is going to keep doing stupid things like this. She is a stubborn wench and won't listen to reason."

"Yes, I've noticed that."

"My mother is afraid she'll hurt herself, but my father and I believe she'll be safe as long as she is in your care."

"Thank you for your confidence. I will do my best."

"Just keep doing what you're doing for now." They approached the great hall and stopped before they entered.

"My lord, just to be clear," said Jonathon softly. "You really want me to keep training Lady Raven in the joust?"

"Yes, that's right."

"I'm not a knight and haven't had any real training. I've taught myself the sport, and honestly, I'm not really that good at it."

"And neither do you need to be. I've seen you in the practice yard with your sword. You're good with weapons, so I'm sure you know enough about the joust to quell my foolish sister's wish to try it."

"True enough," he agreed.

"So, keep her distracted. That is perfect. The knights are going to start arriving for the tournament soon. We don't want her scaring off any of them beforehand, since one of them needs to end up marrying her."

"I understand."

"Good." Rook blew air from his mouth. "Just make her think you're teaching her."

"Then... you want me to lie to Lady Raven."

"Not lie. Just give her whatever it is she wants, and keep her away from the arriving knights," said Rook with a smile. "You see, we want you to keep her happy and distracted at the same time."

"I-I see," said Jonathon, not able to stop thinking about how distracted Raven and he had become in the forge when he was measuring her for her armor. "I think I need to tell you something else, Lord Rook."

"What's that?"

"Lady Raven has asked me to make her a set of armor."

"What?" Rook's eyebrows raised and then he burst out laughing. "What in God's name does she want that for? It's not like she'd ever really need to use it."

"She didn't say why she wanted it, my lord. However, it seemed very important to her. Should I deny her request?" He'd already started making it, but wasn't in a hurry to tell Rook that part.

"Nay, not at all," said Rook with a careless wave of his hand through the air, sounding as if it was too trivial to take his concern. "Go ahead and do it, by all means. Let her live out her addled fantasies now, while she still can. As soon as the tournament is over and we've secured a proper husband for her, it'll be that poor man's job to put an end to all Raven's silly antics. Then you will be free of her once and for all."

"Aye, my lord," said Jonathon, feeling unsettled about how things had taken an odd turn. He didn't think feeding the girl's interest in something she shouldn't have or do was a healthy alternative. Still, he couldn't deny the orders of the lords of the castle either. He also felt upset by Rook telling him he'd be free of her once and for all. He didn't want to be free of Raven. The last thing he wanted was to have to give her up to another man. The knot in his stomach became larger.

"Is something wrong?" asked Rook. "You look as if you're bothered by something."

"Nay, my lord. I was just wondering if Lord Corbett will not find this all... improper?" he asked.

"Oh, of course, my father will think it's not right for my sister to joust or have her own armor, but he'll get over it, I assure you. I will convince him that whatever it takes to get my sister to the altar is well worth it. Right now, all that matters is that you pacify her and keep her away from the potential suitors so she doesn't scare them off before the wedding day. The competitors usually arrive well before the day of the tournament, to pitch their tents outside the castle and to have time to become familiar with the area where the competition will be held."

"Aye," said Jonathon, opening the door to the keep for Lord Rook.

"You're doing a fine job, Jonathon." Rook patted Jonathon's back. "Keep it up and you'll be rewarded greatly when this is all over, I promise."

Jonathon followed Rook into the great hall, feeling uncomfortable and on edge. He didn't see that being paid more as a potential reward for him in the end was a reward at all. The more time he spent with Raven, the more he had feelings for her. Just the thought of her having to marry a noble like Whitehead or Belmouth made him ill. She was a beautiful woman, and much too young and full of life to have all her dreams and desires smothered by the likes of them. Raven deserved someone better for a husband. Or at least someone she half-liked. He actually felt sorry for the girl and wished for her sake that things could be different.

Or mayhap he was really only feeling sorry for himself, since he wished he could be the one marrying Raven. That, he supposed, was a fantasy of his that he needed stifled, since they would never be allowed to marry. She was of noble blood and all he had running through his veins was the soot from the forge.

~

"Raven, I miss ye since ye've been away so much lately," said Lark to Raven the next morning. "I came to England to spend time with ye, and it seems we are never together lately."

"Well, you will be seeing a lot more of me now that Jonathon has refused to train me anymore."

"I think it's a good thing," said Lark, opening the shutter on the window and letting the fresh air and sunshine into the bedchamber. "Ye should be here to greet the knights and nobles as is expected of you. The competitors will be starting to arrive for the tournament any day now."

"Why would I want to greet the knights or even talk to them at all?" Raven sat up in bed and yawned, stretching her arms above her head.

"Raven Blake!" snapped Lark, turning around and putting her hands on her hips. "You are a lady, and lucky enough to be gettin' married to a titled man. Dinna ruin this for yerself with yer bad attitude."

"I'm known for my bad attitude, so why change now? And for your information, I truly wish I could ruin it for myself." She slid to the side of the bed and put her feet on the floor.

"Ye need to spend time with yer potential husbands for the next few weeks and get to ken them."

Raven shuddered. "Don't refer to them as my potential husbands. I don't like that."

"Well, it's true. Ye're goin' to have to marry one of them, so get to ken them now."

"I don't want to get to know them." She stood up and started to dress. "None of them will be to my liking, so why bother?"

"Dinna say that," scolded Lark, hurrying over and helping her dress. "There has got to be a man who is to yer likin' somewhere."

"There is." Raven smiled and looked up at the ceiling in thought, and then pulled the gown over her head. "Jonathon Armstrong is to my liking." Since her head was covered, her voice was muffled as she spoke.

"I couldna hear ye, Cousin. Ye sounded like ye said Jonathon is who ye like."

"I did," she said, sticking her head out of the top of the gown. "Lark, I think I am starting to have feelings for the man. I like spending time with him, and I also enjoy being with his family."

"Nay," said Lark, shaking her head. Her eyes became wider. "That is wrong. It canna be. Ye canna fall for him, Raven. Ye need to find a nobleman instead. It is important."

"I want Jonathon. I don't want any of those stuffy nobles."

"Ye're about to marry one of those stuffy men, in case ye've forgotten."

"I'm not giving up hope yet, Lark. I need to find a way to learn the joust quickly because that will be my saving grace."

"That is ridiculous. Ye're a lady, and ladies dinna joust. Besides, it takes too long to learn and get any good at any new sport. Also, unless ye've forgotten, ye have no one to train ye anymore."

A knock at the door took their attention.

"My lady, I am here to escort you to the great hall," came Jonathon's voice from the other side. Even though he'd been reprimanded more than once for coming up to her room, he still did it. She liked his determination and was glad he was here.

"It's Jonathon!" Raven hurriedly ran to the dressing table and pulled a boar's-bristle brush through her hair. Lark finished dressing quickly. "Just a minute," Raven called out in a sing-song voice. "Lark, are you done dressing?" asked Raven. "If so, open the door, please."

"Me? Ye canna open the door yerself?"

"I don't want to seem too anxious to see him."

"Och, ye are mad, Cousin." Lark went over and pulled open the door.

"Good morning, Lady Lark," Raven heard Jonathon from the corridor. She purposely took her time, not wanting to seem eager.

"Good mornin', Jonathon," said Lark with a smile.

"Lady Raven, we must hurry." Jonathon stuck his head into the room, but was careful not to cross the line by stepping even one foot inside the bedchamber.

"Hurry?" she asked, strolling over to the door. "I don't see why. I have nothing planned for the day."

"If we're going to get in a practice session before the next meal, we'll have to leave as soon as we break the fast."

"Practice? Leave?" Her heart sped up. "What do you mean?"

"I mean–" He looked both ways and then leaned forward, speaking in a low voice. "I mean, I'm going to continue training you in the joust after all."

"Really?" She blinked several times in succession, not sure she'd heard him correctly. "What made you change your mind?"

"Let's just say I'm not good at rejecting persuasion," he answered with a sigh. "Now, are you ready to go? We'll need to get back here early enough so I will have time to work on your armor later. I'm the only one at the castle smithy now, so I might have other jobs to tend to as well."

"Nay, I'm not ready yet." A smile slowly pursed up the corners of her mouth. She looked over at Lark and then back to Jonathon. Mayhap all hope wasn't lost after all. She grabbed Jonathon by the shoulders, reaching up and kissing him on the mouth, and then let go just as fast. "Now, I'm ready," she told him, feeling as if Jonathon was the only man she could trust.

≈

"Again," called out Jonathon, watching and cringing as Raven attacked the quintain, and in return got knocked on her ass. He ran over to help her to her feet. "Are you all right, my lady?" he asked, reaching down and pulling her up to a standing position.

"I-I'm fine." She blew a puff of air from her

mouth, lifting the stray strand of hair hanging in her eyes.

It had been three days now, and still the girl wasn't getting any better at the quintain. She had mastered the rings, but was just too slow, not to mention she also had trouble holding the lance steady. If he didn't do something soon, she was going to really get hurt.

"Jonathon, please just call me Raven when we're not around the nobles," she told him with a smile.

Her silver eyes lit up and she shyly looked up at him. He wasn't sure what was happening here. Ever since he said he'd train her again, she seemed to change dramatically. Instead of her reminding him to use her title, now she was telling him to drop it. And instead of glaring at him menacingly, she was actually acting shy, if he wasn't mistaken. Or mayhap was it flirting? He couldn't be sure.

"I think that's enough for today, my lady."

"Raven. Call me Raven. Please."

He wanted to, but just couldn't bring himself to do it. It went against everything he'd ever learned about how to behave around nobles and how to address and talk to them.

"Lady Raven, I'm sorry but I cannot do that." She looked sorely disappointed that he'd used her title.

"I'm not good at the joust, am I?" she asked. "Be honest with me."

Damn, he was hoping she wasn't going to ask him that question. He didn't want to lie to her, but neither did he want to hurt her with the truth.

"Well, like I said, it takes time to learn the sport. You can't expect to master it so quickly. Plus, remember, it is a sport created for men, not women, so you are at a disadvantage."

"I think we should keep practicing," she decided for them. "I need to be good at it and time is running out."

Jonathon had to stop this nonsense. He figured the only way to do it was to make her think she was good at it even though she wasn't. It was a deceitful thing to do and he hated himself for even considering it, but he had no choice. Mayhap then she'd stop pushing so hard.

He had an idea, but it would take time to prepare. For now, he needed to get her back to the castle. His work was piling up at the castle forge, now that he'd sent Avery and Gerold to help his father.

"I need time to work on your armor," he told her.

"Oh. All right," she said, lowering her head, looking so sad that it about broke his heart.

He reached out and lifted her chin with two fingers. Her eyes met his, causing his heart to skip a beat. God's teeth, this woman was alluring, even dressed in men's clothes with her hair tousled and with dirt on her face. He brushed back her loose strands of hair and proceeded to use his thumb to rub the dirt from her cheek.

"I'm sure by tomorrow after you've rested, you will be able to beat that blasted quintain with your eyes closed."

"Really? Do you really think so?" She looked up to him with all the hope in the world in her gaze. He didn't believe she was ever going to be able to make a clean pass at the quintain, but he didn't have the heart to tell her.

"Time will tell."

"Mayhap I should try just one more time before we go then."

"Nay," he told her. "Not today."

"But I really think—"

Not knowing any other way to distract her or to shut her up, Jonathon reached down and gently kissed her on the lips. It worked. She was suddenly silent. He only meant to kiss her quickly and then walk away. But when her hands came up to his shoulders and her mouth hungrily claimed his again, he got lost in the moment. His arms wrapped around her and he pulled her close. The kiss deepened and he suddenly forgot they were standing out back of his father's shop in town.

Someone cleared their throat, causing Jonathon to snap back to his senses. He quickly released the girl and stepped away. Thankfully, it was only his brother Avery.

"Lady Raven, why don't you go inside and wash up and change back into your gown," said Jonathon. "Then we'll head back to the castle."

"All right," she said, suddenly looking shy again. When her tongue shot out to touch her lips, it about drove him wild. She turned and ran back to the shop, leaving Jonathon and Avery standing there alone.

"You are playing with fire, Brother," said Avery. "What if someone saw you kiss her? Someone besides me?"

"Well, they didn't, so don't worry about it."

He turned and walked over to the quintain with Avery on his heels.

"Still, I don't think it's a good idea to be falling in love with a girl you can never have."

Jonathon stopped in his tracks and turned

around. "Who said I love her, or have any feelings at all for the wench?"

"Well, don't you?"

Jonathon could no longer deny it. Avery would see right through it if he said no, so he didn't even bother to try.

"Aye, I can't help it. I do," said Jonathon with a sigh, looking back over to see Raven talking to his sister Estrilda as they entered the house. The girls were laughing and seemed so relaxed. After Jonathon told his family in secret that Lord Rook approved of this, they knew nothing bad would happen to them, and accepted Raven being here trying to joust once again.

It almost felt as if Raven truly belonged here, but he knew she was only lowering herself to come here in the first place. "She is intoxicating, Avery. I don't know what's the matter with me, but the more I remind myself that nothing can ever happen between us, the more I want it to."

"I agree, she is a real looker," said Avery with a nod. "But you need to stop getting all besotted around her and remember she is a titled lady who is about to be married to a nobleman. Do yourself a favor, Brother. Forget all about her right now."

"That's rather hard to do when we're together most of the day, every day."

"Then at least get her to drop the idea that she is ever going to be able to joust."

"I did, but her brother told me I had to continue with the training to distract her."

"She's going to get hurt and you'll be to blame."

"You're right," Jonathon agreed. "I feel as if she

won't drop the silly notion until she actually thinks she's any good at it."

"Then she's never going to drop it. I know she is great with other weapons, but come on," said Avery shaking his head. "She can barely hold the lance steady. She will never be quick enough, either. She's a girl, for God's sake. No one can expect a woman to be as strong or as skilled as a man."

"Mayhap not, but I do have an idea of how to stop her. I mean—how to make her think she is doing well with the joust, even though she is not."

"That makes no sense. What are you saying?"

"I'm saying, I have a job for you."

"I have enough work to do as it is." Avery frowned, not liking what he heard.

"Nay, this is different. I want you to tighten up the quintain so it doesn't swivel as easily. That will give her the extra moment or two to make it past the swivel-arm before the sandbag swings around and knocks her on her ass again."

"That might work," said Avery with a nod, looking over at the quintain.

"One more thing."

"What's that?"

"I need you to replace the metal collars on the lances with the lightest steel you can find. Mayhap you can hollow out the poles a little or sand them down to help make them lighter."

"I could, but don't you think she'll notice?" asked Avery.

"Not if she's wearing a helm, she won't."

"You made the helm for her armor already? That was fast."

"Nay, I didn't. I'll have her wear one made for a

man. That will block her view a little. Hopefully, she'll be too distracted to notice any differences with the training equipment."

"Now you are starting to sound like her brother and father, wanting to distract Lady Raven from what's really going on. Is it right to do that?"

"It is, since now I can understand her brother's and father's concern. Lady Raven is the kind of woman who needs to be distracted. If not, she'll get hurt, not to mention drive everyone crazy. She'll also scare away any potential husband as well."

"It seems to me you'd like it if she scared away any possible husbands-to-be."

"Mayhap I would, but what difference does it make?" asked Jonathon, looking back toward the house. "Lady Raven and I are from two different worlds. Worlds that can never combine. She'll marry a noble because that is what's expected of her. I will watch and not say a word, because that is what is expected of me."

Just admitting this aloud felt like a blade being twisted into Jonathon's heart. There wasn't a thing he could do about it, because a noble didn't belong with a commoner, and that was never going to change in his lifetime.

CHAPTER 13

J onathon worked well into the night, having had to complete a few repairs for the nobles before he could get back to working on Raven's armor. He enjoyed constructing it, since he had never made armor so fine and detailed before. It was a true challenge. However, it was taking more time to make it as lightweight as possible. Still, it was a challenge that he more than welcomed.

Heating and pounding the sheet of metal, he used a curved anvil to help bend the vambrace, the metal plate that would protect her forearm. Once he got the curve right, he would hinge it to the other half that made up the armpiece.

"Hello?"

He was so busy pounding and working, that he hadn't even been aware that anyone entered the smithy. He turned around to see Raven standing in the doorway with one of her hounds at her side. She wore a long cloak with the hood covering her head. It was late and dark outside. His guess was that it was well past midnight.

"Lady Raven, what are you doing here?"

Raven entered the smithy, being led by Brindy, her male mastiff. Her hounds slept in her bedchamber, so it was easy to sneak out with her dog without the kennelgroom realizing it was gone.

"I couldn't sleep. I heard the pounding so I knew you were still awake."

"Come in," he said with a nod, putting down the hammer and picking up a rag to wipe his hands.

She entered, closing the door behind her.

"I'm sorry, I'm not dressed appropriately, but it was hot in here and I wasn't expecting visitors at this hour," said Jonathon.

Raven's eyes fastened to Jonathon's arms. They were bare. His chest was bare as well. Only the leather work apron covered his top half. Thank goodness he wore trews or she thought she would have swooned. "You look... fine," she said, once more letting her gaze travel down his body. She wanted to say he looked sexy, amazing, exciting, but she said none of those words.

"Brindy, good to see you, boy," said Jonathon, hunkering down and petting the dog. Brindy got a little excited with the attention and knocked him to the ground. Jonathon fell back on the floor laughing.

"Brindy, nay. Bad boy," Raven scolded, hurrying over to pull the dog off of him. "I'm sorry I brought my hound along, but it was late and dark and I didn't want to go out unescorted."

Brindy sat down and whimpered, his tail swishing back and forth over the floor.

"No problem. I think Brindy should have been made your personal guard instead of me." Jonathon jumped up, patting the dog on the head. "I have something for you," he said, walking over to a table.

"I figured sooner or later you'd come to visit and I wanted to make sure you were satisfied." With his back toward her, he picked up something that was wrapped in brown paper.

"Me?" asked Raven, wondering what he had, and how he planned on satisfying her. His comment only made her thoughts go wild.

"Nay, I was talking to Brindy," said Jonathon, pulling out a big bone and handing it to the dog. The dog grabbed it and ran into the bedroom to chew on it.

"Oh," she said, suddenly feeling very foolish.

"I saved that from the last time my mother made soup. I thought it was too good to throw away."

"Of course," she said, flashing him a smile.

"I do have something for you, too," he told her, walking back over to the work area, picking up several pieces of armor.

"My armor!" she exclaimed, nearly running to him, so excited to see it. "It is finished?"

"Naaaay," he said with a chuckle. "I only have the greaves and the plackart finished, and one of the vambraces. I have a long way to go yet."

"The what?" she asked. "I'm sorry, but I'm not really knowledgeable about the names of the different pieces of armor."

"Oh, I'm sorry. I sometimes take it for granted that everyone knows what I'm talking about." He picked up a piece that looked like it was to be worn on the leg. "The greaves protect your shins, and the vambraces, your forearms."

"And the plackart? Isn't that like a breastplate?" she asked.

"Nay, I haven't made the breastplate yet. I need to take another measurement for that before I do."

"Y-you do?" Her heart picked up a beat as she remembered the last time he measured her. It excited her to think he might do that again.

"The plackart is the part that protects your stomach, under the breastplate. Right here," he said, putting his hand over her cloaked body, right below her breasts. "Since you are here, would you mind trying on the pieces I have to see if they fit properly?"

"Try them on?" Her mouth became so dry that she could barely swallow. All she was wearing under her cloak was her night rail. It was thin and a little sheer.

"Give me your leg. I am anxious to check the fit." He bent down before her with his naked chest and back so close to her that she could reach out and touch him. She slowly stuck one leg out from under her cloak.

"I put straps and buckles on the back to hold them in place." His fingers brushed against her bare leg, sending a delightful shiver coursing through her. "Ah, I see the fit is good, but I need to make the back straps shorter so it buckles tighter."

"Yes. Tighter," she repeated, looking down at his beautiful long hair tied with a band and trailing down his neck.

"Let's try the vambrace next. I hope that fits better. Give me your arm." He jumped up with another piece in his hand. He reached out and took her arm, almost causing her to lose her grip on her cloak since she'd only been holding it shut and it wasn't fastened. He slapped the metal piece around her arm, buckling it quickly.

"Is it good?" she asked, feeling her heart beating in her ears.

"Yes, it is a tight fit. Just the way I like it."

Why did that sound like he was talking about something else to her? The rousing thought lodged in her brain and she couldn't shake it.

"Take off that cloak," he commanded, removing the armpiece and picking up the next. "I want to see how the plackart fits now."

"Well, I don't know." She hesitated, not sure she should do it. Especially since he was looking so naked to her right now, and she felt so naked under the cloak.

"It's fine. You won't have to undress. You can try it on right over your gown." He took the edge of her cloak, moving it. When he did, her grip slackened on her covering. The cloak was resting on her shoulders and fell off, pooling around her feet on the ground. "Oh," he said, his eyes fastening to her chest. "I'm sorry, my lady. I thought you were fully clothed underneath, and not in your night clothes." He bent over to get her cloak, but she reached out and touched him on the arm.

"Continue. Please. I want to try it on," she said, giving him the permission to move forward. Slowly, he stood back up, looking the other way.

"I think it would be better to do this at a later time."

"Nay," she objected, reaching out for the plackart. "I'm here now, and you need to get my exact measurements, so let's do it." She tried to put the piece on, but didn't know how it went.

"Nay, my lady. Not like that." Jonathon reached out and took the plackart from her.

"Please," she said in a half-whisper. "Just call me Raven when we are alone. I'd like that."

He suddenly felt as if his tongue were too big for his mouth. All he could do was nod. Carefully, he put the piece on her, reaching around her waist to buckle it from the back.

"It seems to fit?" she said, more as a question than a statement.

"It isn't too snug, is it?" His hands encompassed her waist. And when he did that, he realized because of where it ended, it made her breasts even more noticeable as they stuck out over the plackart. Her night rail was thin and white and very sheer. The plackart pulled the material taut. In the firelight from the forge he saw her hardened pink nipples poking forward, which instantly caused his groin to tighten.

Damn, he wanted her bad. In his bed, on the floor, on the table, it didn't matter. All he could think about right now was making love to this beautiful woman. He couldn't stop wondering how it would feel to plunge his length into her tight, warm...

"Jonathon?" she said, breaking him from his thoughts. His arms were around her waist, and his eyes were still fastened to her breasts.

"I think that's good." He removed the plackart and turned and headed over to the table. "Mayhap it would be better if you left now."

With his back to her, he didn't even hear her coming. She slid her arms around his waist and laid her cheek against his bare back. He could feel her hot body pressed up against his, and he felt as if he were going to combust.

"I don't want to leave," she said in a half-whisper. "I want to spend the night with you."

"What?" He spun around so fast that she fell against him. He reached out and put his hands on her shoulders to steady her. Looking into her eyes he could see her need for him and wondered if she could see his need for her as well. "Nay. You can't stay. If you do, I'm only going to end up doing something we'll both regret in the morning."

"I promise you, I won't regret it. I want to couple just as much as you want to," she boldly came out and admitted.

"Raven, no," he said in a half whisper, shaking his head, using her name without the title. His arms slid from her shoulders. "I can't take your virginity. It's not right. Especially so close to your wedding day."

"I'm not a virgin," she said, surprising him even more.

"Y-you're not?" he asked, running a hand through his hair. What kind of little vixen was she?

"I'm not a whore, either, if that's what you're thinking."

"Nay! I'm not. I wouldn't. I couldn't." He slowly reached up and cupped her cheek in his palm. Her eyes closed and she leaned in to his touch.

"I only made love once before," she told him. "It was a few years ago with the son of a visiting noble."

"You did?" He didn't know what to think of that, nor how to respond.

"I was seduced," she told him.

"So he forced himself on you?" he asked, needing to know.

"Nay," she said, shaking her head. Her eyes remain locked with his. "We both wanted it. I was curious and so was he. I thought it would be exciting and satisfying, but it wasn't."

"It-it wasn't?" he asked, causing her to shake her head.

"I didn't feel anything for the man, and ended up feeling used. Afterwards, we both realized we meant nothing to each other, and that was the end of it."

"Did your father ever find out?"

"He didn't," she said. "However, I did tell my mother about it."

"Oh no," he mumbled. "What did she say?"

"We discussed it and thought it best not to let anyone know. Especially not Father."

"Yes. I agree. That is something that should remain a secret. Forever." Why the hell was she telling him? He didn't want to be privy to this kind of knowledge. He didn't want anything to ruin the perfect angelic image he had of her in his mind.

"Jonathon, please make love with me," she all but begged.

"I don't know. I want to, Raven, honest I do. But I can't."

"Why not?" she asked. "Because I'm a noble and you are a commoner?"

"Yes, that has something to do with it. Plus, the fact that if your father or brother found out, I'd be beheaded. Not to mention, I have no idea what your new husband would do to me or to my family. I just can't take the risk."

"No one has to know." She reached up and kissed him, causing him to lose his resolve.

"I'll know. So will you," he answered, not stopping her when she kissed him once again.

"I don't want to be naught but the grand prize of a silly competition," she told him. A tear streamed down her cheek. He reached up and gently brushed it away.

"Neither do I want that for you," he said softly, feeling the love in his heart swell for this woman. "You deserve so much more."

"I am about to be handed off as the wife to someone who might be horrible, old, ugly, and disgusting," she told him. "What if Lords Whitehead or Belmouth win the competition? I don't want to be either of their brides."

"Nay. Neither do I want that for you."

She was crying now, and Jonathon didn't know how to comfort her. He wanted her so much that if he touched her again, he wasn't sure he'd be able to let go and walk away.

"Raven, darling, stop crying. Please," he told her. It felt odd to just call her Raven without her title. Still, it felt right in a way. They were together and alone, and he didn't want her status to come between them. Even if just for a night, dropping her title would help him cope with the fact that they were so different from each other.

Her arms went around him and she rocked back and forth as she continued to cry. The strong, rebellious, boisterous woman, who seemed afraid of nothing or no one, was now vulnerable and frail and he didn't know what to do.

"At least give me one night of pleasure before I am imprisoned in a loveless marriage for the rest of my life. Please, Jonathon. At least allow me that."

"It's not right, Raven. We don't belong together and you know it."

"I wish I could marry you, not any stupid noble."

"What?" he asked in surprise. "Raven, you don't mean that."

"I do. I think I am in love with you, Jonathon. I have never felt this away about a man before."

"Ohhh," he said, wondering if he could have gotten himself in any worse position.

"Don't you want me?" she asked with a sniffle.

"More than you know," he answered, stepping back, trying hard not to touch her, when all he wanted to do right now was to scoop her up in his arms and take her to his bed.

"Do you love me?" she asked. "Please, tell me the truth. I need to know."

He wanted to lie to her and say he didn't love her. If he could discourage her, mayhap she'd turn and leave right now before it was too late.

"Yes," he said instead, his voice coming out in a breathy whisper. His eyes closed and he found it hard to breathe.

"Then I see no reason to stop ourselves from doing what we both want so badly."

When his eyes flittered open, this time his jaw dropped. Raven stood there completely naked, with her night rail pooled around her feet. Her ebony hair was loose, falling softly over her shoulders. Her perky, but full breasts stood at attention, her hardened nipples begging to be suckled. Raven's waist was small, her hips delectably curvy. And in the juncture of her thighs was a nest of midnight curls that he wanted more than anything to touch.

"God's eyes, what are you doing to me?" he asked in a shaky breath, doing his best to keep from running to her.

"Jonathon, we were meant to be together, and

you know it." She stepped forward, reaching out to touch him. His hand shot out to stop her. He stepped backwards, hitting up against the wooden table.

"Tell me you really want me to leave, and I will," she said, her voice trembling. "Tell me you don't want to give me one night of bliss that will have to last me a lifetime, and I'll go."

Jonathon's apron became tight with his erection poking out from beneath it. He removed the apron and threw it to the side.

"I'm losing control, Raven. I don't know how much longer I'll be able to conduct myself like a gentleman around you."

"I'm not looking for a gentleman tonight," she told him, sounding like a sexy, wanton siren of the sea. She walked up to him and took his hand in hers. "I am looking for a lover." She placed his hand over her bare breast, offering what he so desperately wanted. I love you, Jonathon Armstrong, and I mean it."

Raven moaned when Jonathon's mouth covered her nipple and he suckled her, causing her to feel a vibrating feeling between her thighs. Pressed up against him, she felt his hardened manhood against her belly. She reached out and untied his trews as they kissed, slowly pushing them to the floor. He kicked off his shoes and stepped out of his trews. His eyes devoured her. The man looked so hot, hard, and hungry.

"I don't want either of us to regret this," he said in a sultry voice.

"I know I won't," she assured him. "Will you?"

"Probably," he answered, picking her up in his strong arms. She squealed in surprise and held on to him, breathing heavily. "There is no turning back now," he answered, taking long strides over to the adjoining room where he slept. There was one bed and two pallets on the floor. Brindy lay atop one of the pallets, still chewing on the bone.

He gently laid her down, positioning himself above her. "I must be out of my mind," he whispered, kissing her again, pushing her legs apart with his knee.

"I know I'm crazy, but I don't really care," she told him with a giggle.

He used his hand to ready her, playing with her womanly folds. When he kissed her, he slipped his tongue into her mouth, bringing her more and more to life. Heat spiraled up from her belly. Then his mouth covered one nipple, his teeth grazing over it, before his hot mouth covered it completely. His tongue flicked out, licking her, and then he suckled her hard, causing her to gasp in delight. Her eyes closed and her back arched off the bed. And just when she thought it couldn't feel any better, he surprised her by slipping a finger inside her, making her moan loudly in lust and delight as she squirmed beneath him.

"Ooooh, that feels so good, Jonathon. More. I want more."

He proceeded to slip another finger into her, using his thumb to tease her nub. The action nearly made her scream aloud with unbridled passion. She needed him and wanted him. Her breathing deepened and she saw the rise and fall of her own chest pushing up against his nakedness. It was almost too much to take. The euphoric feeling engulfed her, and she thought she would burst.

"Jonathon, I need to feel you inside me," she said, as he continued to fondle her and kiss her neck. "I need you. I want you. I want you to take me right now." When he didn't answer, she reached down, wrapping her fingers around his engorged form. "Ooooh," she moaned, feeling the thickness of his shaft beneath her fingers. His skin was like silk covering steel and she couldn't get enough.

He pulled back a little, and she could see his eyes close as he bit his bottom lip. Still, she didn't release him. Instead, she slid her fingers down his long shaft, and back up again. Raven's excitement caused a wetness she felt gathering between her thighs.

"Raven, this is wrong," he whispered, breathing just as heavily as she. He still hadn't penetrated her with anything but his fingers, but that wasn't good enough for her. She wanted more.

"In case you haven't noticed, I'm not known for always doing what is right," she said, reaching up to lick his neck. He moaned and his eyes closed again. "I have a mind of my own, and I say this feels so right, that there is no way it could possibly be wrong."

"Still, I-I-" He couldn't seem to finish his sentence. That was fine with her since she didn't want him to talk or change his mind about making love with her.

"If you won't be the aggressor, then I will." She pushed him onto his back and climbed atop him, spreading her legs to take him in. Slowly, she started to lower herself on to him. And just when she felt the tip of his erection at her door, he pushed her to her back and was suddenly on top again.

"If anyone is going to get blamed for being the aggressor, it'll be me, not you."

"Blamed? Not exactly the words I was expecting in foreplay, but it'll do," she told him.

That caused them both to laugh. And when the tension was broken, he slipped his length into her, little by little, until he filled her completely. "Ooooh. Oooooh, Jonathon," she cried out, having never felt anything so wonderful in her entire life. She wanted to feel more of him, and lifted her legs, wrapping them around his waist, not allowing him to go. Not that he would at a time like this, but she still didn't want to take any chances that he'd end up changing his mind.

"Shhhh," he told her, kissing her again. He moved his hips in the dance of love, thrusting into her, making her squirm and scream, then slowly pulling out again. In and out, they found the rhythm, until she felt such excitement well up inside her that she couldn't stop it now even if she tried. Her head fell back with her eyes closed, and colorful stars burst behind her closed lids. Her breathing labored and her entire body tingled and vibrated, making her feel as hot as the fire of the forge. "Yes! Jonathon, yes, yes, yes!" she cried out louder and louder as she reached her climax.

His mouth came down on hers again making her realize he was probably trying to muffle her cries of passion so they wouldn't be heard by the castle guards. Then he growled low in his throat, sounding like a wild beast, exciting her even more. His rhythm didn't stop until he released his seed within her. The thought of it made her so excited that she found her completion a second time, which surprised her since she didn't know that she could.

Spent and exhausted, they separated, lying next

to each other and breathing hard. Brindy let out a groan and rolled over on his back, making them both giggle.

"Thank you, Jonathon. You have made me so happy." She snuggled up against him, never wanting to leave. Here was the man with whom she wanted to spend the rest of her life. She didn't want a noble. She didn't care if she had a title and he did not. All that mattered was that she finally found love in her life, and now she didn't want to ever let it go.

CHAPTER 14

"Raven? Are you in here?"

Jonathon awoke the next morning, hearing someone calling for Raven. It wasn't until he saw Raven's naked body pressed up next to him that he remembered what happened last night.

"Oh, hell," he said, bolting up to a sitting position, quickly pulling on his trews. Brindy got up and stretched and yawned. Raven stirred in the bed.

"Raven?" Lark appeared at the door to the bedroom holding a lit candle in her hand. Copper, Raven's apricot-colored dog was with her. "Oh, my!" exclaimed Lark, when she saw Jonathon get out of bed, half-dressed, and Raven still lying there under the covers.

"Lark?" came Raven's sleepy voice from the bed. "What are you doing here?"

"Me? What are *ye* doin' here?" asked Lark, looking back over her shoulder. "Yer father is lookin' for ye. It's already mornin'. When ye and Brindy weren't there when I awoke, I thought ye might be with Jonathon. But I never thought ye'd be doin' this!"

"Raven, get up," said Jonathon, not bothering to

use her title since they were more than familiar with each other now. He quickly pulled a tunic over his head and jammed his boots onto his feet. "Lady Lark, I'm sorry you had to see this."

"I'm no'," said Lark with a smile. Then her eyes opened wide and she shook her head. "I mean, I'm no' sorry ye did it. Together. I mean—"

"Never mind, Cousin." Raven sprang from bed, trying to pull her night rail over her head. "Father can't see me like this. I need to hide. If he finds me in here in my night clothes, he'll know what happened."

"Here. I brought yer gown." Lark put down the candle and pulled Raven's gown out from a bag she carried over her shoulder.

"Raven? Where are you?" came Corbett's bellow from just outside the blacksmith's shop.

"Damn it," spat Jonathon. "I knew this would happen." He paced back and forth.

"Hurry, Raven," said Lark, helping her dress. "Here, put the cloak back on and mayhap no one will notice yer messy hair."

"Raven?" came Rook's voice next. They were getting closer.

"That's it." Jonathon threw his hands in the air. "I'm going to tell them the truth and take my punishment like a man." He started to leave the room, but Raven grabbed his arm and spun him around.

"You do that and I will never forgive you!" she spat.

"What? I don't understand," he said. "We both knew this might happen."

"We knew, and it did, but that is no reason to act stupid!" She pushed him out the door. "Get over to the forge and crank it up. Fast."

"But –"

"Do it," she spat, and Jonathon didn't argue.

"Raven, ye need to get out of the man's bedchamber," said Lark. "Oh, I'm so frightened for ye."

"Don't be," she said, spying the bone on the ground and scooping it up. "This isn't the first time and it won't be the last."

"What?" asked Lark. "Are ye sayin' ye –"

"Shush, Lark. Now, follow me and let me do all the talking." Raven grabbed Lark by the arm and pulled her into the other room where Jonathon was working the bellows, bringing the flames to life.

"Oh, no. Hide the armor," said Raven, not wanting her father to see it.

"Nay, it's fine," Jonathon told her, making no sense at all.

"Raven? Are you in here?" Rook pushed open the door to the blacksmith's shop.

"Here, Brindy," said Raven, throwing the bone on the ground. The dog sniffed it but did nothing to chew on it. Thankfully, Copper decided she wanted it, and lay down and gnawed on the bone instead.

"I found her," Rook called over his shoulder, entering the shop, leaving the door wide open. The sun streamed in, lighting up the dark room.

"Raven?" Corbett walked in next with Devon at his side. "Where the hell were you? I came to your room this morning and Lark said she hadn't seen you."

Devon, Raven's mother, walked in, keeping to the back of the room and not saying a word.

"I was here," said Raven.

"Doing what?" asked her brother, sounding suspicious.

"Jonathon told me yesterday he had a bone for the dogs. Brindy was acting anxious and I thought it would calm him."

"Really." Corbett looked down to the dogs. "If you're trying to calm Brindy, why is Copper chewing on it and Brindy is yawning?"

"Brindy already had his time with the bone, my lord," said Jonathon, coming to her rescue.

"I see," said Corbett, still looking at them oddly. "Armstrong, why is the forge going this early?"

"He was catching up on orders," said Raven.

"Well, I said you are to stay with my daughter during the day, and only work in the forge at night."

"Aye, my lord. I'm sorry," said Jonathon.

"Carry on," said Corbett, leaving with Rook.

"Whew, that was close," remarked Lark.

"Shhh," said Raven, looking around. "Mother?" she called out.

"I'm here, Raven." Her mother walked out of Jonathon's bedroom, and came up to her and handed her something.

Raven looked down to see it was her night rail. "Oh. So, you know."

"What I know is that you will not be able to fool your father for much longer. I suggest you tell him soon that you've fallen for a man who isn't a noble." She glanced over to Jonathon, but he couldn't meet her gaze.

"Will you tell Father for me?" asked Raven.

"It's not my story to tell. I suggest you figure out what you're going to do before you're married off to a man you don't love or want."

"Father is so adamant about me marrying a noble," said Raven. "I don't want a noble. I want

Jonathon." She looked over to him but he kept busy stoking the flames of the forge.

"Your father is a proud man, Raven. He has worked hard to bring honor back to the family name. He won't take this news easily."

"He must understand what it's like to fall in love with someone beneath one's status," said Raven. "After all, he fell in love with you when he thought you were only a servant."

"Raven, I won't tell you what to do because, for one, I believe in true love over status. But just remember that whatever decision you make, you will have to live with the consequences for the rest of your life. Whatever that might be." With that, her mother left the forge, leaving the room in silence.

"I think I'll leave now, too," said Lark, hurrying out the door with the dogs following right behind her.

Raven glanced over at Jonathon, but he was still not looking at her. He purposely kept busy dousing the fire now that her father told him to do so.

"Jonathon? Say something to me. Please," she begged.

He put down a poker and turned to face her. "I never wanted to be deceptive. I don't like lying."

"It's not lying. We are just... keeping some things quiet. For now."

"Don't deny it, Raven. All you do is lie. And what happens when your mother reveals to your father just what went on between us? What position will that put us in?"

"She said she wouldn't," said Raven. "I believe her."

"Well, what happens when in a few weeks you are

forced to marry whichever noble wins the tournament?" he asked. "What will you do then?"

"I-I won't let that happen."

"What does that mean?" He crossed his arms over his chest. "You can't stop it."

"I have plans, Jonathon. You won't have to worry. I promise."

"Let's hope so," he said, heading to the door. "Because I won't sacrifice my job, my reputation, and my family for a spontaneous decision to have one night of passion."

"I'm ready," called out Raven, sitting atop her horse behind Jonathon's father's shop in town. She was determined that today was the day she'd conquer the quintain. Time was running out. If she wanted to learn this joust and hopefully win the tournament, she needed to get better at it quickly.

She lowered the visor on the helm that Jonathon insisted she wear. It wasn't made for her. It was the helm of a man and too big for her and also too heavy. It kept slipping and it took all her concentration to keep her chin up so she could see where she was going. Still, she felt good about this. The lance in her grip didn't seem as heavy and cumbersome as always. Perhaps she had a newfound strength after making love with Jonathon. Or mayhap all this practice was giving her muscles. After all, swinging the hammer in the forge gave Jonathon those bulging muscles in his arms that she adored.

"Go," shouted Jonathon from the other end of the practice field.

Kicking her feet into the sides of her horse, Raven raced across the field toward the quintain.

"Pick up the tip of the lance. Raise it higher," he shouted. "Focus, focus."

"Faster, faster," yelled Avery. "You need more speed."

"I'm trying," she called back, aiming for the target on the quintain, hitting it and already cringing, ready to feel the air knocked out of her as soon as the sandbag walloped her in the back. To her surprise, she rode right by, hearing the squeaking of the swivel arm, but wasn't hit from behind. She turned her horse to see the sandbag slowly swinging back and forth.

"I did it? I did it!" she screamed, excited that she'd finally conquered the struggle with the quintain. "Did you see that, Jonathon? I did it, didn't I?" She threw the lance down.

"Aye," he said, walking over to meet her. Avery rushed over and picked up the lance. "You did it," said Jonathon, sounding less than enthusiastic.

"I finally beat the quintain." She ripped off her helm.

"Yes, you did. So you're done. Let's prepare to go back to the castle. I have a lot of work to do."

"Nay, wait. I want to try it a few more times to make sure it wasn't just dumb luck."

"All right," he said with a nod. "Two or three times should suffice. Then we're finished with the joust."

"Finished? Nay, I'm not. I've only just started."

"What do you mean?"

"I need to try it in competition. Against a man. For real," she said.

"No, you don't. This is good enough, Raven."

"No, it's not. I am going to learn to joust against someone. You need to fight me, Jonathon."

"What?" His head jerked back in surprise. "Nay. I'm not going to joust against you."

"Why not?" she asked. "I need to practice against a real person. Since I will be rejected back at the castle, you're going to have to do it. I'll be ready in a few minutes." She turned and rode back to the start.

"Nay!" he called after her. "I don't have your armor finished yet."

"I can't wait for it. I'm running out of time and I need to learn the joust right now."

"Damn, she's stubborn," Jonathon said to his brother. "I thought that would be enough to suffice her, but no, she wants to battle against a live person. What the hell is the matter with her? And what is her all-fired hurry?"

Avery shook his head. "The real question is what's the matter with *you* for allowing her to even do this?"

"I'm only trying to make her happy. Plus, her father wants me to keep her distracted so she doesn't scare away all the knights who are starting to arrive for the tournament."

"They're arriving already?" asked Avery. "The tournament isn't for another two weeks yet."

"I know. However, I believe they arrive early to get a good spot to pitch their tents, and also to get used to the tiltyard and practice areas before the tournament starts."

"I'll bet they'll come early to eye up Lady Raven, too," said Avery, getting a scowl from Jonathon in return. "I mean, to see what the prize is, to know if it's —if she's worth fighting for."

"She is, believe me," said Jonathon in a low voice.

"Brother, she thinks she's really good at the quintain now because she doesn't know we rigged it. How are you going to make her think she's mastered the joust so she'll stop this nonsense?"

"I just have to fool her once again, although I hate to do it. I'll let her knock me off my horse a few times. That should satisfy her and mayhap she'll forget all about this silly notion of jousting. I need to make it look believable since everyone knows a girl could never beat a man at the joust."

"Even if it works, you'd better hope she never finds out you're throwing the competition."

Jonathon's head hurt and his gut twisted. He didn't like Raven telling lies, and now he was being no better than she. When would all this deception end? "I don't like all these secrets and all this deceit," said Jonathon. "I feel like going to her father and telling him what transpired between us."

"You do that and you're a dead man, you do know that," said Avery. "Plus, it won't reflect well on the rest of the family either."

"If I say nothing, it'll kill me to sit back and watch her marry a noble instead of me."

"Then ask her father for her hand in marriage."

"I can't. He's trusted me to be her personal guard. I don't want to disappoint him."

"If you just let Raven marry someone else, you'll disappoint her, won't you?"

"Yes, I believe I will. What am I supposed to do? I'm not a noble, dammit. I couldn't marry her even if I begged Lord Corbett on my knees. Any way I turn, I'm doomed, I tell you. I don't like this one bit."

"Mayhap Raven can help where that's concerned."

"I doubt it. Noblewomen don't have a say as to whom they marry. That is determined for them by their fathers."

"Well, it seems to me, her husband is being chosen by fate, not her father. After all, even Lord Corbett doesn't know which man she'll marry until a winner of the tournament is determined."

"Aye, you're right," said Jonathon, just the thought of all this making him feel like he was going to retch. One of the lucky sots entering the tournament would get Raven for his wife. Only nobles were allowed to participate in the tournament, so he didn't even have a chance to compete for her hand in marriage. Nay, he was not that lucky. He had no chance in hell of ever becoming Lady Raven's husband.

CHAPTER 15

"Raven, there are a bunch of the tents goin' up outside the castle walls," Lark reported the next day, looking out the open window of the bedchamber. "Some of those men look pretty handsome from here. Come take a look."

"That's nice," said Raven, not caring at all.

"Dinna ye want to see? Oh, look at that one walkin' right under our window." Lark giggled and waved.

"Get away from the window," snapped Raven, marching over and getting ready to close it. She stopped when she looked over to the practice yard and noticed Jonathon getting atop his horse. "What is Jonathon doing?"

"Where?" asked Lark, stretching her neck, peering out the window.

"He's over there. In the tiltyard," she said. "It looks like he's about to... to joust. With Rook."

"Really?" asked Lark excitedly. "I want to see how good he is."

They watched as Rook and Jonathon jousted. After several passes, Jonathon was evenly tied with

Rook, who was the castle's best when it came to the sport. It was unbelievable that a common man could go up against a knight and hold his own. It was just as unbelievable that her father and brother would allow Jonathon to joust, with all these competitors arriving for the tournament. Rook seemed to be friends with Jonathon now, and any gossip she'd heard earlier about favoring Jonathon seemed to have dissipated.

"He's pretty good, Raven, wouldna ye say?"

"Aye, he is," she said, impressed with Jonathon's skills. "Anyone who can match my brother deserves to be a knight, or at least one of my father's guards."

"I'm surprised they're lettin' Jonathon joust. After all, that's only for knights. Everyone was already gossipin' about him, and this will only make matters worse."

"Yes," said Raven. "However, it seems my brother has become good friends with Jonathon and favors him. Rook always had a way with the rest of the nobles, so he has probably convinced them to accept Jonathon as well."

"Well, I hope his favorin' a commoner isna goin' to cause trouble with the rest of the competitors arrivin' for the tournament."

"Jonathon is only practicing, not competing," Raven pointed out. "I'm sure it doesn't really matter." As Raven watched Jonathon in awe, she wished more than anything that he was really competing in the tournament, and that he would be the one to win her hand in marriage.

～

"Are you ready?" called out Jonathon from the other side of the practice field in town later that day. He sat atop his horse with a lance in hand. There was a short wooden fence serving as the list which they would use so they wouldn't collide. Raven was so excited to finally be jousting for real. The best part was that she'd finally convinced Jonathon to go up against her.

"I am ready," she called back, touching her new breastplate Jonathon had constructed. She also wore the plackart and coverings for her forearms and shins. She didn't have the complete set of armor yet, but she didn't really need it all. She also refused to wear the heavy man's helm while she waited for her own to be finished. "Shouldn't you be wearing armor, too? Or at least a mail shirt?" she called out, since he wasn't protecting his body from potential harm in any way.

"Nay, I'm fine. I won't get hurt. I'm wearing a padded gambeson, so don't worry."

He was wearing one, but she could see that he hadn't bothered to fasten the ties on the front, so it still exposed part of his chest.

"I don't know how you can say that. This is a dangerous sport and you need to be protected." She'd seen him wearing armor when they'd practiced at the castle just that morning. Why would he be so flippant about wearing some now? She knew he had his own armor that he wore when the knights went up against him to test out theirs. The only reason she could think of was that he didn't really believe she'd be able to hit him. Well, she would show him how wrong he was.

"Raven, I'm fine. Now, ready, set, go!" He took off atop his horse, barreling toward her before she could object. She had no choice but to do the same.

She aimed her lance, feeling tense since she was

sure he'd knock his into her and she wasn't sure if it would hurt. After all, when she'd watched him practice, Jonathon broke several lances against her brother.

"Oh, oh, this is scary," she said softly. She wasn't frightened when she practiced swordplay, or even when she worked with other weapons. This, on the other hand, was something that frightened her to death. She'd seen what happened to other knights during a joust when they were hurt, and it wasn't a pretty sight. Raven only hoped for the best now because she had no idea what to expect.

"I don't want to hurt you, Jonathon," she shouted as they got closer.

"You won't," he yelled back. "Now aim, and hit me, damn it."

"All right." She tried to steady the wobbly lance and aim for his chest. It was a real trick to hold up the weight while moving. It was also difficult to even move or breathe wearing this armor. Controlling a horse under her at the same time was taking all her concentration. "Here it goes," she said, reaching out with the lance as he got closer, bracing herself to be hit at the same time.

Surprisingly, his lance only glanced the side of her armor, and she didn't think she even hit him at all. But when she turned to look, she saw Jonathon had lost his balance, and was struggling to stay atop his horse.

"Did I do that?" she asked in surprise, stopping the horse and turning back. Avery watched from the side.

"That was good, Raven," Jonathon told her. "Just

try to aim for my chest," he told her. "You are just a little off."

"All right, but if you at least had a shield, I wouldn't feel so bad about hitting that," she answered, trying it once more. This time, she felt as if the tip of her lance actually touched him, but it didn't seem like it hit him hard. She didn't feel his lance on her at all. When she looked back, he was pulling himself back up atop the horse, looking like he'd almost fallen off.

"Good, good," he called out. "You almost unseated me. I wasn't expecting that. Once more and I think you'll have it."

"Really? That quickly?" she asked, thinking something was odd here. "I didn't even feel you hit me, Jonathon. You're not holding back, are you?"

"Mayhap just a little, but I won't this time."

"All right. Good. Neither will I." As she readied the lance, she saw Avery and Jonathon smiling at each other. It was then that she realized they were playing with her. She had seen Jonathon joust. He was damned good. He must only be pretending to be hit by her, because she knew for a fact she didn't hit him with enough force to almost knock him off his horse twice now. What the hell was he doing?

Angry with the men for fooling her in this manner, she decided this time she would be the one laughing in the end. She was going to hit him with all her might. Hell, she might just break the lance while she was at it. Either way, this time he would know for sure that she hit him.

As they rode toward each other with their lances held high, her anger got the best of her. This time, she put all her weight into the jab, making sure she smashed him dead center on his chest.

"Ooomph," she heard at the same time his lance hit her in the chest too. The tip of her lance shattered. She received a harder blow from Jonathon than she'd expected. She fell back in the saddle, dropping the pole. It wasn't easy to keep riding since it was hard to right herself wearing the armor. Raven lost her balance and couldn't recover. Unfortunately, she fell to the ground.

"Damn it!" she shouted, pushing up to her knees and brushing herself off. When she looked back at Jonathon, he was lying on the ground too, not moving. "You can get up now and stop pretending. I know what you're doing and I don't like it."

"Jonathon! Are you all right?" Avery ran over to his brother.

"Oh, stop the acting," she spat, still angry with the men. "He didn't even bother to wear armor or tie his gambeson closed because he didn't think I'd ever hit him. His phony act of falling off the horse is not believable either." When she heard him moan again, and Avery called out for their mother, Raven suddenly realized that mayhap Jonathon wasn't acting after all. She might have really hurt him. "Jonathon? Jonathon!" she cried, running to him, stopping short when she saw the pain on his face.

"What's the matter?" asked his mother, coming from the house with Estrilda. "Oh, no! He's hurt. Crispin, Jonathon is hurt!" She ran over to her son.

"Jonathon, talk to me," cried Raven, falling to her knees. Tears streamed from her eyes.

"You're better than I thought you'd be," he answered, feigning a smile and then wincing in pain. "I think I should have worn protection after all. These wooden splinters are going to be hell to remove."

"I didn't mean to hurt you," she apologized. "When I realized you were only making me think I was doing a good job when I wasn't, I became angry. After all, I saw how accomplished you are at the joust when you practiced with my brother this morning."

"Oh, damn. You were watching?"

"Yes, I was. That is why I know you are only doing this to make me want to stop jousting."

"You unhorsed me, if you didn't notice. That part was real. Help me up, Avery," said Jonathon.

"Nay. You might have bruised a rib. Don't move," warned his mother.

"The only thing bruised is his pride," chuckled Avery, helping Jonathon to his feet.

"Jonathon? What the hell is going on?" asked Crispin, hurrying from the house with Heathcliff and Gerold right behind him.

"I'm fine. Really," he said. "I know what it feels like to have a broken bone, and this isn't it. I just hit the ground hard, that's all. Not to mention, I took in a few nasty splinters." He reached over and pulled out a shard of wood and threw it to the ground.

"Then you're all right?" asked Raven, jumping to her feet as well.

"I am, but you were right. I must admit that I wanted you to think you learned the joust so you'd stop with all this nonsense."

"It is getting nerve-wrecking for all of us," said his mother. "We are only commoners and not used to this. We live a simple life."

"Your mother is right, Jonathon," said his father. "I've never stopped you from doing what you want, but this isn't a knight's tiltyard. It is my place of business, and needs to be treated as such. My customers have been asking questions about what you're doing out here, and I don't want to tell them. I'm afraid I'm going to get into trouble with the nobles, even though you and Lady Raven said we won't."

"Jonathon, they're right," said Raven. "I suppose I should stop practicing here." This made Raven sad, but she didn't want Jonathon's family to feel as if she were putting them in a bad situation, even if she didn't believe that was so. She had tried to stop before, but then Jonathon insisted he train her again. This time, it would sadly have to end.

"Yes, stopping might be a good idea," said Jonathon, rubbing his chest and shoulder. He pulled out another splinter of wood and threw it to the ground.

"Hello?" came the voice of a man from inside the shop.

"We have a customer," said his father, hurrying inside.

Jonathon and the others followed his father into the smithy. His body ached and his pride was bruised. The damned wench had it in her to actually learn the joust after all. That was actually something he hadn't been expecting. He'd underestimated her, but also admired her at the same time. He didn't think her lance would ever touch him. He'd told her not to hold back and she hadn't, so he supposed he'd gotten exactly what he deserved.

"Guild Master Wilkin," said Jonathon in surprise when he'd entered the shop. "What are you doing here?"

"Who is that?" Raven whispered to him.

222

"This is the guild master to whom I'll be presenting my masterpiece, in order to be judged and hopefully become a master at my craft."

"I've stopped by to collect the dues."

"I-I'm not sure I have all of it right now," said his father.

"I do." Jonathon stepped forward and paid the dues, using some of the money that Rook had given him.

Wilkin recorded it, and stuck the coins into his pouch. "Jonathon, you'll be presenting your piece to me and the rest of the guild in two weeks' time," said the man.

"Two weeks? That soon?" This news was horrifying to Jonathon. He had thought he'd have at least another month or so to decide what to make and to complete it. He couldn't possibly create a masterpiece worthy of becoming a master in that short amount of time.

"Is this a problem?" asked the man.

"It's just that I've been hired to help out Lord Corbett Blake with his upcoming tournament that will happen in a fortnight as well."

"A tournament?" asked Wilkin.

"Aye," said Jonathon. "I've been staying at the castle's smithy."

"Well then, we'll just come to the castle during the tournament to judge your piece."

"But-but can't we wait and do it at a later date? In a month or two, mayhap?" asked Jonathon, feeling suddenly pressured since he hadn't even started on anything yet.

"It's either then, or you'll have to wait until next

year when we return," said the man. "What is your choice?"

"Next year?" That sounded like an eternity to him. "Nay, I don't want to wait that long." Jonathon felt his opportunity slipping away as well as another year of his life. He was already twenty-three. His father couldn't continue to pay two journeymen for long, since Avery was a journeyman now, too. It was crucial that Jonathon have his own shop, but he couldn't do that without first becoming a master. He needed to do this if he was ever going to move forward. It was also time to marry and have a family in his life. He needed and wanted to be a master with his own shop. The problem was, he no longer had the time to make the masterpiece that was required to get to where he wanted to be.

"Then it's settled. I'll tell the other judges and we'll meet you at the tournament in two weeks to judge your masterpiece," stated Wilkin.

"Nay, don't do that." Jonathon needed to make the man understand. "I haven't decided on anything yet or even started on my project."

"You haven't?" asked the man. "Two weeks is not enough time to make anything that is going to be good enough to earn you the title of master, I can guarantee you that. This piece needs to be exquisite and the best work you've ever done. Only the finest quality craftmanship will win you the title."

"I know," said Jonathon, shaking his head in frustration. It all came back to titles again, and him not having one. "I have very limited time at the forge to work on anything, since I've taken this job for Lord Blake. I'm sorry to say I will not be able to complete it in time. I guess I will have to wait until next year."

"That's a shame since I had a good feeling about you. I thought you would make a fine master of your trade, just like your father," said Wilkin shaking his head. "We could use someone like you opening his own shop right now. There are many towns around here who need an armorer. You'd make a lot of money. We have a lot of blacksmiths, but not many armorers at all. Oh well, I guess that isn't going to happen this time. Well, then, good day."

"Thank you. Good day," said Crispin, when Jonathon found himself lost for words. "Thank you for stopping by, Guild Master Wilkin."

"Jonathon, what are you going to do?" asked Avery, after the guild master left. "This is your dream. It's all you've been talking about for years now. How can you give it up so easily?"

"I don't have a choice, Avery," said Jonathon. "Without a masterpiece to present to them, I have no chance of being anything but a journeyman for at least another year."

"Let me get those splinters out of your chest," offered his mother, directing him to a chair.

Raven stood there silently, watching Jonathon's family support him and take care of the wounds that she'd inflicted. Had her obsession to learn the joust and fight in the tournament cost Jonathon his dream? He seemed so downhearted, and she felt as if she were to blame.

It didn't sit right with her. Raven felt stupid and also very selfish. She was only fooling herself thinking she could go up against experienced knights in a tournament. It took years of practice to learn the skill of jousting. Why in the devil's name did she think she could master it in such a short time? Or even at all?

Her foolishness had given her hope, but now she realized there was nothing she could do to change the fact she was going to have to marry whichever man won the blasted tournament. Raven's dream, just like Jonathon's, was gone. Her future was being determined by chance, and there was nothing she could do to change it.

Removing her armor, she placed it on the table, slowly running her hand over it reverently, in a silent goodbye. "Don't worry about finishing my armor," Raven told Jonathon. "I won't need it anymore."

With that, she walked out the door to wait for Jonathon to take her back to her prison—Blake Castle. She saw Guild Master Wilkin mounting his horse, and had an idea of how she could at least help Jonathon.

"Excuse me, guild master," she said, approaching him, sloshing through the muddy street.

"Who are you?" asked the man, looking down at her from his horse.

"I'm-I'm a friend of Jonathon's," she told him, not wanting to reveal her true identity. He would probably never believe she was a noble anyway, since she wore dirty men's clothes and was wallowing in the mud.

"What do you want?" he asked her.

"I want you to give Jonathon another chance to earn the title of master craftsman and to have his own shop. It is his dream. It's everything he ever wanted."

"Well, he'll still have a chance but it'll have to wait until next year."

"Nay. He can't wait that long. Isn't there something you can do to help him?"

"I wish there was, but unfortunately it looks as if Jonathon has no masterpiece to present to the guild, and no time to make anything impressive enough in that short of a time."

"Oh, but he's a wonderfully skilled craftsman," she assured the man.

"I don't care how skilled his is. If he doesn't have a presentation piece, then he won't be considered for the position of master this year."

"He does have something," she blurted out in desperation, certain Jonathon could get something together in time if he just stopped wasting his time with her.

"He does?" The man's ears perked up. "Then why did he say he didn't?"

"It's only because he is being modest."

"He said he has no time to make anything."

"He doesn't think he has time to finish, but I assure you after today he'll have much more time to complete his project for you. Just please give him another chance. I will promise you it won't be a waste of your time. You'll see."

"Well, I don't know." The man didn't seem as if he were going to agree, so she realized she would have to say something even more to change his mind.

"It's something that you and the others have never seen before." That wasn't really a lie, she decided, since no one had seen it before since he hadn't made it yet.

"Really?"

"It is unique. Plus, Jonathon only does quality work."

"Like his father," said Wilkin.

"Yes, just like his father. You won't be disappointed."

"That sounds intriguing," said the man. She had finally got his attention. "What is the piece?"

"The piece? What's the piece?"

"Aye. I'd like to know what I'll be coming to judge."

"I-It's a surprise. I don't think Jonathon would want me to tell you. After all, it is not my story to tell," she said, repeating her mother's words when she told Raven to tell her father she was in love with Jonathon. "Just give him a chance, please. I'm sure he'll be finished by the time the tournament starts."

"Well... all right then, I will. Only because I know what wonderful work Jonathon does, and this mystery piece really intrigues me."

"Oh, thank you," she said, feeling elated. Mayhap Jonathon's dream would come true after all, even if she had to give up hers.

"I will return with the rest of the guild masters to judge his piece. We'll do it during the tournament, right there at the forge at Blake Castle, since he said he is employed there for now."

"Yes, that will be fine," she said with a smile. "I'm sure you won't be disappointed."

"We'd better not be," stated the man. "Please remind Jonathon that his masterpiece needs to be complete upon our arrival. If it isn't, he will have ruined his chance of becoming a master armorer."

"Until next year," she said with a nod. "I understand."

"Nay, I don't think you do," said the man, making a sour face. "Now that the date and place is set, there is no turning back."

"What do you mean?" she asked.

"We will arrive to judge his masterpiece. Our trip is far and it will keep us from doing other important things. Therefore, if for some reason he doesn't have a presentation, or if it isn't finished, it's over."

"What's over? I don't understand."

"If he fails at completing it in time and we travel here and see nothing, then I am afraid he will have ruined his chance of ever becoming a master, because it will never come again. Good day."

With that, the man turned and rode away, making Raven feel as if perhaps she hadn't helped Jonathon but instead hurt him more, if that were even possible. When she told the guild master Jonathon had a unique piece, she only made it up to give him more time to make something. All she wanted to do was to give Jonathon another chance at his dream and not have it diminished because he deserved it. She hadn't realized that in trying to help him, she might have just sealed his fate as a journeyman forever.

CHAPTER 16

I t was only a week before the tournament now, and honestly, Jonathon couldn't wait for it to be over. More and more knights had arrived in the last few days, and all of them wanted something from the blacksmith.

Some wanted their armor fastenings strengthened, and others wanted new shoes for their horses. They even expected Jonathon to sharpen their swords and polish their armor. It had become too much for him to work only at night. Having no other choice, he called for his brother and Gerold to return to the castle smithy to help him keep up with the orders.

Jonathon pounded out his frustration on a horseshoe, having gotten little sleep. He arose early to get some work in before he had to waste the entire day following Raven around, doing absolutely nothing. She was still sneaking off at every opportunity to practice with her weapons, not wanting to accept the fact she was to be a lady and married to a noble.

That was something else that bothered him. In his dreams he somehow hoped there would be a way for him to marry Raven, even though he knew it was impossible. As an armorer, he made decent money most of the year. He had hoped if he could become a master, mayhap Lord Corbett would see him in a different light. It no longer mattered now, since he had no presentation piece to put before the guild masters anyway. He would have to wait for an entire year to even have a chance again. By then, Raven would be married and will have forgotten all about him.

Every day Raven seemed to bother him, begging him to make something for the guild masters, but he told her he had no time to do so. Besides, he'd already lost his chance to present to them, so what did it matter? Still, the determined wench never seemed to stop trying to get him to change his mind.

"Brother, it's a little hard to sleep with you pounding away, making so much noise," complained Avery, emerging from the bedroom, rubbing his eyes.

"It's morning and we have a lot to do," grumbled Jonathon. "If we're going to ever get caught up, I have to get something done before I spend the day with Raven."

"Aye, what's happening with that?" asked Avery with a yawn, walking over and pulling the string that worked the bellows. "I thought that after you spent the night with her, things would change between you."

"Shhhh," said Jonathon, stopping his banging, looking over at the door. "Forget that it ever happened. I don't want to talk about it, and neither do I want her father or brother to ever find out about it. Or her husband-to-be," he said under his breath, picking up the horseshoe with long tongs and taking it over to the forge. "It was a mistake. I never should have allowed myself to get involved with someone I knew I could never have."

"Does she want you?" asked his brother.

"I-I'm not really sure anymore," he answered.

"So she hasn't given you any impression that she feels the same way about you as you do about her?"

"Yes, but she lies so much that I'm not sure I believe her." Jonathon turned the horseshoe as it started to glow red.

"What do you mean?"

"I mean, she said she wants to marry me and that she loves me."

"Really?" Avery worked the bellows once more. "Well then, what's the problem?"

"The problem is, I'd like to believe it is what she honestly feels in her heart, but I'm not convinced."

"What is there not to know? You make no sense, Brother."

"I think she might only be saying this because she is so adamant about not wanting to marry the winner of the tournament. She's got a very rebellious nature, you know."

"I've noticed. Then, you think she only went to bed with you to hopefully scare off the nobles when they find out she might be pregnant with a commoner's baby?"

"What?" Jonathon looked up so quickly that he almost dropped the tongs. "I-I never considered the fact I might have... fathered her child. Damn it, what was I thinking? God's eyes, I'm going to hang now for sure."

"A little too late to worry about that, I suppose."

Jonathon put the horseshoe back on the anvil and started pounding on it with his hammer again. "You don't think she'd really... I mean, would she do that to me?" asked Jonathon. "Do you think she might actually be pregnant?"

"I don't know, but like you said, the wench is pretty rebellious and sneaky. I suppose you could ask her if she's pregnant, but it's probably too soon to know."

"Yes. Too soon," repeated Jonathon, feeling his world crashing down around him. "Oh hell, Avery," he said, stopping his work and wiping his brow with a rag. "I'm in over my head, and I don't know what to do."

"Wish I could tell you, but I can't," said Avery with a shrug, crossing his arms and leaning against the brick edge of the forge. "You play with fire and you're eventually going to get burned. Ow!" he said, jumping up, rubbing his backend. "Guess I got too close to the flames."

"Now you know how it feels."

"Jonathon, guess what I just saw?" Gerold ran into the shop, having already been up and around early. The boy was always up before anyone else.

"I don't have time right now," said Jonathon, taking off his apron.

"It was Lady Raven. You should have seen her!" the boy said in excitement, crawling atop a stool.

"Did you say Lady Raven?" Jonathon looked over to the boy in question. "She's out of bed already? Damn. I had hoped she'd sleep late so I'd have more time at the forge. Bid the devil, I can't get a break." He hung up the apron and donned his tunic.

"She's over by the archery range with her bow and arrows," said Gerold.

"She is?" asked Jonathon, wondering what she was up to now.

"Aye, and you should see her." Gerold's eyes lit up with excitement as he rocked back and forth on the stool. "She's a better shot than any of the knights I've seen practicing that have already arrived for the competition."

"Stop rocking on that stool, Gerold, you're going to fall," said Jonathon, having stepped in as the role of the boy's father lately. "Don't forget about your chores."

"I won't," said Gerold, hopping off the stool and grabbing a broom. "I'm going to do my chores fast so I can go watch Lady Raven again." He started sweeping quickly, raising a cloud of dust.

"Slow down or we'll choke to death," he told Gerold.

"But I want to go watch Lady Raven!"

"There will be nothing to see because I'm about to stop her."

"Aye, you'd better go after her," agreed Avery.

"I will," Jonathon answered with a sigh, changing his shoes. His gaze fell on Raven's armor in the corner. He'd still been working on it late at night, even though she told him not to. When Jonathon made a promise, he wanted to see it through. Besides, this would be all Raven had to remember him by shortly, and he never wanted her to forget him, so he was doing an extra good job on it.

"I need to get her out of there before the competitors awake and see what she's doing," he mumbled. "It won't bode well with her suitors to know she's a better shot than them. Plus, her father is going to kill me for not keeping a tighter lead on her."

Jonathon headed out the door at a brisk pace, making his way over to the archery range. Some of the competitors who had arrived for the tournament were already up and about. He hoped to hell he wasn't too late.

~

"Raven, we need to go now," said Lark, looking over her shoulder. "The knights are startin' to wander over. Ye dinna want them to see ye."

"Actually, I do," said Raven, reaching over her shoulder to pull another arrow from the quiver on her back. "I've decided to purposely practice in front of them to scare them off."

"Och, nay," said Lark. "Yer father isna goin' to like that."

"I don't care," said Raven, nocking the arrow and pulling back the bowstring. A few of the men who had pitched their tents in front of the castle saw her and headed in her direction. "If I can't have Jonathon, then I will do everything in my power to keep any of the other men from wanting me for their bride." She loosed the arrow and it hit the target, just off center. "Damn," she spat aloud, pulling out another arrow. "I need to be perfect at this."

"Cousin, stop yer cursin'. Someone might hear ye."

"I hope they do," she answered, wanting to do anything in her power to push these men away.

"Ye're no' still thinkin' about really enterin' the tournament, are ye?" Lark asked in a low voice.

"Shhh." Raven's eyes scanned the area and she

leaned in closer to Lark. "I already have," she said, smiling.

"Ye have? How?"

"As you know, the competitors have been signing up as they arrive."

"Aye. So?"

"So, yesterday, when Jonathon went to work in the forge, I volunteered to watch over the table with the sign-up sheet for the tournament."

"Ye did?"

"Aye. Just for a while. My father thought I wanted to meet my potential husbands. Actually, I wanted to sneak another name onto the list. Sir Jonathon Nevar of Lyon, France. I sent the master of ceremonies to fetch me a drink, and when he'd gone, I wrote the name down on the sheet. I even made up a crest and have been constructing it in the ladies' solar. I will sew it on my tunic and wear it during the tournament." She smiled proudly at Lark.

"Please tell me ye dinna," said Lark, looking as if she were going to swoon.

"I most certainly did, and it was easier than I thought," she said, still smiling. "I used Jonathon's first name since I like it. And Nevar is my name spelled backwards." She giggled at her cleverness.

"Nay!" Lark's eyes opened wide. "Ye shouldna have done that. It is insane. Ye canna go forward with this foolish plan."

Raven scowled. "Neither can I agree to marry whichever fool wins the contest, when I'm in love with Jonathon."

"Och, Raven. This is bad. Very bad," said Lark shaking her head.

"Don't say a word about it to anyone. Only Albert

knows, because I've convinced him to act as my squire."

"Yer father will have both yer heads."

"Nay. I'll take care of that, don't worry. I will smooth things over with my father once I've won the competition."

"How are ye plannin' on winnin'? Ye will be goin' up against strong men. Accomplished knights. Soldiers. Plus, ye'll have to joust."

"I thought about that, and figured out the answer. I only need to win both the archery and sword-fighting rounds. If I do, it won't matter about the joust because it will never have to happen. The way my father set up the tournament, the two winners of these first events are the only ones to move on to the joust. So, if I win both of them, the tournament is over and I am proclaimed the winner."

"I'm afraid ye'll be hurt. I canna let ye do this."

"You can and you will. You know as well as I how important it is to marry the right man."

"I'm scared for ye, Raven."

"Don't be. I'll be fine." She spotted Jonathon hurrying toward them from the smithy. "Damn it, Jonathon's here. He's going to make me stop. I don't have much time to practice."

"Ye need to tell Jonathon the truth. Be honest with him," said Lark, trying to change her mind.

"Nay, I can't. If I tell him, I'm sure he'll inform my father and it'll be over before I even have a chance to try. Now, stay silent. I mean it."

"Lady Raven, what are you doing?" Jonathon hurried to her side. Some of the competitors started to stare.

"What does it look like I'm doing? I'm practicing archery," she answered.

"Whatever for?" He seemed nervous and kept glancing over his shoulder at the knights and nobles who were starting to wander over.

"I was bored. Plus, you know I like to practice with my weapons."

"Not now. Not here." He reached for the bow. "Come, let's go to the great hall."

"Nay!" she said. "Not until I am finished."

"You are finished," he said. "I am supposed to be guarding you. Now stop this."

"Guarding me from what?" she asked, pulling back the bowstring and letting the arrow fly. It landed dead center of the target.

Jonathon's eyes opened wide when he saw it. "That was... that was good," he told her, sounding impressed.

"I know," she said with a smile. "I have bested every man at the castle, including my own father, when it comes to archery."

"Well, that's nice, but you need to stop it now." He reached for her bow once more but she moved it away from him. "How are you at archery, Jonathon?" she asked him curiously.

"Me?" He lowered his hand. "I-I'm all right at it, I guess. I mean, I've been hunting since I was a lad, so the bow is no stranger to me."

"Compete with me," she said, urging him to do it.

"What? Nay. I can't. I'm a just a commoner, Raven," he reminded her under his breath. "I don't belong here and we both know it."

"I saw you jousting with my brother," she said, letting another arrow fly. Once again, she hit the center of the target. The competitors hanging around noticed and moved in closer to watch her. "Compete with me as well," she told him.

Jonathon's heart raced. The competitors who were here for the tournament and to try to win Lady Raven's hand in marriage were noticing Raven's skills and moving in closer. He needed to stop her. He was hired to keep her out of trouble, and to act like a lady, not a man. If word of this got back to Lord Corbett, he wouldn't be happy.

"All right," he told her in a low voice. "I'll compete with you, but only if you promise to stop this nonsense."

"It's not nonsense. Now pick up that bow and arrows," she said, nodding to the equipment right behind him.

Jonathon hadn't used a longbow before. Only the bow and arrows he had for hunting. Still, it couldn't be that hard, could it? "If I can beat you, two out of three shots, then you'll agree to put down the bow and stop this," Jonathon told her, not asking.

"Done," she said, raising a corner of her mouth, looking and sounding so cocky. "And if not, we continue until you can. Even if we're here all day."

"Fine," he spat through gritted teeth, just wanting to beat her and get her out of here before she created more of a spectacle of herself. He picked up the long bow and an arrow, feeling as if this wasn't going to be as easy as it looked. God's eyes, what had he agreed to? This woman was like a siren and he a bewitched sailor. Anything she asked, anything she said, he ended up agreeing to it, although he wasn't sure why. He nocked the arrow and pulled back the bowstring, aiming at the target.

"You might want to wear an armguard or gloves," she told him, just as he was about to shoot.

"What?" He jerked, with her distracting him, and his arrow hit the target, but off to the side. It wasn't a very good shot at all. "Damn it."

"Perhaps an armguard or gloves would help."

"Nay, I don't need them, now stop distracting me," he growled.

"I'm just trying to help."

"My hands and arms are toughened up from working in the forge, so I'm fine. Now shoot."

"Of course," she said, using perfect form and hitting the target dead center. "That's one for me, none for you," she told him, holding up her pointer finger.

The men watching started talking quietly amongst themselves about Raven's skill. This wasn't good. He needed to get her out of here quickly.

Once again, it was Jonathon's turn to shoot. Now that he had tried it with the longbow, he felt more comfortable this time and knew what to expect. He was determined not to let the wench distract him. He maintained his focus and this time his arrow hit the target dead center.

"Beat that," he said smugly, lowering his bow.

"Gladly." When she was ready to shoot again, he thought he'd pay her back the favor. He leaned in close and spoke in a low voice.

"You should really use a chest guard, my lady."

"I don't need it."

"I'd beg to differ with you since I know the size of your..."

"Oh!" she exclaimed, being so flustered that she missed the target completely.

More comments went up from the crowd.

"One for me now, so we're tied," he gladly pointed out.

"Stop that," she said with a snarl. "I know what you're trying to do and it won't work."

"Really." He grinned and raised one eyebrow, taking his shot before she could distract him again. He hit the target once again, dead center.

"You're not bad at archery," she commented. "But I'm better." She lifted the bow and took her shot, hitting the center of the target as well.

"Damn," said Jonathon. "We're even. My lady, I don't think we should go another round." He eyed the crowd starting to gather. This wasn't good at all and he was becoming very uncomfortable.

"Normally, I would disagree with that," she told him. "However, I have some things to do today, so I think I'll stop for now."

"Och, thank goodness," said Lark, rushing to her side.

"You have things to do?" asked Jonathon, handing the bow to one of the competitors, since they all seemed to want to practice now. "Like what?"

"I have a bit of sewing to do," she told him, as they walked to the great hall. "I'll be in the ladies' solar, and you aren't allowed to be there. So, after the meal, why don't you work on finishing my armor while I sew?"

"Y-you're going to sew?" asked Jonathon, surprised to hear that she even knew how to do it. After all, she didn't partake in too many things that were expected of a lady.

"How close are you to finishing my armor?" she asked.

"I've worked on it. A little. I just haven't had much

time to even think about it since all the competitors have started showing up, needing me to do things for them," he explained.

She stopped in her tracks and cocked her head. Lark stood by silently. "Are you saying the competitors are more important than me?"

"Nay. Of course not, my lady. However, they need things done before the tournament starts," he explained.

"I need my armor done by then, too, I told you that at the start."

"I thought you no longer wanted or needed it, since you realized ladies can't joust."

By the look on her face, he realized he shouldn't have spoken his thoughts aloud. It only made her angry.

She leaned in close to him this time, speaking directly into his ear in a low voice. "The deal was, you make my armor, or I tell my father what we did."

He looked at her from the corner of his eyes. "Nay, that's not right. It was so you wouldn't tell him we kissed," he corrected her.

"Well, you wouldn't want him to find out anything else, either. Would you?"

"I don't believe you'd tell him... everything," he said, not thinking she was that bold or dumb.

"Are you willing to bet on it?" she asked, making no sense to him at all. Why the hell would she want to tell her father she made love to a man right before she was about to be betrothed? Still, with Raven, one never knew, and he couldn't take the chance that she might not be bluffing.

"Are you... pregnant?" he asked, holding his breath while waiting for her answer.

"Nay!" Her eyes opened wide. "Or at least, I don't think so."

"Good," he said, almost thinking she was and that was what she planned to tell her father.

"Now, about my armor?"

"I'll make the helm next, as well as the pauldrons," he told her, talking about the helmet and the shoulder coverings. "I'm not sure I'll have time to finish the gauntlets or sabatons though. That's the gloves and shoe coverings," he explained, when she looked confused.

"I know what they are," she spat.

He was sure she knew what a gauntlet was, but didn't think she knew the term of sabatons. She obviously just didn't want to admit it.

"Will that be a problem, my lady?"

"Nay. I don't need them. Just do a good job on the rest of the pieces, please."

"I will," he said, curious as to why she was making such a stink about getting her armor. After all, once she was married, she'd never even have a chance to use it. No knight would be daft enough to let his lady wife even dress that way.

Unless it was him, he realized sadly, more than eager to see Raven fully dressed and wearing his creation.

CHAPTER 17

R aven sat in the corner of the ladies' solar later
that day, sewing a phony crest onto a surcoat
that she would be wearing for the tournament in the
guise of Sir Jonathon Nevar. She decided the crest
would be a raven with a sword in its claw. The irony
of it made her silently chuckle. It kind of reminded
her of a combination of herself and Jonathon. She was
the bird and he represented the sword, being a
swordsmith, or blacksmith, or armorer, or whatever
he was calling himself.

"Raven, ye canna do this. Now please stop before
it's too late," begged Lark, embroidering a pillow covering. The rest of the noblewomen worked on pieces
while making small talk between them, however they
were at the other end of the room.

"I cannot just stand by and watch my life go up in
flames," said Raven.

"It'll be in flames when the truth comes out. Ye
canna deceive yer father nor the noblemen competin'
for yer hand in marriage."

"Well, it's not like I can tell them the truth of
what I did, either." She pushed the needle through

the tunic and pulled the long thread. She didn't normally sew and wasn't that skilled at it. Most of her time growing up had been spent practicing with her weapons or watching her father and brother fight the other knights. "If I did that, my life would be ruined. I'd have a bad reputation and no one would ever want me. I'd be like—" She stopped short, looking up at her cousin.

Lark's eyes became glassy and she looked like she was about to cry. "Ye'd be like me. That's what ye were goin' to say, wasna it?" She put down her stitching and got up.

"Lark, you know I didn't mean anything by that. It just slipped out." Raven cursed herself inwardly for not using more discretion when talking with Lark. The poor girl had a hard life and was very vulnerable. Raven just wasn't used to keeping her thoughts to herself.

"I'm goin' for a walk," said Lark. Her tone was a cross between anger and humiliation with a little sadness thrown in.

"I'm sorry, Lark. Please don't go. You're not angry with me, are you?"

Lark let out a deep sigh before answering. "I ken ye speak the truth, but I canna undo the damage that's already been done in my life. Ye need to remember that. Dinna hurt Jonathon. He doesna deserve it."

"I'm not going to hurt him. Don't you see? My plan will help him instead."

"How?" she asked. "Do ye really think that even if ye do win the tournament, which is addled to even believe ye can, that yer father will let ye marry who ye want?"

"Why not? The winner is supposed to get me as their bride. If I'm the winner, I should be able to choose."

"Choose who?" she asked. "No knight will want a bride who beat him at a tournament. And if ye think ye can choose Jonathon, that is a lie, too. Besides, after he discovers what you want that armor for, ye'll make him look like a fool. He willna want ye either."

"Don't say that!" she spat, but Lark was already walking away. Raven clenched her jaw, knowing that what her cousin said was the truth. She was doomed either way. And the last thing she wanted to do was to hurt Jonathon.

"Raven?"

Raven looked up to see her mother enter the solar. When she dismissed the rest of the ladies before coming over to talk to her, Raven knew she was in trouble.

"Mother," she said, hiding the tunic she was sewing, picking up Lark's needlepoint and pretending she was doing that instead. "What brings you here?"

"Raven, I sent the rest of the ladies away because I wanted to speak to you in private."

"I noticed. What's troubling you?"

"You are, Daughter. I'm worried about you."

"Me?" She looked up and smiled, shrugging her shoulders. "I'm acting like a lady sitting here sewing. Why are you worried?"

"You know why I'm concerned—now stop pretending." Devon sat down in Lark's vacated chair.

"You'll have to be more specific, Mother." She held out Lark's stitching, pretending to be inspecting her work.

"How long are you going to let this go on before you speak to your father?"

"About what?"

"About you and Jonathon. You've got to tell him. You're not being fair about this."

"Father isn't being fair to me either, making me the prize of a stupid contest. Besides, it wouldn't make a difference if I did tell him about Jonathon. He's already decided I will marry a noble and will never change his mind even if the man is older than him and bald and has no teeth. I hate it!" She dropped the needlework on her lap.

"If you really love Jonathon, then you're not being fair to him either."

"What am I supposed to do?" asked Raven, feeling the tears in her eyes. "Mother, mayhap you can talk to Father for me? I'm scared to do it."

"Raven, you are an adult now and no longer a child. You are also the best female warrior I've ever seen. Yet you fear confronting your father?"

"You know better than anyone how stubborn he can be. You are the only one who can get through to him."

Her mother looked as sad as Raven felt at the moment. "Your father prides himself on winning back respect for his family name," she explained. "His dream is to have each of his children marry worthy nobles, strengthening the honor of the Blake name. He had a hard childhood, losing everything and more or less everyone he loved. This is very important to him."

"He didn't lose everyone he loved. He found his siblings again, Mother."

"True, but it took a long time. Those years

without them can never be replaced. Plus, he didn't have a mother or father to go to with all his problems. He had only the sorcerer, Orrick, until he disappeared for a while, too."

"So, Father was raised by the sorcerer?" asked Raven. "He never speaks about it."

"It's a long story. Mayhap you can ask him about it someday. The point is, I didn't have parents to guide me, either. Yet, we both became stronger because of what we went through. It was what helped us to endure and to survive, and to become the people we are today."

"So what are you saying?"

"I am saying, I won't get involved in your life, Raven. As much as I want to help you, if I do, you will never learn your lessons and you will never change."

"I don't want to change. I like the way I am now."

"Does Jonathon like the way you are, too? And what about the man you will marry? What will he think about it?"

"It doesn't matter, because I am not marrying a noble, I tell you."

"So, you plan on marrying Jonathon then? Does he want to marry you, Raven?"

"I-I think so. But he doesn't think he can."

"He can't," said her mother, placing her hand on Raven's arm. "As long as he comes from below the salt, he will never be allowed to marry you, and nothing can change that. Mayhap you should have thought long and hard about this before you made love to the man."

Her head snapped upward. "You don't know that I did that. Not really."

"I do know. I'm your mother, and I can see it in

your eyes, not to remind you that I found your night rail in his bed. Thank God it was I and not your father who found it." She stood up, looking down at the needlework on her lap. "Raven, if you are going to pretend to be doing needlework, then at least have the proper needle and thread in your hand." Devon headed for the door.

"Mother, wait!" Raven shot to her feet. "What am I going to do? How can I make this end the way I want it to?"

"Mayhap you can start by not thinking so much about yourself. Instead, think of how your decisions are going to affect others." She stopped in the doorway, turning around. "I have faith in you, Raven. I always have. You are a defiant young lady, just as I once was, but I know you will do the right thing in the end."

"The right thing? What do you mean? Is the right thing doing what is expected of a noblewoman? And isn't it too late for that?"

"I can't answer those questions, Daughter. You need to look into your heart and you will know just what to do."

She left the solar, closing the door behind her.

Tears streamed down Raven's cheeks. Her anger got the best of her as usual. She picked up the pair of shears and flung them at the closed door. Just when she did, someone opened it from the other side.

The tips of the shears stuck into the wood of the door as Jonathon poked his head inside the room, only making her want to cry even more.

Jonathon jerked backward, not able to believe that Raven just flung a pair of shears at him!

"I guess I should have knocked first, but your

mother just told me you were the only one in here and that it would be all right to enter. I'm sorry." He started to close the door.

"Nay, wait, Jonathon," she called out, and he slowly opened the door again.

"My lady?"

"I'm sorry about the shears. I wasn't aiming for you."

He scanned the room, seeing that Raven was indeed there alone. "Then who?" he asked.

"Come in." She ran over and yanked the shears from the wood.

"I'm not sure I should. I don't believe it's proper for me to be in here when you're unchaperoned, my lady." He was hesitant to step inside.

"Don't be silly. I'm the only one here."

"My point, exactly."

"My mother gave you permission." She reached out and pulled him into the room, closing the door behind him. "Jonathon, I need to talk to you."

"About what?" His eyes went to her hand holding the shears. "Can you put those down first?"

"I'm sorry." She pulled him farther into the room and placed the shears on the table. "I don't want to marry any of the noblemen competing in the tournament," she told him.

"I know that. You've only mentioned it now like a hundred times," he said, feeling choked by the notion that it was exactly what she had to do. "However, my lady, I don't see as if you have a choice."

"Stop calling me *my lady*. I told you, call me Raven in private."

"I can't," he told her. "It's not proper, and it certainly won't be tolerated once you are married. Can we go now?"

"Nay. I'm not done." He could see her becoming upset. If he wasn't mistaken, her cheeks looked wet.

"Have you been crying?" he asked, stepping closer, reaching out to wipe away a stray tear.

"Oh, Jonathon." She fell into his arms weeping. His arms closed around her, and he tried to comfort her, but was afraid someone might walk in and see them. He dropped his arms to his sides and pulled away.

"Why did you do that?" she asked with a sniffle.

"I did what is expected of me. Just as you need to do what is expected of you." It hurt him to say it, but he knew it could never be any other way.

"Jonathon, don't you understand? I don't want any nobleman. I want *you*."

"Me," he said, biting the inside of his cheek, feeling so pathetic right now. She was a titled lady with everything she could want waiting in her future. He was a simple man whose biggest dream was to have enough money to eat the next day, and someday possibly own his own business. He had hoped to become a master at his trade, but that wasn't going to happen any time soon. He had absolutely nothing to offer her that she didn't already have for herself.

"Say something, Jonathon." She looked up to him with those sad, glassy eyes that now looked scared and vulnerable. "Tell me what to do."

Who was he to tell her anything? His opinion didn't matter. All he wanted was to protect his family. Nothing he could do would change the outcome, and he'd be a fool to even think it could.

"Jonathon, speak to me. Please," she begged.

"You don't want me," he told her in a low voice.

"Yes, I do. You're the one I love."

"Nay," he said, becoming angry now. He grabbed her by the shoulders and shook her. "Snap out of it, Raven. You are living in such a dream world that you're only hurting those who care about you."

"W-what do you mean?"

"We can never be together, and you know it. Making love was a big mistake that is only going to come back to haunt us and hurt a lot of people in the end."

"You think making love with me was a-a *mistake*?" she asked, blinking away her tears.

He sighed and looked the other way. What he really wanted to say to her was that he was head over heels in love with her, and that he wanted to marry her more than anything in the world. But how could he say that? It would only make things harder for her, and put a wedge between Raven and her father. Jonathon knew how important it was to Lord Corbett to have all his children marry nobles, and he couldn't blame him. If Jonathon were in his place, he would feel the same way.

"I can't give you what you need," he told her, clenching his jaw, trying to hold back his emotions.

"What I need from you is your opinion on how I can change things, so we can end up together."

"Why?" he asked.

"Why?" She blinked in succession again. "I would think you'd want this as much as I do, but you are starting to sound as if you really don't."

"Raven. Sweetheart," he said, reaching out for her, but she wrapped her arms around herself and backed away. "I have nothing, and I mean nothing to offer.

Don't you see that? I am a common man who works by the sweat of my brow to get what little I have. I live a simple life, and none of that is ever going to change."

"But you love me, don't you?"

He wanted to tell her he did, because if he said anything else, he'd be lying. However, if he told her that, then she would never stop trying to change a future that was predetermined from the day she was born. He didn't want her to suffer because of him. What she needed was a strong knight who would give her all she needed, while she gave the man royal heirs. Raven was a lady and supposed to live in a castle, not in a smoky, dirty forge with half a dozen barefooted, snot-nosed children. If she married him, that is what she would get.

"Your father is expecting us in the great hall. The competitors who have arrived want to meet you, and he wants you to act like a perfect hostess and lady."

"I see," she said, turning suddenly cold. She went over and picked up the sewing basket, sticking it under her arm.

"Your needlepoint looks nice," he told her, trying to compliment her and make small talk. "May I see it?" He reached out for it, but she slapped his hand away, daggers shooting from her eyes now.

"Nay, you cannot. You shouldn't be in the ladies' solar in the first place, and you shouldn't be touching something that isn't yours." She turned and ran for the door, leaving Jonathon standing there wondering if she meant the needlework... or herself.

CHAPTER 18

"Let's see how your helm fits," said Jonathon the day before the tournament was to begin. He, as well as his brother and little Gerold, had been so swamped with requests from the competitors, that Lord Corbett had told him to work in the forge instead of guarding Raven.

Raven, of course, had been glad not to be guarded. He, on the other hand, missed her, since these were his last days to spend with her before she got married. Still, he realized it was probably for the best.

After the other day in the ladies' solar, Raven had barely spoken to him at all except to ask about her armor. He knew what she wanted concerning the two of them, but wasn't able to give it to her. She wanted him to help her find a deceptive way to ensure that none of the nobles would marry her. Raven had also had a daft notion that he could help her find a way to marry him instead.

If only that were true.

"I'm excited that you're done with my armor," said Raven, looking down at the entire set, including her favorites, which were the gauntlets.

With the extra time he was allowed to work the forge, he'd been able to not only fill all the orders from the knights, but also finish and add etchings and even little engraved hearts on the breastplate and up and down the arm and leg pieces, too. "Wait. What's this?" she asked, pointing at the etchings.

Jonathon smiled. She'd be so happy with his addition. It was just his way of trying to etch the memory of him on her mind. "It's just a little something extra I put on the armor for you. I hope you like it."

"Hearts? And are these etched flowers on the helm too?"

"Yes, they are," he said proudly, holding it out and admiring it. "I thought it would make your armor look more feminine."

"It certainly does that." By the tone of her voice, it didn't sound like she liked it. Mayhap he should have etched dragons and ogres on it instead.

It was late at night, and Avery and Gerold had already gone to bed. Everyone in the castle was sleeping as well. They were excited about the big tournament tomorrow that would start at sunrise and wouldn't end until sundown. A huge feast and celebration were planned for afterwards, with fancy food, music, and dancing that would last far into the night.

"This armor fits you like a glove," he said, finishing dressing her. He held pride in his work. It was one of the best things he'd ever constructed. Still, Raven didn't seem happy with it at all.

"What's the matter?" he asked. "Is it not everything you wanted, and even more?" He couldn't help admiring his work.

"Nay, not exactly, but it'll have to do," she answered with a sigh, pulling off her helm.

"I'm sorry I wasn't able to please you, my lady." He had no idea anymore what would make this girl happy.

"Stop calling me *my lady*," she snapped at him. "Help me take it off. I need to go to sleep and get my rest for tomorrow."

"You're leaving the forge? So soon?" His heart dropped. He had hoped to spend just a little more time with her, and mayhap even sneak in another kiss or two before she got married and they never saw each other again.

"It's very late, Jonathon. We both know I shouldn't be out here without a chaperone."

"It never stopped you before. Besides, I'm your chaperone," he said, still hoping she would stay. At least for a little while.

"That's not the same."

Once her armor had been removed, Jonathon put it all in a large bag and handed it to her. "I still don't know why it is so important that you get this armor. It's not like you're ever going to be able to use it."

"It's something I need." She barely even looked at him when she spoke.

"Need? Want, mayhap. But why in the world would a lady need armor?"

"You're right. I should have said *want*," she corrected herself. "My mistake. Well, I'll be going now."

He grabbed her arm to stop her. "Raven, wait." He used her name without the title, because it was probably the last time he'd ever be able to do so.

"What is it?" she asked.

"I-I just thought since this will be the last time

we're together before you're married, that mayhap you'd want to stay a little longer, that's all."

She looked at him and sighed. "Jonathon, doesn't it even bother you that tomorrow I'll have to marry a noble? I mean, another man besides you? Or are you totally fine with that?"

"Nay, of course, I'm not fine with it, and yes, it bothers me more than you'll ever know."

"Then why don't you do something about it?"

"I can't. It wouldn't make a difference if I did. You know that. We are from two different walks of life. We can't be together, as much as we want to." He took her in his arms and kissed her atop her head. Her body stiffened. It was obviously not the answer she wanted to hear.

"I have to go now." She pulled away from him.

"Wait, Raven. Please. You need to understand that I want to marry you more than anything in the world. But it just... can't be."

"I'm a fighter, Jonathon, and have always been. Now, you need to fight for what you want as well."

"I can't give you what you want. I am only a commoner. I have nothing at all to offer."

He saw the tears in her eyes, as well as aggravation. It confused him and made his heart break at the same time.

"The only thing I wanted from you, Jonathon, was your love."

With that, she hurried out the door, leaving Jonathon standing there feeling as if his life was over. He turned around to see Avery and Gerold watching him from the entrance to the bedroom.

"Go to sleep," he told them, dousing the fire on the forge. "There is nothing to see here."

"You're just going to let her go?" asked Avery.

"Damn it," spat Jonathon, throwing an iron poker across the room. "What the hell am I supposed to do?"

Avery and Gerold didn't say a word. Probably because there was nothing to say. Nothing Jonathon said or did would do anything to change the outcome of tomorrow.

Or would it?

~

Raven bolted into her bedchamber, slamming the door behind her. Lark was up and pacing the floor, waiting for her to return.

"Cousin, what's the matter?" she asked, running over to Raven. "Did ye get yer armor?"

"I got it," she said, opening the bag and dumping it on the bed. "However, it's not what I wanted."

"Och, that is bonnie." Lark ran over and held up the helm in the firelight. "I love the flowers and little etched hearts."

"Well, I don't," she complained, plopping down on a chair to remove her shoes.

"Why not? I think it's the bonniest armor I've ever seen."

"Exactly. That's why." She pulled off a shoe and threw it across the room. "I need people to believe I'm a man tomorrow at the tournament. No man would ever have little flowers and hearts etched on his armor."

"Oh, I see what ye mean." Lark giggled and put the helm down on the bed.

"It's not funny, Lark. Tomorrow is my only chance

to keep myself from having to marry a noble, and hopefully to be able to choose Jonathon to marry instead."

"What do you mean?" Lark sat down on the bed, pulling the breast plate over to inspect it. "Ye're goin' to ask to marry Jonathon?"

"Aye. Well, I mean, I want to. That was my plan. Right after I won the tournament."

"Ye're goin' to ask yer father that right in front of everyone?" Lark looked horrified by the thought.

"I know it'll make Father angry, but I was hoping if I did it in front of everyone, he wouldn't be able to say no. I only wish Jonathon would have approached him first. I'm starting to wonder if he really wants to marry me after all."

"Dinna be angry with Jonathon," said Lark. "Ye need to realize that he has too much to lose if he asks and yer father says no."

"Lose? Like what?"

"Well, his customers, for one. No nobleman, or even Uncle Corbett is goin' to get work done in his father's shop after hearing that! And if anyone finds out that ye two made love, there's a chance that Jonathon might lose his life. His family might suffer too. Ye canna blame him for not wantin' to stick his neck out regardin' this. Dinna ye see that?"

Raven stopped and thought about it for a moment. Just like her mother told her, she needed to stop thinking about her own wants and needs, and think about how her decisions were going to affect those she cared for or loved. "I suppose you're right. But that still won't stop me from trying." She finished undressing and blew out the candle. "I just hope everything goes the way I plan tomorrow."

CHAPTER 19

"**B**rother, wake up. You're missing the archery competition that has already started."

"What? Nay." Jonathon had fallen asleep at the table last night, fully dressed. He'd been dreaming of Raven all night long... married to another man. It was the worst nightmare of his life. "I need to talk to Raven's father. Where is he?"

"He's sitting up on the platform watching the competition," said little Gerold.

"Out of my way." Jonathon hurried to the door.

"Wait! Why do you want to talk to him?" asked Avery.

"I have to stop this competition. I'm going to tell him that I want to marry his daughter."

Jonathon raced out to the practice yard, trying to dodge the many people who had showed up to watch the tournament. How the hell did he sleep through all this? It must have been from his lack of rest while making Raven's armor. He'd been so exhausted. If not, he never would have overslept.

Strolling minstrels dressed in parti-colored clothes wandered the courtyard playing lutes, and passing the hat for coins. Not only the nobles and competitors were there, but also the servants and the villagers, since everyone was invited to watch the spectacular competition that would determine which man would win Raven for his bride.

The thought sickened him. He should have gone to Lord Corbett days ago, weeks ago, asking for Raven's hand—she was right. Being a commoner, he knew this would only mean trouble for him, but he had to try. If not, he would never forgive himself.

The noise level within the castle walls was heightened. He could hear the spectators cheering from the area where the archery competition was already in progress. Children ran by chasing each other, and he almost stumbled over a few stray dogs and even a goat and pig.

"Damn it," he mumbled to himself, not able to move quickly or even see what was happening through the crowd.

"Fresh pies. Get your fresh pies," called out a vendor carrying a tray over her head with small hand pies filled with fruit.

"Two herrings for a shilling," called out a fishmonger.

There were many vendors with their carts set up in the courtyard today, trying to make a living.

"Ale or wine. Ale or wine," called out a man with a long tray filled with mugs of the drinks. He carried them high over his head.

"Jonathon, wait for us," called Avery from behind him. Jonathon stopped, trying to look through the crowd to find Raven, but he didn't see her. His brother and Gerold caught up to him. Avery held a hand pie in one hand and a mug of ale in another.

"Care for something to eat or drink?" asked Avery, taking a bite of the fruit pie and holding it out to him.

"Nay," said Jonathon still not seeing Raven anywhere. He could see Lord Corbett and Lady Devon up on the wooden dais watching the sport, but oddly, Raven wasn't with them. "Why didn't you wake me, Avery? I don't have time to stop this now. I'm already too late."

"Brother, you were up pining over Lady Raven most of the night, so I thought you'd want to sleep late today. The last thing I figured you'd want to do is to watch the competition."

"I'm going to sneak through the legs of everyone and make my way to the front to watch the archery," said Gerold.

"All right, go on," said Avery. "I wish we could get close enough to at least see what's happening. There is such a crowd here. And so many competitors."

"Don't remind me," growled Avery, knowing each one of those competitors was a potential husband for Raven. Right now, Jonathon felt like killing them all.

"Jonathon, I was looking for you and wondering where you were."

Jonathon turned around to find Rook standing there with one arm around a serving girl, clutching a tankard of ale in the other.

Why did no one ever say a word when a nobleman wanted to have a fling with a peasant, but if a noble*woman* did it, she was punished severely and sometimes even killed?

"Get back to work," said Rook with a chuckle, hitting the girl on the rump. She giggled and blushed and hurried off through the crowd.

"I'll catch up with you later, Brother," said Avery, following the girl.

"I wanted to give you your pay now, since you're no longer needed as my sister's personal guard. After today, she'll be betrothed, and hopefully her husband will keep her in her place. You won't have to worry about it anymore." He handed a pouch of coins to Jonathon, but Jonathon didn't take it.

"I don't want the money," he told Rook.

"You don't?" Rook seemed surprised. "Well, what is it you want?" he asked, lifting up the tankard to his mouth to drink.

"Flowers, buy a flower for your lover?" asked an old lady missing her front teeth. She held out a basket of flowers to him.

"Nay. Not now," he said, shooing the woman away. Once she left, Jonathon continued. "Rook, I want... I want to... I want to marry your sister."

Rook spit a stream of ale from his mouth, almost choking. Then he laughed. "You are jesting, right?"

"Nay. I love her and want her as my wife."

Rook's smile slowly faded. "Don't be saying things like that so loud. Someone might hear you." He stuck the pouch of coins back in his pocket.

"I don't care who knows. I was on my way to find your father to ask him for Raven's hand in marriage."

"We need to talk." Rook downed the rest of the ale and plopped the tankard down on the tray of a passing vendor. "Come," said Rook, leading the way to the mews.

Jonathon could hear a man at the archery range calling out the competitors' names.

"Sir Jonathon Nevar from Lyon, France, is now in the lead," shouted the man who was the castle's herald and also served as the master of ceremonies for the tournament.

Rook entered the mews with Jonathon right behind him.

"Leave us," Rook told the falconer, who promptly left as commanded. "Now, what is this foolish notion that you, a commoner, could ever marry a noble? Are you mad?"

"I know it's insane, but I have to try. I love Raven and can't let her marry another man. I should have said something to your father sooner."

"Nay, I don't think that would have been a good idea. It still isn't," he said. "My father has worked hard over the years trying to bring respect back to the Blake family name. After his father was stripped of his title for marrying a commoner, he is determined that his children will never make the same mistake. He almost made that mistake with my mother when he thought she was just a servant, and before he discovered she was noble. However, I believe he would have married her either way. After all, love does change a man, I hear."

"Yes, it does," said Jonathon, feeling suddenly panicked. He could see that the talk he wanted to have with Raven's father would do nothing at all to change the outcome after all. Or at least, he didn't think so.

"I suggest you forget all about my troublesome sister, and go back to your father's shop in town and live your life. Nothing you could possibly say to my father would make him change his mind once he's already decided on something." Rook turned and headed to the door.

"We made love," he blurted out. His words caused Rook to groan and turn around.

"Please tell me you're jesting."

"Nay. It happened. We made love and honestly, for all I know, she might be carrying my child within her right now."

"Oh, hell, this is just great!" said Rook in a half-laugh, half-yell. "This will kill my father."

"Mayhap, he doesn't have to find out?"

"Think what you're saying, fool," spat Rook. "Noblemen don't want a bastard child. They need heirs of their own blood, not a commoner's whelp. If my sister marries the winner of the tournament today and she's already pregnant, it'll cause a battle between the winner and Blake Castle. That can't happen. Marriages are done for the sake of alliances. Don't you get it?"

"I didn't say she *was* pregnant. I just said... I suppose it's a possibility."

Rook's fist hit Jonathon hard in the jaw, the force knocking him to the ground."

"Ow, what was that for?" asked Jonathon rubbing his aching jaw. His lip was split and bleeding.

"That's just a sample of what's to come when my father finds out," growled Rook. "Only instead of punching you, he'll have you strung up from the gallows. What is the matter with you? How could you take my sister's virginity?"

"I didn't. She wasn't a virgin," Jonathon said in his defense, still on the ground.

"What?" asked Rook.

"She said she lost that to an actual nobleman who visited years ago."

"Bloody hell! Who is he? I'll string him up myself." Rook paced back and forth.

"I don't know," he told Rook. "All I know is that I love your sister."

"And that gives you the right to lure her to your bed?"

"Well, actually... I didn't want to tell you, but she was the one luring me. At first."

"Why am I not surprised?" mumbled Rook. "God's eyes, we've got to stop this tournament." He extended his arm and helped Jonathon to his feet.

"My thoughts exactly," said Jonathon.

"We need to stop the competition, but it'll never happen," stated Rook. "It is already underway, and there are just too many people here. My father would never turn them away. That would be bad for his reputation. Plus, the nobles would make his life hell."

"What can we do?" asked Jonathon.

"We?" Rook paced back and forth. "You will do nothing. I have to figure this out on my own."

"Nay. I want to help. Certainly there's something I can do," said Jonathon.

"You've already done too much, believe me."

"Can I enter the competition, and fight for Raven's hand?" asked Jonathon.

"Nay. It's against the rules. Only nobles can compete." Rook crossed his arms over his chest. "However, there is no rule saying *I* can't enter the tournament."

"You?" asked Jonathon, making a face. "You're her brother."

"I know that," said Rook. "However, if I win, then it'll keep any other nobleman from winning."

"Can you do that?" asked Jonathon, feeling excited that this might just work.

"I am the son of the lord of the castle. No one would stop me from being in the tournament. They'll think I'm just doing it for sport and naught else."

"What if you don't win?" asked Jonathon, fearing the worse. "Then it will have been all for naught."

"Not win?" Rook laughed. "I am the best at tournaments in all of England. Plus, I have an advantage since it is taking place at my home and I'm already comfortable with the setting. There's no way I can lose. Now come on. I need to hurry. You can act as my squire. I'll have to compete in the archery competition, and get there before it's over. Let's just hope to hell this works or it's not going to be pretty in the end."

~

Dressed in her hooded cloak and her surcoat, pretending to be Sir Nevar, Raven shot another arrow, hitting dead center once again. It looked like she won. Or at least she thought so. Then the herald made a surprise announcement.

"Before I declare Sir Nevar as the winner of the archery competition, we have one late entrant. Lord Rook Blake."

"Rook?" she said aloud, turning quickly to see her brother picking up a bow right next to her. Jonathon was with him, acting as some kind of fake squire.

"Hello," said Rook, nocking his arrow. "I am Lord Rook of Blake Castle. I don't believe I know your name."

Damn it, she didn't need this. What the hell were they doing? They were going to ruin everything.

She kept her face hidden under the hood, glancing over to Albert who was dressed as her squire. He shrugged.

"I am Sir Jonathon Nevar," she said, trying to use a low, fake voice. Jonathon looked up when she said his name. Now she wished she had used another name instead.

"From France?" asked Rook. "You don't sound French."

"*Oui*," she answered, wishing her brother would just shut up.

"Is this your first tournament?" Rook asked in French.

Her brother was fluent in French. Raven, on the other hand didn't know that language that well, since she hadn't paid much attention during her studies. However, thankfully, she did understand what Rook just said.

"Nay, of course it is not my first tournament," she answered, trying hard to have a French accent. "And I prefer to speak in English while I'm here."

"He sure is a small one," her brother said in a low voice to Jonathon. "This should be a breeze."

Raven wasn't too worried. While Rook was a good archer, she was far better at it than he. Rook had never beat her in an archery competition, and wouldn't do so today either.

Thankfully, the final round was in her favor. She beat Rook and was declared the winner of this leg of the competition.

"The winner is Sir Jonathon Nevar of France," called out the herald.

"Let's get out of here," she whispered to Albert, taking off through the crowd before Rook decided to shake her hand and congratulate her.

"What about your prize?" asked Albert from behind her, following on her heels. Each winner of each round of the tournament was awarded with a bag of money.

"I don't care about it," she said, rushing to a shed behind the mews where Lark would be waiting for her. "Take watch and make sure no one sees me." She slipped into the storage shed.

"Ye won!" said Lark, hugging her. "Good job. Was it hard?"

"Nay," she said, undressing. "It was a breeze, as my brother would say." She needed to put on her gown and get back to the dais platform before her father became suspicious. "The worst part was when Rook showed up to compete with Jonathon as his squire."

"What?" asked Lark in surprise. "Why would your brother enter the tournament?"

"I have no idea. However, I can't let him win. I need to win in order to secure my future." She tied the bodice of her gown. "All right, let's go. I'll have Albert guard the shed until we return to change for the hand-to-hand combat part of the competition."

"Raven, I'm worried for ye."

"I'll be fine."

"Mayhap for now. But what will ye do when ye're required to joust?"

"Hopefully, I'll win the next round, too, and won't have to joust. With two wins under my belt, I'll win the tournament without even having to put myself in that position."

"What if you don't win the sword fight?"

"I will. I have to. If not, my life will be over."

"Ye mean when ye have to marry a nobleman ye dinna care for?"

"That, and the fact that I will probably actually be killed attempting to joust."

CHAPTER 20

Jonathon hurried over to the nobles' platform, hoping to talk to Raven, telling her his plan. When he got there, the herald was already announcing the knights who would fight in the first round of the hand-to-hand combat using their swords.

"Raven. Lady Raven," called Jonathon, waving, trying to get closer to the platform.

Raven and Lark had just seated themselves next to her parents when she heard Jonathon calling out to her from the crowd.

"What does he want?" whispered Lark.

"I don't know, but we need to get rid of him before it's my turn to compete again."

"Raven? I think your friend Jonathon is trying to get your attention," said her mother.

"I see him," she said, waving back, just to be polite.

"Why don't you invite him to sit up here with us to watch the competition?" asked Devon.

"An armorer, on the nobles' platform?" asked her

271

father, overhearing their conversation. "Nay. It's not allowed."

"I think after all he's done for us lately, you could make an exception, dear," Devon told her husband.

"Nay. Father's right," interrupted Raven. "It wouldn't look good. Besides, he's acting as Rook's squire in the tournament so he'll be busy."

"Aye, that's right. He's busy," agreed Lark.

"Father, why is Rook even competing?" asked Raven.

"Yes, that is a little odd, considering the winner is to marry Raven," agreed Devon.

"I didn't know he was competing," said Corbett. "I'll put a stop to this at once." He got up, but just then the sword-fighting began and he sat back down. "Mayhap I'll send a squire to find him. I don't want to miss this."

"I'll find him," said Raven, using this as an excuse to leave.

"Nay, you'll miss the sword-fighting competition," said her father. "You already missed the archery since you were at the garderobe so long."

"Nay. I saw it," said Raven.

"You did?" Her father turned to face her. "How?"

"From down there," she told him, nodding with her head. "I wanted to get a better view, so I stayed down there. I'll watch the sword-fight from there too, as soon as I find Rook."

"Raven, you sit back down and stay here," ordered Corbett. "The knights are competing for your hand in marriage. It doesn't look good if you keep disappearing."

"But I—"

"I said, *sit!*"

"Yes, Father." She sat back down, just as Jonathon came up to the front of the raised platform.

"Raven, I need to tell you something. Hurry," he said, waving her closer.

"What is it?" she asked, feeling trapped, aggravated, and anxious right now.

"Lean forward. I don't want everyone to hear this."

Just as she leaned forward, Rook walked up.

"Jonathon, come on. I'm up next," he said, urgency in his tone.

"Rook? What are you doing competing?" growled Corbett.

"I have a good reason, Father. I'll tell you later."

"What reason could you possibly have to enter this tournament?" he asked in challenge.

"I-I can't say. Not right now."

"He's probably only doing it to embarrass me somehow," spat Raven. She needed Rook out of the way if she was going to win. Her brother was better at sword-fighting than she was, and she worried he might beat her. If so, she'd be forced to compete in the joust, and that couldn't happen. Not if she valued her life. "Father, tell him to withdraw from the competition right now. I don't want him in it. He's going to ruin everything."

"Nay, Raven," said Jonathon. "You don't understand."

"You need to call her Lady Raven. Use her title, armorer," snapped Corbett.

"Lord Rook will fight against Sir Whitehead now," called out the announcer. "Gentlemen, make your way over to your spots to compete."

Corbett stood up and called out. "My son, Rook,

withdraws from the competition. Carry on without him."

"Father, nay!" shouted Rook. "You need to let me compete. You don't know what you're doing."

"There is no reason in the world why you need to be out there. This tournament is to find your sister a husband, not for you to show up every one of the competitors. Now sit down and be quiet. Your place is up here with me."

"I-I will be back," said Raven nervously, having no excuse to leave now.

"Nay. You'll stay right here, too," said Corbett. "The competitors need to see you."

The herald announcing the competition spoke up. "Since Lord Rook has withdrawn from the games, Sir Whitehead will compete against the next man in line instead."

"Raven," said Jonathon, pulling at the hem of her skirt from the ground. She leaned forward to look over the edge of the raised dais and to hear him. "Your brother was going to win the competition so you don't have to marry a noble. He can't do that now."

"What?" she asked, not able to hear him clearly with all the noise. She thought he said something about Rook wanting to help her?

"Rook knows everything that went on between us. I told him," continued Jonathon.

"Nay! Why the hell would you do that?" she spat, having no idea why Jonathon would do such a stupid thing. It could only hurt them in the end.

Everyone clapped and shouted as Sir Whitehead made his way to the center of the field, holding his sword high over his head.

The announcer continued. "Sir Whitehead of Liverpool will fight Sir Nevar of Lyon, France. Sir Nevar, take your place."

"Oh!" Raven's head snapped upward. She needed to get to the shed to change and get out to the field before she was disqualified.

"Who is that Frenchman?" asked Corbett. "Rook, did you invite him to compete?"

"Nay," said Rook. "I don't know him. I thought you invited him, Father."

"Excuse me, I'm not feeling well." Raven stood up and bolted from the dais.

"Where the hell is she going now?" growled her father. "I told her to stay here."

"I'll get her," said Lark, running after her.

"I will make sure she returns," said Jonathon, following, trying to see the women through the crowd. Unfortunately, he lost them. He wandered over to the practice yard where the sword-fight was about to begin.

"Sir Nevar, come to the field," called out the announcer. "You have one minute to show up before you're disqualified."

"No one can beat me," called out Sir Whitehead, holding his sword in the air and getting the crowd to cheer for him again.

Jonathon already despised this man who thought he was so important. He dreaded the thought that Raven might actually have to marry him.

"Sir Nevar, this is your last call," yelled the herald.

"I'm here," came a strange voice from behind Jonathon. A small man darted past, knocking into him. He wore a long cloak and oddly enough his hood was pulled up over the helm he wore on his head.

"Excuse me," said Jonathon, knowing he needed to apologize since he was only a commoner. Even if it wasn't his fault, he needed to show respect for all nobles.

The knight didn't answer, and neither did he even look at Jonathon. He was very rude.

"Sir Whitehead will now compete against Sir Nevar," called out the herald.

Jonathon watched the small Frenchman pull his sword from his scabbard, to fight the huge man that towered over him. Jonathon had never seen such a small knight in his life. He looked thin and frail.

As their swords clashed together, the Frenchman's hood fell, exposing his helm that shined in the sun. Jonathon couldn't see it clearly from where he stood, but the craftmanship of the piece seemed exquisite.

Then he heard Whitehead heckling the French knight.

"You are no match for me. No knight with roses and hearts on his helm is going to best me in a fight. I will beat you into the ground."

"Roses? Hearts?" Jonathon repeated, pushing his way to the front. "God's eyes, nay!" cried Jonathon, gripping the wooden fence that held back the onlookers. He realized now why the knight was so small, and also why the helm caught his attention. It was the helm he made. That was Raven in disguise, fighting Whitehead!

"Jonathon, did you find my sister?" asked Rook, coming to join him. The onlookers moved out of the way since Rook was a noble.

"Unfortunately, I did," he mumbled, his heart racing and his eyes focused on Raven as she fought

276

with Whitehead. She was good, but how long could she keep it up, fighting a strong man twice her size? This was ludicrous and he needed to do something to stop it.

"Where is she?" asked Rook, looking around.

"You're watching her fight Whitehead," said Jonathon.

"What are you saying?" asked Rook, confused.

Jonathon turned to face Rook. "Your sister is in disguise as the Frenchman Nevar."

"Huh?" Rook looked over to the men fighting. "You're wrong. That is not Raven."

"Do you know the Frenchman?" asked Jonathon.

"Nay," said Rook, shaking his head. "Neither does my father."

"And doesn't it seem suspicious that the man's name is Jonathon Nevar?"

"I don't understand what you mean."

"She used my name, and spelled her name backwards for the surname. Plus, she is wearing the armor I made her. Raven joined the competition in disguise for some odd reason, but she is going to get hurt or even killed."

"She's holding her own for now, but you're right," agreed Rook. "If she has to joust, she will get killed. She can't compete against trained men. Not in the joust. I'm going to end this right now." He started forward, but Jonathon stopped him.

"Nay. You will embarrass her as well as your father," said Jonathon.

"Why is she doing this?" asked Rook.

"My guess is that she is trying to win the tournament so she won't have to marry one of the nobles."

"My sister is a fool! I'm going to strangle her, I swear."

Raven noticed them. When she glanced their way, Jonathon swished his hands through the air, trying to silently tell her to leave the competition. He realized his mistake as soon as he did it. Taking Raven's attention for that one moment caused her to lose focus. Whitehead unarmed her and knocked her to the ground. Then he put his foot on her chest and raised his sword in the air. The crowd cheered, and the announcer proclaimed him the winner of this hand-to-hand combat.

"Sir Whitehead will move on," said the herald. "Sir Nevar, please leave the field."

"I'll kill him for touching her," snarled Jonathon watching Whitehead with his foot on Raven's chest and his sword raised in the air. Jonathon was ready to jump the fence and punch the man, but Rook stopped him.

"Don't," warned Rook. "She doesn't seem hurt. Just let her be."

Raven jumped to her feet, grabbing her sword and hurrying from the field. She ran past Rook and Jonathon without saying a word to them.

"Let's follow her," said Jonathon.

"You go. I need to tell Father about this," said Rook.

"Can you wait?" asked Jonathon. "I mean... give me a minute to talk to Raven first."

"Fine," said Rook with a sigh. "Convince her to withdraw from the competition. If she does it now, no one has to know what she did."

"I'll try my best," said Jonathon. "Let me talk with

her. Then I'll meet you at the platform and let you know what she said."

Jonathon saw Raven sneak into a shed. He also noticed Albert standing outside of it.

"Albert?" he asked. "You're part of this deception?"

"I didn't want to be, but had no choice," said the boy.

"Step aside, I'm going in."

"Lady Raven told me to guard the shed. I'm not supposed to let anyone enter."

"I'm trying to save her life, now move aside." He pushed past Albert, entering the shed, stopping in the doorway.

Raven was standing there in her shift and Lark was helping her dress in her gown. The helm and the fake French surcoat were on the ground. He saw a bag with the rest of her armor in it.

"Jonathon!" Raven held her gown in front of her. "What are you doing here?"

Jonathon stepped inside and closed the door. "I know what you're doing, Raven, and it is a foolish thing. You need to stop now, before you're hurt."

She continued dressing. "I suppose you're going to tell my father now? I saw you and Rook talking. It's your fault I was distracted and lost the sword fight."

"Rook was going to tell Lord Corbett, but I stopped him. I figured you deserved a chance to explain."

"There is nothing for me to explain." She bent down and slipped her shoes onto her feet. "I am going to win this tournament, and then I won't have to marry whichever fool is the winner."

"Don't you think that will anger your father? And embarrass both of you?"

"I no longer care."

"Raven, fast, put on your cloak." Lark handed it to her.

"Since you didn't win two events in a row, you will now be forced to compete in the joust," Jonathon told her.

"That's right," she answered, sounding terrified if he wasn't mistaken.

"You are going to get yourself killed out there. This is not a game."

"Yes, it is a game," she told him.

"You know what I mean."

"Don't worry about me, Jonathon. I will be fine since I have my armor to protect me."

"Nay. You can't do this. I won't let you." He was not going to let her risk her life like this.

She walked over to him and smiled. Then she reached up and kissed him on the mouth. "You can't stop me, and you know it. Besides, I'm doing this for us."

"Nay. There has to be another way."

"What way?" she asked, sounding huffy now. "You are not a noble and cannot compete, so I am the one who has to do it."

"Rook was going to win to ensure you didn't have to marry anyone, but you convinced your father to remove him from the competition."

"If you two fools had told me the plan, I would have known what to do."

"If you had told me your plan to enter the tournament using a guise—"

"Then what?" she asked. "You and my brother

would have never let me do this. Just admit it."

"Well, no, I guess not. But still—"

"Stop worrying. You taught me how to joust. I'll be fine." She left the shed with Lark, leaving him standing there alone.

Now he wished more than anything that he had taken the time to train Raven properly. The joust was a brutal sport, and meant for men. No lady, good with weapons or not, would ever survive it. Especially not Raven, since he'd never seen anyone as bad at the joust as she.

Rook stuck his head inside the shed. "I saw my sister leave. Did you convince her to withdraw from the tournament?"

"Nay, I couldn't," said Jonathon.

"Well, we can't let her joust. I guess it is time to tell my father and let him handle this."

"I wish you wouldn't. There has to be another way." If they did this, everything would blow up and everyone's lives would be affected. Jonathon couldn't have that.

"Then tell me how, because I'm not seeing it," said Rook.

Jonathon was about to leave the shed when his gaze fell on the bag with the armor in it. "If Raven doesn't have her armor, she won't be able to compete in the joust, will she?"

"Nay," said Rook. "It is in the rules that every man competing in the joust must have proper protection."

"Then I'm taking it back," he said, shoving the helm in the bag and picking up the armor.

"How is that going to solve the problem? She'll still end up marrying the winner of the competition. And since I didn't participate in the second event, I can't joust, or even be in the tournament at all. It is a rule that to proceed to the final event, you have to have competed in the first two. Which I haven't."

Jonathon saw the tunic with the fake crest on the ground and picked it up. "You haven't, but Sir Jonathon Nevar has."

"What are you thinking?" asked Rook.

"I'm going to take over the guise of the Frenchman."

"Nay." Rook shook his head. "You aren't allowed to compete. Besides, you don't have armor, and I know you won't fit in Raven's since it was made for a lady." He nodded at the armor Jonathon held.

"Nay, I won't fit in that. I do have my own armor, but it is back in town and there is no time to get it. However, we're about the same size. Since you're not going to be using your armor, let me wear it."

"You? You're going to win a joust? Hah!" Rook found the thought amusing.

"Mayhap I won't win, but I have to at least try. I won't give up Raven without a fight."

"As soon as everyone discovers who you are, you'll be imprisoned for posing as a knight. Think of what you're doing."

"I no longer care," he said. "If I have the chance of helping Raven, I will risk my life to do it."

"How the hell is this going to help her? Even if you did win for some odd reason, you still won't be able to marry her. You're a commoner, Jonathon, or have you forgotten?"

"I wish I could," he said, looking down at the tunic with the French crest in his hand. "I should have spoken to your father earlier like Raven wanted me to. I was a fool, and now I know I'm going to lose her."

"Then why even do this?" asked Rook. "You will lose everything if you do."

"I have to do it to prove to Raven how much I really love her. And as for possibly losing everything, it no longer matters. Because without Raven in my life, I will have lost everything that really matters."

CHAPTER 21

R aven was furious that Jonathon had distracted her, causing her to lose the sword fight to Sir Whitehead. Whitehead had gone on to win the complete round. If she had won, there would have been no need for the joust. Now she would be required to joust with Whitehead in the finals since she won the archery round.

This tournament was set up a little differently than usual. Her father said the winners of the first two rounds would be the only ones to compete in the joust for Raven's hand in marriage. Afterwards, there would be an opportunity for each of the competitors to joust, but the prize—meaning her—was off the table. Any other prizes would be money only.

"Well, Daughter," said her father. "In just a short while you will be betrothed to either Sir Whitehead or Sir Nevar. Which one do you fancy?"

"Oh, Sir Nevar, without a doubt," she said, sitting on the platform next to Lark.

"Quit your scowling, Raven. You're going to scare them both off," said Corbett.

"I can't help it. I told you, I don't want to get married. Not to either of them."

"Corbett, mayhap you should listen to Raven," said Devon. "You don't want her to be unhappy, do you?"

"I have a feeling there is nothing that would make our daughter happy," answered Corbett.

"I think mayhap she doesn't want to marry the winner because she already has her eye on another man." Devon looked over at Raven and nodded. "Raven, is there anything you'd like to say to your father? Now might be a good time to do it."

"Shhh, not now," said Corbett holding up his hand. "The joust is about to begin."

"Raven," said Lark, leaning over and whispering. "What are ye goin' to do? Ye canna really joust."

"I have no choice," said Raven, looking from the sides of her eyes at her father. "We have to go." She got up to leave, but stopped when she saw two knights riding out to the tiltyard.

"W-who's that?" she gasped and pointed.

"I told you, that is Sir Whitehead and Sir Nevar," said Corbett. "Haven't you been paying any attention at all?"

"We have to leave. Right now," whispered Raven, not knowing what was going on. She needed to get into her armor and out to the tiltyard so she could win this competition.

"Raven, look," said Lark, grabbing her arm. "They are both ridin' this way to ask for yer favor."

"Get your sleeve or ribbon ready," said Corbett. "You can give your favor to whichever one you want to win, but remember, it still doesn't mean a thing. You will be wedding the winner."

"My lady," said Whitehead riding up with his

helm in his arm and holding out his lance to hopefully win her favor.

"My lady," repeated the imposter, riding over and holding out his lance to her as well. This man was wearing a helm, covering his face. He also wore the tunic with the phony French crest on it that she'd constructed. Who was he?

"Raven, you must give one of them your favor so the joust can begin," said Devon.

"Before I do, I want to see Sir Nevar's face." She untied a ribbon from her hair and waited.

"Please, Sir Nevar," said Corbett. "It seems no one here really knows you, and I'd like to see your face too."

"Damn it, Raven," she heard the imposter mumble from beneath his helm. Her heart jumped. Then the man raised his visor, but looked at Raven only.

Lark saw Jonathon's face as well. "Raven, that's—" started Lark, but Raven dug her nails into Lark's arm. "Och, that hurts."

"I've seen enough, put your visor down, Sir Knight," she said, hurriedly slipping her ribbon over the tip of Jonathon's lance. "Go now and joust. Go. Shoo," she told the men, waving her fingers. They slowly turned and rode back to the lists.

"Raven! That was rude," said her father. "These men are our guests, so show them some respect. Especially since one of them will be your husband."

"Raven," whispered Lark. "Are ye goin' to let Jonathon joust?"

"I don't have a choice," she answered. "He's my only hope now. I assure you, he has a much better chance of winning than I did."

"Raven?" It was her mother. She moved away from Corbett and sat down next to her. "I tried to give you a chance to tell your father about Jonathon and you didn't do it. That means you will have to marry one of those two men out there."

"That's what I'm hoping for," said Raven. "However, I only want one of them, Mother."

"What are you saying? I thought you wanted to marry Jonathon."

"I do. And if he wins the joust, I'll be the happiest girl ever."

Devon slowly turned and looked at the two men preparing to joust. "Oh, Raven. Don't tell me that Frenchman that no one seems to know has been your lover all along."

"Nay, Mother. For the last two rounds I was Sir Nevar."

"You?" Her mother's brows raised and then she scowled. "How can you do this to your father? Do you realize the position you will put him in if Jonathon wins?"

"Aye. He'll have to let me marry him. Those are the rules."

"On the contrary, he will have no choice but to throw Jonathon in the dungeon and make Whitehead the winner."

"Nay!" said Raven. "He wouldn't do that."

"You will have left him no choice. With all the nobles here today, if he let Jonathon get away with it, he would probably be stripped of his title and mayhap even his lands and castle."

"That wouldn't happen."

"Oh really? Well, what do you think is going to happen once the rest of the nobles tell the king what your father did? You are putting him in a very uncomfortable position."

"Oh no," said Raven, feeling the tears welling in her eyes. "I never asked Jonathon to do this, I swear. I don't even know why he is out there."

"Could it be because he loves you and is trying to keep you from getting hurt or possibly killed?" asked her mother in a knowing manner.

Raven's attention flashed back to the tiltyard. She saw the men charging at each other in the first pass. Jonathon's lance broke on Whitehead and he was awarded a point. Everyone cheered and she breathed a sigh of relief.

"Do you really think that is what will happen if he wins?" asked Raven, not wanting to believe it.

"I know so," answered Devon. "I had hoped you would talk to your father and handle this in your own way, but now I see I should have intervened."

"Mother, what am I going to do?" Raven felt terrified, and not for herself. In her haste she had been selfish, and wasn't thinking about Jonathon's future without her. "I might have just condemned the man I love to death."

Jonathon felt so alive that nothing could bring him down at this moment. He had scored the first point against Whitehead and it felt damned good. He wasn't a knight. Far from it. But he had been a mercenary for a long time. And in that time, he'd learned fighting skills to keep him alive. This time he wasn't fighting for himself. He was fighting for Raven.

He rode over to Rook who was waiting for him with a fresh lance. Raising the visor, he laughed.

"Did you see that?" he asked Rook. "Who would have ever imagined I could do that?"

"It was quite impressive," said Rook, handing him the lance. "Do you think you can do it a few more times?"

"I'll do whatever it takes to make sure Whitehead doesn't win Raven's hand in marriage."

"Jonathon, stop," called out Raven, rushing over to him. Lark was a little ways behind her. "Don't do this. You need to forfeit right now."

"Damn it," grumbled Jonathon, seeing Raven heading over to him. "Rook, you need to keep her quiet and away from me."

"Like I can?" asked Rook raising his palms in the air.

"Stop," said Raven once again, approaching Jonathon out of breath, since she had run all the way down here. "I can't let you do this."

"Just try to stop me. I'm on fire," said Jonathon, flipping down the visor. The horn sounded and he was off.

"Nay!" she shouted, tears dripping down her cheeks. "Rook, you can't let him win," she told her brother.

"Sister, you make no sense. I thought you wanted Sir Nevar to win the tournament," said Rook. "Wasn't that your plan all along?"

"I wanted it when I was Sir Nevar. Jonathon never should have taken my place."

"It would be me out there right now if you hadn't convinced Father to stop me from competing."

"I only did so because I knew I couldn't beat you

at the sword fight. If I had won both events, there would be no need for a joust, don't you understand? If I had won both, this stupid tournament would be over right now, and I'd be happy."

"Jonathon is only doing this to keep you from being killed out there. Also to prove his love for you," said Rook.

"He might be imprisoned for this."

"He knows that."

"And yet it still continues?" Raven's heart hurt. This man truly did love her after all.

"Look, Raven!" Lark approached, pointing at the tiltyard.

Whitehead's lance hit Jonathon so hard that it not only splintered but it knocked Jonathon off balance and he almost fell from the horse.

"Oh!" Raven held her hand to her mouth and watched as Jonathon somehow managed to pull himself back up. If he was unhorsed, he'd be automatically disqualified and Whitehead proclaimed the winner. As the crowd cried out, Jonathon rode back to Rook to prepare for the last pass.

"Jonathon," she said, ducking under the list and running over to the side of his horse. "Are you all right?" she asked.

"I'm seeing a few stars right now, but I'll live," he said, flipping open the visor and smiling.

"You've got to lose this competition," she told him. "Please, do it for me."

"Lose? Nay, my love. I am going to win so you don't have to marry that ogre Whitehead. Rook, give me another lance."

"Nay, you can't do this," said Raven.

"I'm doing it to show you I love you."

"If you really loved me, you would lose, and let me marry Whitehead."

"What?" he asked, looking down at her. "Raven, have you lost your mind?"

"Not yet, but I swear I will if anything happens to you."

"I'll be fine."

"Not if you win, you won't. If you win, my mother explained to me that my father will have no choice but to imprison you for this deception. You might even be condemned to death for pretending to be a noble."

Jonathon's smile quickly faded. "If it means you are free from being a prize at a competition, being treated no better than a side of beef, then I don't care." He reached down and put his fingers beneath her chin. "I will go to my death knowing that I did everything I could to try to help you and to show you my undying devotion. I truly love you, Raven. I will go to my death with those words on my lips."

Raven was really crying now. Everyone would see her, and she didn't really care.

"Please, stop this madness, Jonathon. I love you and don't want to lose you," she tried to convince him one last time.

"I will live on in your heart," he told her, lowering the visor. "Rook, give me my last lance. I need to make this my best run. I'm about to win this entire tournament."

"Aye," said Rook, picking up the lance.

"Nay, let me give it to him," said Raven, taking the lance from her brother. When she handed it to Jonathon, she walloped him with all her strength right in the gut. His hand went out to stop her, his arm getting hit hard in the process. The horse became spooked and reared up, causing Jonathon to lose his balance, bringing him to the ground. When he tumbled from the horse, he fell on his right arm, and cried out in pain.

"God's eyes, what the hell is the matter with you, Raven?" snapped Rook, running over to help Jonathon.

"I can't let him win. That's all there is to it," she said, staring straight ahead.

"Och, Raven, here comes yer father and he looks madder than a wet hornet," said Lark.

"Can you get back up on the horse?" asked Rook. "Can you finish the joust?"

"Aye," said Jonathon, pulling himself atop the horse but wincing in pain. "Nay. I think my arm is broken. I'm not sure I can hold the lance."

"What the hell is going on over here?" shouted Corbett, approaching them with Devon running to keep up. "Raven, did I just see you knock Sir Nevar off his horse with the lance?"

"Yes, you did," she answered nonchalantly. "I decided I didn't want him to win after all."

"I will not let you get away with treating a nobleman this way," spat Corbett.

"Sir Nevar is not noble," explained Raven. The crowd was in a frenzy and thankfully no one else could hear their conversation.

"What the hell are you talking about?" asked Corbett.

"I wanted to win the tournament so I wouldn't have to marry the winner," she told him. "So I entered the competition as Sir Nevar."

"Quit lying. I am looking right at the knight."

"She's not lying, my lord." Jonathon flipped up the visor to let Corbett see his face.

"You?" asked Corbett in confusion. "What the hell are you doing up on that horse? You can't enter the competition. You have to be a noble."

"Father, listen to me," said Raven. "I have something to say."

"I'm not going to be made a fool of, Armstrong. I have no choice but to imprison you." Corbett was doing exactly what they thought he'd do, but Raven couldn't let him. Jonathon didn't deserve it.

"Father, listen to me," she cried.

"Corbett, I think you'd better give your daughter your ear," said Devon. "After all, she is in love with Jonathon, and he is the one she wants to marry."

"What? You knew about this?" Corbett now glared at Devon.

"In Mother's defense, she didn't know that I, or Jonathon, entered the competition," said Raven.

"What about you?" Corbett asked Rook. "If you're helping the armorer, you must have known as well."

"I just found out today and tried to help Raven," said Rook. "I wanted to win so she didn't have to marry a fool like Whitehead." Whitehead used this delay to his advantage, holding his lance high and getting the crowd to cheer for him. "Then you disqualified me and ruined that plan," finished Rook.

"That's why I'm jousting," explained Jonathon from atop the horse. "I'm doing it to save Raven from having to marry a man she doesn't love."

"And from getting killed, since she can't joust worth a damn," added Rook.

"I'd normally be angry at you for that comment, Brother, but unfortunately it's true," Raven told Rook before turning back to her father. "I love Jonathon, Father. I would do anything to marry him."

"You can't marry him." Corbett's anger grew. "He's just a commoner. He's a goddamned armorer."

"He's also a mercenary and good fighter," said Rook, coming to Raven's defense. "Father, I have to disagree with you on this one. Raven should be allowed to marry Jonathon if she loves him."

"Thank you, Rook." Raven smiled at her brother.

"Nay. This can't be happening." Corbett ran a hand through his hair. "All I ever wanted was for my children to marry nobles. Is that too much to ask?"

"It is, when it is someone I don't love," said Raven. "Father, please. I want to marry Jonathon."

"My lord, I know I have nothing to offer," said Jonathon, looking over to Raven now, holding his hurt arm. "That is, I have nothing but my love to offer your daughter. I will do anything to protect her, and try my hardest to give her the life she needs, I promise. Just give me the chance is all I ask."

"I don't need anything but you, Jonathon." Raven looked up at Jonathon, holding on to his leg. "I'm so sorry I hurt you."

"Nothing could hurt as much as watching you marry anyone but me," Jonathon answered.

"All right, that's enough," said Rook. "Remember, we're still in the middle of a tournament here."

"Nay. Nay, I can't agree to it," said Corbett through gritted teeth. "Raven, you are to marry a noble at the end of the tournament, and I won't change my mind about it so don't try to stop it again."

"We've already coupled," said Raven, getting ready for her father to pull Jonathon off the horse and strangle him with his bare hands. "I can't marry another man. What if I'm already pregnant?" she asked.

"You what!" Corbett's eyes bore fire. "Keep your voice down," he ground out. "God's eyes, I will kill you, armorer, for touching my daughter."

"I initiated it, Father," Raven admitted, raising her chin. "And I want you know that I lost my virginity long before I ever knew Jonathon."

The herald called out that it was time for the final pass. They were tied in the score and this pass would determine the winner of the competition.

"Raven, you will be the death of me yet," said Corbett looking ready to explode.

The crowd cheered and roared, wanting to see the end of the competition.

"I'm sorry, Father. I didn't mean for anyone to get hurt." Raven truly did feel sorry for everything. She hadn't really thought about how her decisions would affect so many others in a bad way.

"Do you understand what kind of position you put me in?" asked Corbett.

"I do now," she answered. "That is why Jonathon needs to withdraw from the competition."

"Aye, I agree," said Corbett. "I cannot let this charade go on any longer."

"Father? You aren't really going to declare Whitehead the winner, are you?" asked Rook.

"Well, I can't declare Jonathon the winner, because if I did, it would bring doom to us all," said Corbett. "I will not do anything to bring about the downfall of my family."

"Corbett, don't make our daughter marry a man she doesn't love," said Devon. "Have a heart."

"I have no choice, Devon," he told her. "The purpose of this tournament was to find a husband for our daughter. I can't let a commoner get away with impersonating a knight, and I certainly cannot let him win the competition."

"You can't proclaim Whitehead the winner," spat Raven. "Please."

Corbett looked over at Raven next. "It no longer matters because Jonathon can't compete anymore now that you've broken his arm. He has no choice but to withdraw. I'll tell the herald to announce that Sir Whitehead is the winner."

Corbett left to talk to the herald.

"Nay," cried Raven, running over and clinging to her mother. "Mother, do something. Please, change Father's mind."

"I don't know what I can do, but I'll try to talk to him," said Devon. "I only wish you would have gone to him in the first place like I asked you to. Now, there isn't anything any of us can do to change the outcome."

She followed her husband.

"Well, I guess that's it, then," said Jonathon, holding his arm and wincing in pain. "Rook, can I ask you to help me from the horse? I'm in a lot of pain and don't want to fall again."

"Of course," said Rook, helping him dismount. "Well, at least, now no one has to ever know Sir Nevar's true identity."

"I suppose it's better this way," said Jonathon. "Raven, the last thing I ever wanted was to put you or your family in such a horrible position. I'll pack up my things and leave at once."

"Nay," cried Raven. "I don't want you to go."

"Sir Nevar has withdrawn from the competition

with a broken arm, having nothing to do with the blow from his competitor," called out the herald, causing the crowd to hush. "Therefore, Sir Whitehead of Liverpool is declared the winner of the tournament by default. He has won the hand of Lady Raven in marriage. Please join your husband-to-be up at the nobles' platform, Lady Raven."

"Nay," cried Raven, terrified to go.

"Sister, go. If you don't, it will only be more problems for all of us," Rook told her.

"I won't go. I won't leave Jonathon." Raven's world was crashing down around her and it was all her own fault.

"Cousin, ye must," said Lark. "I'll go with ye."

"I'm not going," she said stubbornly.

This time Rook grabbed her by the arm. "We have all been through hell and back for you, little sister, but it has come to an end."

"I told you, I'm not your little sister. We're twins, you fool. Let go of me." Raven struggled under his grasp.

"Raven, please go. It will be the best for all," said Jonathon sadly. "Do it for me."

"I'll go, but this is far from over," said Raven, letting her brother lead her away.

Jonathon gave the horse's reins to Albert, and made his way back to the smithy, feeling like his life had come to an end. He'd tried everything in his power to help Raven, but there was nothing more he could do. He loved her and didn't want to leave, but he had no other choice.

He was a commoner.

She was a noble.

They would never be together again.

CHAPTER 22

Jonathon stopped by to see the castle's healer who put his arm in a sling. Thankfully, it wasn't broken after all, but it was severely sprained. He wouldn't be able to swing a hammer in the smithy for at least a month. This was going to really hurt their business.

He returned Rook's armor to the armory, and headed back to the blacksmith's shop within the castle's walls. It was hard to ignore the happy people who were celebrating Sir Whitehead's win. Raven should be *his* wife, not another man's. He cursed her silently and then he cursed himself. Why in the devil's name did he have to fall in love with a woman who was off-limits to him? This was the first time he knew love—*real* love in his life. Sadly, now that love would die inside him, because he couldn't let it blossom and bloom. He and Raven were two people from two different walks of life and that is all they would ever be.

"Brother, did you see what happened?" Avery ran up to him with Gerold at his side. "Lady Raven broke

298

a knight's arm because she decided she didn't want him to win the tournament after all."

"Nay, that's not true," said Jonathon softly, heading to the shop. "She only sprained it."

"How do you know?" asked Avery. "Hey, what happened to your arm?"

"I sprained it."

"Just like the knight did," said Gerold.

"Oh, no. Please don't tell me that was you?" Avery looked horrified at the thought.

"It was," he admitted. "I only did it to help her, but now nothing matters."

"You didn't really think you had a chance with her, did you, Brother? Or for that matter, even have a chance to win a joust against a seasoned knight?"

"I suppose not."

Gerold opened the door and entered the shop but stopped and turned around.

"There are two men here that I've never seen before," said the boy.

"Well, they'll have to go somewhere else to get their armor fixed or polished," said Jonathon. "I can't work until my arm heals. Plus, I am packing and leaving right away."

"Leaving? We're leaving already?" asked Avery, sounding like he didn't want to go.

Jonathon stepped around the boy, but stopped in his tracks when he realized who had come to see him.

"Jonathon, there you are," said one of the men.

"Guild Master Wilkin? Guild Master Shroud?" asked Jonathon, surprised to see the masters from the armorers' guild in the shop. "What are you doing here? Did you come to watch the tournament?" God, he hoped not. He never wanted them to know his part in this big deception.

"Jonathon, offer them a seat." Avery stepped forward and moved the bag with Raven's armor in it, putting it on the floor. "Please, won't you sit down, guild masters?" he asked.

"Hrmph," snorted Shroud, taking a seat. Wilkin remained standing.

"We are here because that woman at your shop in town begged us to give you another chance," said Wilkin.

"What woman?" asked Jonathon. "I don't understand. I told you I had no piece to present and also no time to make one."

"Gerold, get them some ale," Avery interrupted again, working diligently to please the guild masters. "I'll start a fire to warm the room."

"After the last time I saw you in town, that woman dressed like a man followed me outside," explained Wilkin. "She assured me you would have a final project to present to us that was unique and like nothing we've ever seen before. That is why I agreed to it."

"Raven," said Jonathon under his breath. He hadn't thought the day could get any worse, but he was wrong.

"I told her we'd be here the day of the tournament. Didn't she relay the message to you?" asked Wilkin.

"I guess it must have slipped her mind," grumbled Jonathon, knowing now why Raven had kept trying so hard to get him to work on his masterpiece.

Gerold poured two tankards of ale and gave one to each of the men.

"Where is your masterpiece?" asked Shroud. "We have been here for a while and need to leave, so please present it to us for judging."

"Yes, we'd like to see it now," said Wilkin, taking a sip of ale. "We have a very busy schedule."

"Masters Wilkin and Shroud, I'm sorry to say that you have been brought her under false pretense, and I knew nothing about it until now."

"False pretense? What do you mean?" asked Shroud, sounding less than pleased.

"Aye, explain yourself, Armstrong. Do you have your presentation piece or not?" asked Wilkin becoming impatient.

"Nay, I do not," Jonathon answered directly, wishing he could say otherwise. "I have nothing to show you, because I have taken on two jobs here at the castle and didn't have time to prepare my masterpiece. I'm sorry."

"Nothing?" asked Shroud.

"At all?" asked Wilkin. "If not, you know that this will ruin your chances of ever becoming a master craftsman. We traveled here because we were promised you were ready to present. If you have nothing to show us, then you will not get another chance. Instead, you will be naught but a journeyman for the rest of your life."

"That's right," said Shroud. "It's a shame, but now you will never have the opportunity of owning your own shop."

"I know," said Jonathon with a sigh, sitting and rubbing his hurt arm. "I am sorry to have wasted your time, but I have no masterpiece to present to you."

"Armstrong, you don't know what a mistake this was. Word will spread about this and you will be blacklisted from now on. Respect is too important to the guild to ignore this incident." Wilkin plunked the cup down on the table. "Let's go, Guild Master Shroud."

"It's a shame," said Shroud, getting to his feet. "I had such high hopes for you, Jonathon."

Jonathon felt like crawling into a hole and dying right now. His life had gone from bad to worse so quickly. Now he had nothing to look forward to in life at all. Part of him almost wished he had been thrown in the dungeon, because at least that punishment would have been something he deserved. Now his dream of becoming a master craftsman was doused, just like the flame of the forge each night, and he'd had nothing to do with the dastardly outcome.

"Oh, hello, there," said Raven, walking into the shop just as the guild masters were about to leave. "Guild Master Wilkin, is it?"

"Yes, my lady," said Wilkin with a slight bow. "And this is Guild Master Shroud."

"My lady," said Shroud, bowing as well.

"Hello," she said to the second man.

"We were just leaving," Wilkin explained.

"Leaving? Already?" she asked. "Why?"

Wilkin and Shroud exchanged looks and then Wilkin was the one to speak up. "Excuse me for speaking so freely, my lady, but you look familiar although I've never met you before."

"Oh, we have met, at Jonathon's father's shop in town," said Raven. "I followed you outside to talk to you when you were about to leave. Don't you remember?"

"That was you dressed in dirty clothes and looking like a man?" Wilkin gasped.

"Yes, that was me," she answered.

"My lady, you told us Jonathon would have a masterpiece to present to us and he doesn't."

"We travelled a long way for nothing," said Shroud.

"Oh, nay, that's not true," said Raven. "He does have a presentation piece, I assure you."

"Raven, please," groaned Jonathon, getting to his feet. "No more lies."

"I'm not lying." She looked around the room and headed over to the corner. "There it is. I've been looking everywhere for it."

"My lady, we are on a tight schedule," complained Wilkin.

"Jonathon is being too modest," said Raven, picking up a bag and heading over to the table. "This is his masterpiece to present to you for judging. I am sure it is like nothing you have ever seen before." She spilled the armor out onto the table.

Jonathon's mouth fell open. Raven was using the armor he made for her as his presentation piece for the guild masters. It was an ingenious idea. Why hadn't he thought of it? It was sure to impress them. Still, it wasn't right, and he couldn't make them believe this is what he'd planned all along when it wasn't true. The lies stopped here and now.

"Nay, guild masters. That's something I made, but is not my presentation piece," he told them.

"Let me see that." Wilkin hurried over and picked up the helm. Shroud inspected the chest plate.

"These are exquisite," said Shroud.

"This armor. It is so small and lightweight," said Wilkin in surprise.

"It's for a lady," Raven told them. "Actually, Jonathon made it for me."

"Armor for a lady?" asked Shroud. "I have never seen or even heard of anything like it before."

"Look at this fine work and attention to detail," said Wilkin, turning the helm around and around in his hands. "Little etched hearts and roses?"

"Aye. That was just an afterthought," said Jonathon. "I thought Lady Raven would like it."

"I do like it," said Raven. "As a matter of fact, I love it. Guild masters, I've already worn the armor, and it works wonderfully."

"Now this is something worth waiting to see." A large smile spread over Wilkin's face.

"But it's not my masterpiece," said Jonathon, just wanting to be honest.

"Well, why the hell not?" asked Wilkin. "It should be. I say it is. Now, excuse us for a moment, we need to talk in private."

"You can use the bedroom," offered Avery, showing them the way.

"Raven. Why are you here?" asked Jonathon, once the men went into the other room. The pain in his hurt arm was becoming unbearable and he needed a strong drink.

"I wanted to tell you I was sorry for hurting your arm. Is it broken?" She reached out to touch it, but he held up his other hand to stop her.

"Nay, it isn't broken. However it is too sprained for me to be able to swing a hammer. I'm afraid I won't be able to work in the forge for at least a month or more until it heals."

"Well, Jonathon Armstrong, that will give you plenty of time to start your own shop," said Wilkin, having overheard their conversation. The two men returned.

"Pardon me?" asked Jonathon. "What did you say?"

"We've decided your exquisite, unique work has earned you the title of Master Armorer," announced Shroud.

"Yay!" shouted Gerold, jumping up and down and clapping his hands.

"That's great, Brother. Congratulations!" said Avery, going to shake his hand, but stopping since it was in a sling.

"Jonathon, your dream came true," said Raven, smiling from ear to ear. "That is wonderful."

Jonathon should have been ecstatic but instead he felt sullen. "Thank you, guild masters, but I don't feel as if I deserve the title."

"Why ever not?" asked Shroud.

"I don't understand," said Wilkin. "You will be recorded as a master now, and will be able to open your own shop and employ your own journeyman."

"Thank you," said Jonathon, not wanting to sound ungrateful. "However, I don't have the money to open a shop of my own, and I know that is a prerequisite. Right now, I can't even work in the forge because of my hurt arm. I don't feel it would be right to use the title until it fits me."

"Oh, that's a shame," said Shroud. "Being made a master means you need to open your own shop."

"As well as be married," Wilkin reminded him.

"Would this help with opening your shop?" Rook entered the room, handing him two pouches of coins.

"What's this?" asked Jonathon, taking the pouches from him.

"One pouch is the money Raven won in the archery competition, and the other is your pay. We had a deal, remember?" said Rook.

Jonathon's eyes flashed over to Raven.

"Rook told me everything, don't worry about it," said Raven. "You were only doing your job. And I can't collect the prize money, so it might as well be yours."

"Thank you. I will take the money, but not to put toward my own shop," said Jonathon. "I will give it to my father instead so he can hire another man to cover my position until I am healed."

"I don't understand," said Raven. "Jonathon, this is what you've always wanted. Why are you dismissing it as if it doesn't even matter? You've just been made a master. You deserve your own shop."

"It's what I used to want," Jonathon told her, feeling a gaping hole in his heart. "Nothing has been the same since... since I met you, Lady Raven," he said, making her blush.

"What's going on in here?" Corbett ducked to enter through the doorway, walking into the small shop, followed by Devon.

"Father? Why are you here?" asked Raven.

"I came to talk to you about Sir Whitehead, Raven."

"Your betrothed," said Jonathon, the words dripping off his tongue.

"We'll be on our way then," said Wilkin.

"Wait," said Raven. "Father, we don't have a castle smith anymore. Jonathon is the best one we've ever had. Can't he stay here at Blake Castle as our new blacksmith and armorer? He's just been made a master by these men."

The men nodded and bowed, being introduced to Corbett and Devon.

"I think that is a wonderful idea," said Devon. "Doesn't a master craftsman have his own shop though? This can be yours, Jonathon."

"We've been meaning to expand it," said Rook. "Mayhap this would be a good time to do so."

"If you need a journeyman and an apprentice, you've got them right here," said Avery, motioning to himself and Gerold.

"I would like you to stay, Jonathon," said Gerold. "I'm lonely since my father died. It's been nice having you here with me. You are like a second father to me. Avery too."

Avery reached over and ruffled the boy's hair.

"Should we write that in our notes then, Master Armstrong?" asked Shroud.

"Aye. Will your new shop be inside the walls of Blake Castle then?" asked Wilkin.

"I-I'm not sure," said Jonathon, still rubbing his arm. "I don't think I'd feel comfortable living and working here at Blake Castle." He looked over to Raven. "Not anymore. Besides, I'd have to be married, and I'm not."

"We'd give you time to find a girl to marry," said Shroud.

"I just don't know," said Jonathon. "I'd have to think about it, I guess."

"Well, when you decide where your shop will be set up, send us a missive to let us know," said Wilkin. "We have another appointment, and need to leave."

"Congratulations, Master Armstrong," said Shroud, as the two men made their way out the door.

Raven knew exactly what Jonathon meant when

he said he wouldn't be comfortable staying there. She would be married to another man, and he didn't want to have to see that. It didn't make her any more comfortable, but she couldn't just let him walk out of her life like this. Her days wouldn't be the same without him. She wouldn't give up so easily. She and Jonathon needed to be together.

"Before you decide, Jonathon, give me a moment to talk to my parents, please," said Raven.

"Raven?" asked Corbett. "What's this all about?"

She pulled her parents over to the side. Her brother, being nosey, joined them too.

"Father," she said in a soft voice. "Are you sure you can't do something so Jonathon and I can be married?"

"Now Raven, you know the rules. The winner of the tournament claims your hand in marriage."

"But the tournament was forfeited," said Raven. "It was never really finished, so no one actually won."

"That's right," agreed Devon. "Sir Whitehead was only proclaimed the winner because his competitor pulled out."

"Thanks to you, Sister," added Rook.

"I did it to save Jonathon's life," said Raven.

"Corbett, do something. This is your only daughter," said Devon. "Don't let things end this way."

"Well, what am I supposed to do?" Corbett crossed his arms over his chest. "It's not like we can have a rematch now, can we?"

"He's right, Raven," said Rook. "Jonathon would have to be a knight or at least a noble to legitimately go up against Whitehead again."

"Can't you make him a knight or something?"

asked Raven, already knowing the answer, but having to try.

"Not on your life," said Corbett. "It doesn't work that way and you know it. He wasn't even supposed to be out on the field during a tournament. I can't let him get away with that."

"Now, Corbett," said Devon. "We're the only ones who know Sir Nevar's true identity, so what does it matter what Jonathon did or didn't do?"

"And Raven. Don't forget Raven pretended to be the French knight first," added Rook. "You'll have to punish her too," he said, getting a nasty glare from Raven.

"Well, couldn't you at least make Jonathon a lord, Father?" Raven kept on trying. "Give him an honorary title mayhap?"

"The only way for a commoner to be titled is if they are married to a noble," said Corbett.

"Like me?" asked Raven. "Oh please, Father, let us be wed. Then you can give him a title. Please, do it. I don't want to marry anyone else but Jonathon."

"You're not going to leave this alone until I agree, are you?" asked Corbett.

"If you make me marry Lord Whitehead, I will not only keep fighting with my weapons, but I will find every opportunity to run away from him."

"Don't threaten me, young lady," warned Corbett.

"I'm sorry, but I'm trying to tell you how I feel," said Raven.

"Dear, I don't think it's really a threat," said Devon. "It is just who our daughter is, and I believe she will do just what she said. I think we need to stop trying to change her and just accept her for who she is."

"Rebellious," said Rook, adding his opinion to the conversation with one word.

"Are you two really in love?" asked Raven's father with a sigh.

"Oh, we are," she answered. "We really are."

"Will you help them, Corbett?" asked Devon. "Remember, when we fell in love it was rather uncommon and forbidden as well. Still, it all turned out for the best."

"Yes, I remember, dear," said Corbett. "And also remember that my parents are living proof that true love can cause a lot of problems, too."

"It can solve problems as well," said Raven. "Just give us a chance to show you."

"I'm not sure what you plan on showing, but I don't want to see it," said Rook jokingly.

"Stop it, Brother." Raven hit Rook on the arm.

Corbett glanced over to Jonathon and then back to Raven. "If you two really feel this strongly about each other, then this is what I'll do."

CHAPTER 23

J onathon couldn't imagine what on earth Raven
and her parents were talking about for so long.
He was excited to have actually been made a
master at his craft, but suddenly it didn't seem as important as it had before. His one true dream was no
longer bettering his occupation. Now Jonathon's
dream was only to be married to Raven.

"Jonathon, it's settled," said Raven with a big
smile, walking over with the others to join him.

"What's settled?" he asked.

"You will have your own shop right here inside
the castle's walls, and it is going to be expanded to
give you plenty of room to do everything you want to
do," she told him.

"Plenty of room for us, too," said Gerold, looking
over at Avery.

"Now, Raven, I don't think that is a good idea."
The last thing Jonathon wanted was to be watching
Raven with her new husband, never able to get away
from his agony of seeing them together.

"Of course, you'll be living inside the castle
during the construction of your new shop," said Cor-

bett. "And afterwards too. Although Gerold and Avery will have to live at the smithy."

"Excuse me?" asked Jonathon, trying to be polite. "I have no idea what you mean."

"Father, tell him," said Raven, looking as if she were about to burst.

"Jonathon Armstrong, I have decided to agree to let you marry my daughter, even if I know I'll regret it later," said Corbett.

"What?" Jonathon's brows raised. "I don't understand. She already has a betrothed. Whitehead."

"Not yet. Not really," said Corbett. "I haven't signed a contract with Whitehead, so nothing is in writing. Besides, as my family pointed out, he didn't really win the tournament because you had to withdraw from the competition."

"I don't understand, my lord. I am a mere commoner, not a noble. How am I allowed to marry your daughter?"

"You will be my new weapons advisor, as well as the castle smith and my master armorer. For that, you'll need a title, so you will be Lord Jonathon Armstrong from now on, even if you are not really a noble by blood."

"A-a courtesy title?" asked Jonathon, not believing his ears.

"That's right. Plus, I won't allow anyone married to my daughter to be called anything but a lord."

"Jonathon, this is wonderful, isn't it?" asked Raven. "Now we can be married, just like we wanted."

"Not to mention you're a master now and will have your own shop," said Avery. "Father will be so proud."

"Everything is happening so fast my head is spinning," said Jonathon. "What about Sir Whitehead?" he asked. "Won't he be angry?"

"Nay. I will be able to handle him," said Corbett, clearing his throat.

"Dear, tell them the rest of it," said Devon.

"The rest of what?" asked Raven.

"Oh, let me tell her, please," said Rook.

"Go on." Corbett nodded.

"When Sir Whitehead saw you knock Sir Nevar off the horse and try to break his arm, he wanted nothing to do with you," said Rook, with a chuckle. "I can't say I blame him."

"Really?" asked Raven. "He said he didn't want to marry me?"

"That's what he said, dear," answered her mother. "However, your father was ready to hold him to it."

"Whitehead was frightened off by you, Raven," explained her father. "He only really wants the money awarded for winning the tournament. He told me he wouldn't have a bride who might try to kill him in his sleep."

That made everyone in the room laugh.

"Raven, your obnoxious ways actually did you a favor this time," said Rook. "Who would have thought it?"

"When I marry Jonathon, I'm going to act more like a lady. I'm going to be a good wife," Raven promised. "Jonathon, say something. Do you still want to marry me? You have my parents' blessing now."

"Mayhap *he* doesn't want a wife who might try to kill him in his sleep, either," said her brother, receiving another punch to the arm from Raven.

"Raven," said Jonathon, walking over and reaching out to hold her hand. He got down on one knee. "I would love more than anything to be your husband. That is my dream now and nothing else matters. But do you really want me? I'm just a common man."

"Jonathon, get up," she said, seeming embarrassed. When he stood, she threw her arms around his shoulders and kissed him hard on the mouth.

"Mmph," he said, feeling more pain in his arm, but her kisses outweighed it, so it didn't matter.

"Of course, I'll marry you, Jonathon, and you are far from common, believe me. Father, how soon can we have the wedding?" asked Raven. "Can we have it right away?"

"Let's wait until everyone from the tournament leaves first," said Corbett with a chuckle.

"Yes, Raven," agreed Devon. "You are our only daughter and we want this wedding to be special. It will take a little while to plan."

"I don't want to wait," said Raven.

"Raven, I agree," said Jonathon. "If we wait for a month, it will give my arm time to heal."

"It'll also give more time for construction to get underway on Jonathon's new shop," added Avery.

"Then it's decided," said Corbett. "Let me go pay Whitehead some money and tell him he is off the hook."

"Father!" said Raven with a scowl.

"I mean, I'll tell him that he'd be better off with another bride," said Corbett.

"Thank you, Mother and Father," said Raven, holding Jonathon's hand.

"Lord Corbett," said Jonathon stopping him before he left.

"Aye?" Corbett turned around.

"I realize I've done some things that are less than honorable and I am sorry. I will willingly accept any punishment that you see fit."

"Nay. You will not be punished," said Corbett.

"That's right," said Rook. "Marrying my sister is the worst punishment a man could ever have." He ducked out the door after his parents, most likely so Raven wouldn't punch him again.

CHAPTER 24
ONE MONTH LATER

"I pronounce you man and wife," said the priest, blessing Raven and Jonathon, while the crowd in the courtyard of Blake Castle watched.

Avery was Jonathon's best man, while Lark was Raven's bridesmaid.

It was late spring and the weather was getting warmer. An arch woven with wildflowers curved above Raven and Jonathon's heads. Big vases of flowers were placed throughout the courtyard. Trestle tables were set up outside, filled with food for the feast that would follow.

"Is this the part where I get to kiss the bride?" asked Jonathon, wrapping his arms around Raven, kissing her passionately in front of everyone.

"Hurry up. I want to eat," called out his younger brother, Heathcliff, making everyone laugh. He held two of the four pups that Copper had given birth to, while Gerold held the other two. Copper was with them, watching over her pups. Raven had told the boys they could each choose one puppy to keep as their own. That was a week ago, and they still hadn't been able to decide. Heathcliff and Gerold were good friends now. Gerold spent most of his time at Jonathon's father's shop as an apprentice. But now that Jonathon's new shop was almost finished, the boy would help out at the castle on occasion, too. He considered Jonathon his new father, and both Raven and Jonathon liked that.

"Who wants Mountain Magic?" called out Lark's father, Storm MacKeefe, who came from the Highlands for the wedding. All of Raven's relatives were at the wedding, including her younger brothers, Tolin and Daegel.

"I want some," called out Heathcliff.

"Nay, ye dinna," said Lark. "It's whisky that is so strong it'll knock ye out."

"Just the way I like it," said Storm, taking a tankard from one of the servers.

"Throw the flowers, Lady Raven." Raven's hand-maid, Emma, was starting to get very big now with her pregnancy. She held on to her husband's hand. Raven had already talked to her parents and secured Emma's position at the castle, even after she birthed her baby.

"All right," said Raven, turning around and throwing the bouquet over her shoulder.

"Ouch, that hurt, Sister."

Raven turned around and laughed. Rook had the bouquet in his hands. He quickly tossed it over to Lark and wiped his hands on his trews.

"Thank ye, Cousin," said Lark, smiling and sniffing the flowers. "Mayhap this means I'll find a husband soon."

"I think I'm going to enjoy this new life," said Avery in a low voice, eyeing up two of the comely kitchen wenches walking by with trays of food.

"Are you talking about the food or the wenches?" asked Jonathon with a chuckle.

"Both," he said. "Excuse me." He hurried away after the girls.

Jonathon's entire family was there as well. They'd even invited the townsfolk, since they were Jonathon's friends. It was a good way to bring the nobles and the commoners closer together.

Jonathon had yet to meet all of Raven's relatives, since there seemed to be many. Remembering all their names would take some time.

"Everyone, take a seat," called out Corbett. "The wedding feast is about to begin. Afterwards, my daughter and her husband, Lord Jonathon, will have the first dance."

"It's going to take a while for me to get used to hearing the title of *lord* attached to my name," Jonathon told Raven as they walked hand-in-hand to the wedding table. Brindy followed at their heels, becoming attached to Jonathon ever since he gave the dog that bone.

"Don't you like it?" Raven looked over to him with sparkling eyes that always made him want her.

"Oh, I didn't say that," he answered, stopping for a second to pet Brindy on the head. "It just doesn't feel real. Just like this marriage to you."

"It's real, I assure you," said Raven, as they took their seats at the raised dais in the courtyard. Lark and Rook, as well as Raven's parents and Jonathon's parents, joined them at the dais today.

"Lord Corbett, this is a fine setup you have here," said Crispin, looking around.

"Father, that's not the right thing to say," Jonathon told him in a low voice.

"Nay, he's right," said Corbett, taking a goblet of wine from the cupbearer. "Crispin, Blake Castle is the best place to be, and I am happy that your son is now my son-by-marriage."

"I want to make a toast," said Rook," standing up with his goblet of wine in his hand. "I wish my sister and her new husband happiness," he said, getting cheers and clapping from the crowd. "And I hope my dear cousin Lark will be the next one married, since she needs a husband desperately."

"Och, Rook, hush," Lark told him, still sniffing the flowers with a smile on her face.

"Rook, sit down," said Corbett. "Lark won't be next to marry, it'll be you."

"Me?" Rook chuckled, sitting down. "Nay, not me. I haven't found the right girl yet."

"Your father has found one for you," said Devon.

"Who?" asked Rook, taking a swig of wine. "And why wasn't I told about this?"

"It doesn't feel good, does it, Brother?" asked Raven, totaling enjoying seeing her twin brother squirm in his chair.

"I'm betrothing you to a noblewoman, but we'll talk about that later," Corbett told him. "Today is all about Raven and Jonathon, so let us focus on them."

"Who is she? What does she look like? Where is she from?" Rook continued to fire questions at his father. "I want to know."

"Not now, Rook," said Devon. "You heard your father. We are celebrating Raven's wedding. Now, calm down."

"To Raven and Jonathon," said Avery, already having tasted the Mountain Magic and being affected by the strong brew. He sat down at a trestle table and almost missed the chair.

Jonathon drank in the beauty of Raven, not able to believe she was really his wife. She wore a beautiful bright-blue gown with long silk tippets that made her look like a queen. On her head she wore a tiara of colored gemstones that glittered in the sun. Her long black hair was braided, and the braids were wrapped in circles over each of her ears.

Jonathon wore a tunic with the Blake crest on it, at Raven's request. He still didn't feel comfortable in it, but did it to please his new wife.

"Kiss, kiss, kiss," called out someone from the crowd, that sounded a lot like Jonathon's sister, Estrilda.

"I wouldn't mind if I did," said Jonathon, kissing Raven once again.

"I can't wait until we consummate the wedding," whispered Raven.

"I think we'd better wait until the festivities are over," he told her, picking up her hand and kissing the ring on her finger. It was a simple gold band for now, but once Jonathon's business started growing, he promised to buy Raven the biggest diamond ever.

"Jonathon," said Raven, taking a cup of wine from the cupbearer. "Did you ever think that someday we'd be married?"

"Never," he said, taking a sip of wine.

"Did you like me when we first met?"

"I have to admit, I've been smitten with you from the first time I saw you, but I also have to admit something else," he told her.

"What's that?" she asked.

"I was a little afraid of you, too. Just like most of the men in town."

She giggled. "I'm sorry again about hurting your arm."

"It's just about back to normal, and I know you did it to save me from being imprisoned. I still can't believe you entered the tournament under the guise of being a French knight. You amaze me, Raven. You are bold, determined... and a little bit crazy as well."

"Now, how can you say that? I did everything for love."

"I need to know something, Raven."

"Anything. What is it?"

"Would you really have jousted if I hadn't taken your place in the tournament? It's such a dangerous sport, and face it, you're no good at it at all."

She giggled once again. "Yes, I would have," she told him.

"You might have been hurt or even killed."

"It was a risk worth taking since I was trying to stop my marriage to anyone who wasn't you." She kissed him once again, and the crowd cheered. Avery started making strange noises and that caused the dogs to bark. The children all laughed.

"I suppose I should be thanking you," said Jonathon. "For more things than I can even list."

"I suppose you should." She looked up at him and winked. "I have to admit something to you now."

"What?" he asked.

"When I discovered you were making me think I was good at the joust even though I wasn't, it made me angry but also made me want you even more."

"Really? Why?" he asked.

"Oh, I don't know. I suppose I wanted you because I knew I wasn't supposed to have you. Same reason for wanting to joust, I guess."

"So you were being rebellious."

"Nay, not at all."

"Then what would you call it?" he wanted to know.

"Let's just say I'm a competitor and probably always will be. When a challenge is thrown down at my feet, you will always find me *Picking up the Gauntlet.*"

FROM THE AUTHOR

I hope you enjoyed Jonathon and Raven's story and will take the time to leave a review for me.

In medieval times, men and women were often betrothed as children. They married extremely young, as soon as they hit puberty. Maybe that is because people only lived to be about 30 years of age back then.

Of course, you won't find anything crazy like that in my books. What you will usually find is very strong women who speak their minds and can even wield a sword. (Of course, back then, men treated their dogs better than the women, but I choose to empower women instead.) I usually write very alpha males who need a good woman to help them find their softer side.

In my *Below the Salt Series*, I chose to push the envelope once again, as I am known to do. Nobles would never marry a commoner, but in my world, love is stronger than status. In this series, I take my readers to parts of a medieval world not usually seen in most romances.

I am intrigued with life beyond the castle walls. I found my research of medieval towns and guilds so interesting, that I knew I had to write about it. Most of us know what life was like inside the castle for the nobles who sat above the salt. But what about the rest of society? Those sitting below the salt? (Salt was expensive and that is why it was a luxury of the nobles.) Nobles depended upon the commoners for lots of things, such as food, clothes, weapons, and more. I think they were very important.

This story touched on the life of an armorer. Blacksmiths usually repaired things, and made horseshoes, tools, and nails. A swordsmith made swords and weapons, and an armorer made and repaired armor. (My hero is a jack-of-all-trades. He does all these things and also has the skills to fight like a soldier.)

The guilds were similar to unions nowadays, but they still had their pecking order. You needed to follow rules, and to be accepted in order to get in. The guild masters decided what materials could be used and also how much could be charged for the products and services of the tradesmen. There were inspections by the guild masters to make sure the work was of quality, and there were also dues to pay.

One would start out as a boy of about twelve, working as an apprentice to a master craftsman. They learned the craft, but were not paid. This lasted about seven to ten years. Then he would become a journeyman, who got paid for his work and often journeyed to other towns to get jobs. This lasted about three years, or for some, a lifetime.

The next step was becoming a master craftsman. The journeyman would have to present a masterpiece to the guild masters to prove he was skilled and worthy of this title. (I say 'he' because women were not really allowed to be in a guild, unless they were married and their husband was a guild member. If the husband died, the widow was usually allowed to take over the business.) The masterpiece would be judged by the guild masters, and depending on the presentation piece, the journeyman would either be accepted or not. Being a master usually meant having your own shop, so the journeyman had to be debt-free and have enough money to start his own business. While journeymen were required to be single, masters were supposed to be married.

You will find out more about the working class in the rest of my *Below the Salt Series*. Next up is Raven's brother, Rook, in *A Rose Among Thorns*.

This series follows the generations of the Blake family. If you'd like to read about Corbett Blake and his wife Devon, you can find their story in **Lord of the Blade**, book 1 of my **Legacy of the Blade Series**. Be sure to read the **Legacy of the Blade Prequel**, to find out what makes Lord Corbett Blake such a hardened man. The stories of his long-lost siblings can be found in **Lady Renegade**, **Lord of Illusion**, and **Lady of the Mist**. Orrick the sorcerer's story, from the Legacy of the Blade Series, is the last book and one of my favorites, called **Keeper of the Flame**.

Stop by and visit my **Website**. You can follow me on Amazon, **Bookbub**, **Goodreads**, **Facebook,** and **Twitter**. I also have a **Private Readers' Group** on Facebook that I invite you to join.

FROM THE AUTHOR

Thank you,

Elizabeth Rose

About Elizabeth

Elizabeth Rose is an award-winning, bestselling author of over 100 books and counting. She writes medieval, historical, contemporary, paranormal, and western romance. Her books are available as EBooks, paperbacks, and some audiobooks as well.

Her favorite characters in her works include dark, dangerous and tortured heroes, and feisty, independent heroines who know how to wield a sword. She loves writing 14th century medieval novels, and is well-known for her many series.

Elizabeth loves the outdoors. In the summertime, you can find her in her secret garden with her laptop, swinging in her hammock working on her next book. Elizabeth is a born storyteller and passionate about sharing her works with her readers.

Please be sure to visit her website at **Elizabethrosenovels.com** to read excerpts from any of her novels and get sneak peeks at covers of upcoming books. You can follow her on **Twitter, Facebook**, **Goodreads** or **BookBub.** Be sure to sign up for her **newsletter** so you don't miss out on new releases or upcoming events.

Click to join **Elizabeth Rose's Readers' Group.**

ALSO BY ELIZABETH ROSE

Medieval Series:
Legendary Bastards of the Crown Series
Seasons of Fortitude Series
Secrets of the Heart Series
Legacy of the Blade Series
Daughters of the Dagger Series
MadMan MacKeefe Series
Barons of the Cinque Ports Series
Holiday Knights Series
Highland Chronicles Series
Pirate Lords Series
Highland Outcasts

Medieval/Paranormal Series:
Elemental Magick Series
Greek Myth Fantasy Series
Tangled Tales Series
Portals of Destiny

Contemporary Series:
Tarnished Saints Series
Working Man Series

Western Series:
Cowboys of the Old West Series

And More!

Please visit http://elizabethrosenovels.com